Always and Forever, Lara Jean

Jenny Han

Published in the UK by Scholastic Children's Books, 2021
Euston House, 24 Eversholt Street, London, NW1 1DB, UK
A division of Scholastic Limited.

London – New York – Toronto – Sydney – Auckland
Mexico City – New Delhi – Hong Kong

First published in the US by Simon and Schuster BFYR, 2017
First published in the UK by Scholastic Ltd, 2017

ISBN 978 0702 30782 9

A CIP catalogue record for this book is available from the British Library.

Printed by CPI Group (UK) Ltd, Croydon, CR0 4YY
Papers used by Scholastic Children's Books are made
from wood grown in sustainable forests.

1 3 5 7 9 10 8 6 4 2

www.scholastic.co.uk

For my dear readers. This one's for you.

"I don't know what lies around the bend,
but I'm going to believe that the best does."

—L. M. MONTGOMERY, *Anne of Green Gables*

1

I LIKE TO WATCH PETER WHEN HE DOESN'T know I'm looking. I like to admire the straight line of his jaw, the curve of his cheekbone. There's an openness to his face, an innocence—a certain kind of niceness. It's the niceness that touches my heart the most.

It's Friday night at Gabe Rivera's house after the lacrosse game. Our school won, so everyone is in very fine spirits, Peter most of all, because he scored the winning shot. He's across the room playing poker with some of the guys from his team; he is sitting with his chair tipped back, his back against the wall. His hair is still wet from showering after the game. I'm on the couch with my friends Lucas Krapf and Pammy Subkoff, and they're flipping through the latest issue of *Teen Vogue*, debating whether or not Pammy should get bangs.

"What do you think, Lara Jean?" Pammy asks, running her fingers through her carrot-colored hair. Pammy is a new friend—I've gotten to know her because she dates Peter's good friend Darrell. She has a face like a doll, round as a cake pan, and freckles dust her face and shoulders like sprinkles.

"Um, I think bangs are a very big commitment and not to be decided on a whim. Depending on how fast your hair grows, you could be growing them out for a year or more.

But if you're serious, I think you should wait till fall, because it'll be summer before you know it, and bangs in the summer can be sort of sticky and sweaty and annoying. . . ." My eyes drift back to Peter, and he looks up and sees me looking at him, and raises his eyebrows questioningly. I just smile and shake my head.

"So don't get bangs?"

My phone buzzes in my purse. It's Peter.

```
Do you want to go?

No.

Then why were you staring at me?

Because I felt like it.
```

Lucas is reading over my shoulder. I push him away, and he shakes his head and says, "Are you guys really texting each other when you're only twenty feet away?"

Pammy crinkles up her nose and says, "So adorable."

I'm about to answer them when I look up and see Peter sweeping across the room toward me with purpose. "Time to get my girl home," he says.

"What time is it?" I say. "Is it that late already?" Peter's hoisting me off the couch and helping me into my jacket. Then he pulls me by the hand and leads me through Gabe's living room. Looking over my shoulder, I wave and call out,

JENNY HAN

"Bye, Lucas! Bye, Pammy! For the record, I think you would look great with bangs!"

"Why are you walking so fast?" I ask as Peter marches me through the front yard to the curb where his car is parked.

He stops in front of the car, pulls me toward him, and kisses me, all in one fast motion. "I can't concentrate on my cards when you stare at me like that, Covey."

"Sorry," I start to say, but he is kissing me again, his hands firm on my back.

When we're in his car, I look at the dashboard and see that it's only midnight. I say, "I still have an hour until I have to be home. What should we do?"

Of the people we know, I'm the only one with an actual curfew. When the clock strikes one o'clock, I turn into a pumpkin. Everyone is used to it by now: Peter Kavinsky's Goody Two-shoes girlfriend who has to be home by one. I've never once minded having a curfew. Because truly, it's not like I'm missing out on anything so wonderful—and what's that old saying? Nothing good happens after two a.m. Unless you happen to be a fan of watching people play flip cup for hours on end. Not me. No, I'd much prefer to be in my flannel pajamas with a cup of Night-Night tea and a book, thank you very much.

"Let's just go to your house. I want to come inside and say hi to your dad and hang out for a bit. We could watch the rest of *Aliens*." Peter and I have been working our way down our movie list, which consists of my picks (favorite movies of mine that he's never seen), his picks, (favorite movies of his that I've never seen), and movies neither of us have seen. *Aliens* was Peter's pick, and it's turning out to be quite good. And even though once upon a time Peter claimed he didn't like rom coms, he was very into *Sleepless in Seattle*, which I was relieved for, because I just don't see how I could be with someone who doesn't like *Sleepless in Seattle*.

"Let's not go home yet," I say. "Let's go somewhere."

Peter thinks about it for a minute, tapping his fingers on the steering wheel, and then he says, "I know where we can go."

"Where?"

"Wait and see," he says, and he puts the windows down, and the crisp night air fills the car.

I lean back into my seat. The streets are empty; the lights are off in most of the houses. "Let me guess. We're going to the diner because you want blueberry pancakes."

"Nope."

"Hmm. It's too late to go to Starbucks, and Biscuit Soul Food is closed."

"Hey, food isn't the only thing I think about," he objects. Then: "Are there any cookies left in that Tupperware?"

"They're all gone, but I might have some more at home, if Kitty didn't eat them all." I dip my arm out the window and let it hang. Not many more nights left like these, where it's cool enough to need a jacket.

I look at Peter's profile out of the corner of my eye. Sometimes I still can't believe he's mine. The handsomest boy of all the handsome boys is mine, all mine.

"What?" he says.

"Nothing," I say.

Ten minutes later, we are driving onto the University of Virginia campus, only nobody calls it campus; they call it Grounds. Peter parks along the side of the street. It's quiet for a Friday night in a college town, but it's UVA's spring break, so a lot of kids are still gone.

We're walking across the lawn, his hand in mine, when I'm hit with a sudden wave of panic. I stop short and ask, "Hey, you don't think it's bad luck for me to come here before I'm actually in, do you?"

Peter laughs. "It's not a wedding. You're not marrying UVA."

"Easy for you to say, you're already in."

Peter gave a verbal commitment to the UVA lacrosse team last year, and then he applied early action in the fall. Like with most college athletes, he was all but in, so long as his grades stayed decent. When he got the official yes back in January, his mom threw a party for him and I baked a cake that said, *I'm taking my talents to UVA* in yellow frosting.

Peter pulls me by the hand and says, "Come on, Covey. We make our own luck. Besides, we were here two months ago for that thing at the Miller Center."

I relax. "Oh, yeah."

We continue our walk across the lawn. I know where we're going now. To the Rotunda, to sit on the steps. The Rotunda was designed by Thomas Jefferson, who founded the school, and he modeled it after the Pantheon, with its white columns and big domed top. Peter runs up the brick steps Rocky-style and plops down. I sit down in front of him, leaning back and resting my arms on the tops of his knees. "Did you know," I begin, "that one of the things that makes UVA unique is that the center of the school, right there inside the Rotunda, is a library and not a church? It's because Jefferson believed in the separation between school and church."

"Did you read that in the brochure?" Peter teases, planting a kiss on my neck.

Dreamily, I say, "I learned it when I went on the tour last year."

"You didn't tell me you went on a tour. Why would you go on a tour when you're from here? You've been here a million times!"

He's right that I've been here a million times—I grew up going here with my family. When my mom was still alive, we'd go see the Hullabahoos perform because my mom loved a cappella. We had our family portrait taken on the lawn. On sunny days after church, we'd come picnic out here.

I twist around to look at Peter. "I went on the tour because I wanted to know everything about UVA! Stuff I wouldn't know just by living around here. Like, do you know what year they let women in?"

He scratches the back of his neck. "Uh . . . I don't know. When was the school founded? The early 1800s? So, 1920?"

"Nope. 1970." I turn back around and face forward, looking out onto the grounds. "After a hundred and fifty years."

Intrigued, Peter says, "Whoa. That's crazy. Okay, tell me more facts about UVA."

"UVA is America's only collegiate World Heritage UNESCO site in all of the United States," I begin.

"Never mind, don't tell me more facts about UVA," Peter says, and I slap him on the knee. "Tell me something else instead. Tell me what you're looking forward to most about going to school here."

"You go first. What are you most excited about?"

Right away, Peter says, "That's easy. Streaking the lawn with you."

"*That's* what you're looking forward to more than anything? Running around naked?" Hastily I add, "I'm never doing that, by the way."

He laughs. "It's a UVA tradition. I thought you were all about UVA traditions."

"Peter!"

"I'm just kidding." He leans forward and puts his arms around my shoulders, rubbing his nose in my neck the way he likes to do. "Your turn."

I let myself dream about it for a minute. If I get in, what am I most looking forward to? There are so many things, I can hardly name them all. I'm looking forward to eating waffles every day with Peter in the dining hall. To us sledding down O-Hill when it snows. To picnics when it's warm. To staying up all night talking and then waking up and talking some more. To late-night laundry and last-minute road trips. To . . . everything. Finally I say, "I don't want to jinx it."

"Come on!"

"Okay, okay . . . I guess I'm most looking forward to . . . to going to the McGregor Room whenever I want." People call it the Harry Potter room, because of the rugs and chandeliers and leather chairs and the portraits on the wall. The bookshelves go from the floor to the ceiling, and all of the books are behind metal grates, protected like the precious objects they are. It's a room from a different time. It's very hushed—reverential, even. There was this one summer—I must have been five or six, because it was before Kitty was born—my mom took a class at UVA, and she used to study in the McGregor Room. Margot and I would color, or read. My mom called it the magic library, because Margot and I never fought inside of it. We were both quiet as church mice; we were so in awe of all the books, and of the older kids studying.

Peter looks disappointed. I'm sure it's because he thought I would name something having to do with him. With us. But for some reason, I want to keep those hopes just for me for now.

"You can come with me to the McGregor Room," I say. "But you have to promise to be quiet."

Affectionately Peter says, "Lara Jean, only you would look forward to hanging out in a library."

Actually, judging by Pinterest alone, I'm pretty sure a lot of people would look forward to hanging out in such a beautiful library. Just not people Peter knows. He thinks I'm so quirky. I'm not planning on being the one to break the news to him that I'm actually not that quirky, that in fact lots of people like to stay home and bake cookies and scrapbook and hang out in libraries. Most of them are probably in their fifties, but still. I like the way he looks at me, like I am a wood nymph that he happened upon one day and just had to take home to keep.

Peter pulls his phone out of his hoodie pocket. "It's twelve thirty. We should go soon."

"Already?" I sigh. I like being here late at night. It feels like the whole place is ours.

In my heart, it was always UVA. I've never really expected to go anywhere else, or even really thought about it. I was going to apply early when Peter did, but my guidance counselor, Mrs. Duvall, advised me against applying early action, because she said it would be better to wait so they could see my senior mid-year grades. According to Mrs. Duvall, it's always best to apply at your peak moment.

And so I ended up applying to five schools. At first it was just going to be UVA, the hardest to get into and only fifteen minutes from home; William and Mary, the second hardest to get into and also my second choice (two hours away); and then University of Richmond and James Madison, both only an hour away, in a tie for third choice. All in state. But then Mrs. Duvall urged me to apply to just one out-of-state school, just in case, just to have the option—so I applied to the University of North Carolina at Chapel Hill. It's really hard to get into out-of-states, but I picked it because it reminds me of UVA. It has a strong liberal arts program, and it's not too far away, close enough to come home in a hurry if I needed to.

But if I had the choice, I would still pick UVA every time. I've never wanted to be far from home. I'm not like my big sister. Going far away, that was her dream. She's always wanted the world. I just want home, and for me, UVA is home, which is why it's the college I've measured all other colleges against. The perfect storybook campus, the perfect everything. And, of course, Peter.

We stay a bit longer, me telling Peter more facts about UVA and Peter making fun of me for knowing so many facts about UVA. Then he drives me home. It's nearly one a.m. when we pull up in front of my house. The downstairs lights are all off, but my dad's bedroom light is on. He never goes to bed until I'm home. I'm about to hop out when Peter reaches across me and stops me from opening the door. "Give me my good-night kiss," he says.

I laugh. "Peter! I have to go."

Stubbornly he closes his eyes and waits, and I lean forward and plant a quick kiss on his lips. "There. Satisfied?"

"No." He kisses me again like we have all the time in the world and says, "What would happen if I came back after everyone went to sleep, and I spent the night, and left really early in the morning? Like, before dawn?"

Smiling, I say, "You can't, so we'll never know."

"But what if?"

"My dad would kill me."

"No, he wouldn't."

"He'd kill you."

"No, he wouldn't."

"No, he wouldn't," I agree. "But he'd be pretty disappointed in me. And he'd be mad at you."

"Only if we got caught," Peter says, but it's halfhearted. He won't risk it either. He's too careful about staying in my dad's good graces. "You know what I'm really looking forward to the most?" He gives my braid a tug before saying, "Not having to say good night. I hate saying good night."

"Me too," I say.

"I can't wait until we're at college."

"Me too," I say, and I kiss him one more time before jumping out of the car and running toward my house. On the way, I look up at the moon, at all the stars that cover the night sky like a blanket, and I make a wish. *Dear God, please, please let me get into UVA.*

2

"*SHOULD I DUST MARIE'S WIG WITH PINK* glitter or gold glitter?*" I hold up an Easter egg to my computer screen for Margot's inspection. I've dyed the shell pale turquoise blue and decoupaged it with a cameo of Marie Antoinette.

"Hold it up closer," Margot says, squinting into the camera. She's in her pajamas; a sheet mask clings to her face. Her hair has grown just past her shoulders, which means she'll probably cut it soon. I have a feeling she'll always keep her hair short now. It really suits her.

It's night in Scotland, and still afternoon here. We are five hours and 3,500 miles apart. She's in her dorm room; I'm sitting at our kitchen table, surrounded by Easter eggs and bowls of dye and rhinestones and stickers and fluffy white feathers that I saved from when I made Christmas ornaments a few years ago. I've got my laptop propped up on a stack of cookbooks. Margot's keeping me company while I finish decorating my eggs. "I think I'm going to do a pearl border around her, if that helps inform your decision," I tell her.

"Then I say go with the pink," she says, adjusting her sheet mask. "Pink will pop more."

"That's what I was thinking too," I say, and I get to work

dusting glitter with an old eye-shadow brush. Last night I spent hours blowing the yolks out of the shells. This was supposed to be a fun thing for Kitty and me to do together like the old days, but she bailed when she was invited over to Madeline Klinger's house. An invitation from Madeline Klinger is a rare and momentous occasion, so of course I couldn't begrudge Kitty that.

"Only a little while longer before you find out, right?"

"Sometime this month." I start lining up pearls in a row. Part of me wishes I could just get this over with, but another part of me is glad to have this time of not knowing, of still hoping.

"You'll get in," Margot says, and it's like a proclamation. Everyone around me seems to think that my getting into UVA is a foregone conclusion. Peter, Kitty, Margot, my dad. My guidance counselor, Mrs. Duvall. I'd never dare say it out loud, for fear of jinxing anything, but maybe I think so too. I've worked hard: I got my SAT scores up by two hundred points. My grades are almost as good as Margot's were, and Margot got in. I've done everything I'm supposed to do, but will it be enough? At this point, all I can do is wait, and hope. And hope and hope.

I'm in the middle of hot-gluing a little white bow to the top of my egg when I stop to cast a suspicious look at my sister. "Wait a minute. If I get in, are you going to try to convince me to go somewhere else, just so I can spread my wings?"

Margot laughs, and her sheet mask slips down her face. Readjusting it, she says, "No. I trust you to know what's best."

She means it, I can tell. Just like that, her words make it so. I trust me too. I trust that when the time comes, I will know what's best. And for me, UVA is best. I know it. "The only thing I'll say is, make your own friends. Peter will be making tons of friends because of lacrosse, and the people he'll be friends with aren't necessarily the kinds of people you'd pick to be friends with. So make your own friends. Find your people. UVA is big."

"I will," I promise.

"And make sure you join the Asian association. The one thing I feel like I've missed out on by going to school in a different country is an Asian-American group. It's definitely a thing, you know, going to college and finding your racial identity. Like Tim."

"Tim who?"

"Tim Monahan, from my class."

"Oh, *Tim*," I say. Tim Monahan is Korean, and he was adopted. There aren't all that many Asian people at our school, so we all know who each other are, at least tangentially.

"He never hung out with Asians in high school, and then he went to Tech and met a ton of Korean people, and now I think he's the president of an Asian fraternity."

"Wow!"

"I'm glad Greek life isn't a thing in the UK. You're not going to join a sorority, are you?" She is quick to add, "No judgment if so!"

"I hadn't thought about it."

"Peter will probably join a fraternity, though."

"He hasn't said anything about it either. . . ." Even though he hasn't mentioned it, I could easily picture Peter in a fraternity.

"I've heard it's hard if your boyfriend's in one and you're not. Something about all the mixers and stuff, like it's easier if you're friends with the girls from the sister sorority. I don't know. The whole thing seems silly to me, but it could be worth it. I hear sorority girls like to craft." She waggles her eyebrows at me.

"Speaking of which." I hold up my egg for her. "Ta-da!"

Margot moves closer to the camera to look. "You should go into the egg-decorating business! I want to see the other ones."

I hold up the egg carton. I've got a dozen blown-out eggs, pale pink with neon pink rickrack trim, brilliant blue and lemon yellow, lavender with dried lavender buds. I was glad to have an excuse to use that dried lavender. I bought a sack of it months ago for a lavender crème brûlée, and it's just been taking up space in our pantry.

"What are you going to do with them?" Margot asks.

"I'm bringing them over to Belleview so they can put them on display in the reception area. It always looks so dreary and hospitaly there."

Margot leans back against her pillows. "How is everyone at Belleview?"

"Fine. I've been so busy with college apps and senior year stuff, I haven't been able to go by as much as I used to. Now that I don't officially work there anymore, it's a lot harder to find the time." I spin the egg in my hand. "I think I'll give this one to Stormy. It's very her." I set the Marie Antoinette egg down on the rack to dry, and I pick up a lilac egg and begin affixing it with candy-colored gemstones. "I'm going to visit more, from here on out."

"It's hard," Margot agrees. "When I come home for spring break, let's go over there together. I want to introduce Ravi to Stormy."

Ravi is Margot's boyfriend of six months. His parents are from India, but he was born in London, so his accent is as posh as you might imagine. When I met him over Skype, I said, "You sound just like Prince William," and he laughed and said, "Cheers." He's two years older than Margot, and maybe it's because he's older, or maybe it's because he's English, but he seems very sophisticated and not at all like Josh. Not in a snobby way, but definitely different. More cultured, probably from living in such a grand city, and going to the theater whenever he wants, and meeting dignitaries and the like because his mother is a diplomat. When I told Margot that, she laughed and said it's just because I haven't gotten to know him yet, but Ravi's actually a huge nerd and not at all smooth or Prince Williamish. "Don't let the accent fool you," she said. She's bringing Ravi home with her over spring break, so I suppose I'll see for myself soon enough. The plan is for Ravi to stay at our house for two nights and then fly to Texas to see relatives. Margot will stay here with us for the rest of the week.

"I can't wait to meet him in real life," I say, and she beams. "You're going to love him."

I'm sure I will. I like everyone Margot likes, but the truly lucky thing is that now that Margot's gotten to know Peter better, she sees how special he is. When Ravi's here, all four of us will be able to hang out, true double dates.

My sister and I are both in love at the same time, and we have this thing we can share, and how wonderful is that!

3

*THE NEXT MORNING, I PUT ON THE POPPY-*colored lipstick Stormy likes me in, gather up my Easter eggs in a white wicker basket, and drive over to Belleview. I stop at the reception desk to drop off the eggs and chat with Shanice for a bit. I ask her what's new, and she says there are two new volunteers, both UVA students, which makes me feel a lot less guilty about not coming around as much.

I say good-bye to Shanice and then head over to Stormy's with my Easter egg. She answers the door in a persimmon-colored kimono and lipstick to match and cries out, "Lara Jean!" After she sweeps me into a hug, she frets, "You're looking at my roots, aren't you? I know I need to dye my hair."

"You can barely tell," I assure her.

She's very excited about her Marie Antoinette egg; she says she can't wait to show it off to Alicia Ito, her friend and rival. "Did you bring one for Alicia, too?" she demands.

"Just you," I tell her, and her pale eyes gleam.

We sit on her couch, and she wags her finger at me and says, "You must be completely moonstruck over your young man since you've barely had time to visit with me."

Contritely I say, "I'm sorry. I'll come visit more now that college applications are in."

"Hmph!"

The best way to deal with Stormy when she's like this is to charm and cajole her. "I'm only doing what you told me, Stormy."

She cocks her head to the side. "What did I tell you?"

"You said to go on lots of dates and lots of adventures, just like you did."

She purses her orangey-red lips, trying not to smile. "Well, that was very good advice I gave you. You just keep listening to Stormy, and you'll be right as rain. Now, tell me something juicy."

I laugh. "My life isn't that juicy."

She tsks me. "Don't you have any dances coming up? When's prom?"

"Not till May."

"Well, do you have a dress?"

"Not yet."

"You'd better get a move on it. You don't want some other girl wearing your dress, dear." She studies my face. "With your complexion, I think you ought to wear pink." Then her eyes light up and she snaps her fingers. "That reminds me! There's something I want to give you." Stormy hops up and goes to her bedroom and she returns with a heavy velvet ring box.

I open the box and let out a gasp. It's her pink diamond ring! The one from the veteran who lost his leg in the war. "Stormy, I can't accept this."

"Oh, but you will. You're just the girl to wear it."

Slowly, I take the ring out and put it on my left hand, and

oh, how it sparkles. "It's beautiful! But I really shouldn't . . ."

"It's yours, darling." Storm winks at me. "Heed my advice, Lara Jean. Never say no when you really want to say yes."

"Then—yes! Thank you, Stormy! I promise I'll take good care of it."

She kisses me on the cheek. "I know you will, dear."

As soon as I get home, I put it in my jewelry box for safekeeping.

Later that day, I'm in the kitchen with Kitty and Peter, waiting for my chocolate chip cookies to cool. For the past few weeks I've been on a quest to perfect my chocolate chip cookie recipe, and Peter and Kitty have been my steadfast passengers on the journey. Kitty prefers a flat, lacy kind of chocolate chip cookie, while Peter likes his chewy. My perfect cookie is a combination of the two. Crunchy but soft. Light brown, not pale in color or flavor. A little height but not puffy. That's the cookie I've been searching for.

I've read all the blog posts, seen the pictures of all white sugar versus a mix of brown and white, of baking soda versus baking powder, vanilla bean versus vanilla extract, chip versus chunk versus chopped bars. I've tried freezing in balls, flattening cookies with the bottom of a glass to get an even spread. I've frozen dough in a log and sliced; I've scooped, then frozen. Frozen, then scooped. And yet, still, my cookies rise too much.

This time I used considerably less baking soda, but the cookies are still vaguely puffy, and I am ready to throw the entire batch out for not being perfect. Of course I don't—that would be a waste of good ingredients. Instead I say to Kitty, "Didn't you say you got in trouble for talking during silent reading last week?" She nods. "Take these to your teacher and tell her you baked them and you're sorry." I'm running low on people to give my cookies to. I've already given some to the mailman, Kitty's bus driver, the nurses' station at Daddy's hospital.

"What will you do when you figure it out?" Kitty asks me, her mouth full of cookie.

"Yeah, what's the point of all this?" Peter says. "I mean, who cares if a chocolate chip cookie is eight percent better? It's still a chocolate chip cookie."

"I'll take pleasure in the knowledge that I am in possession of the perfect chocolate chip cookie recipe. I will pass it down to the next generation of Song girls."

"Or boys," Kitty says.

"Or boys," I agree. To her I say, "Now go upstairs and get a big Mason jar for me to put these cookies in. And a ribbon."

Peter asks, "Will you bring some to school tomorrow?"

"We'll see," I say, because I want to see him make that pouty face I love so much. He makes the face, and I reach up and pat his cheeks. "You're such a baby."

"You love it," he says, snagging another cookie. "Let's get the movie started. I promised my mom I would stop by the store and help her move some furniture around." Peter's mom owns an antiques store called Linden & White, and Peter helps her out as much as he can.

Today's movie off our list is *Romeo + Juliet*, the 1996 version with Leonardo DiCaprio and Claire Danes. Kitty's already seen it a dozen or so times, I've seen bits and pieces, and Peter's never seen it at all.

Kitty drags her beanbag cushion downstairs and arranges herself on the floor with a bag of microwave popcorn beside her. Our wheaten terrier mix Jamie Fox-Pickle immediately plants himself next to her, no doubt hoping for a falling popcorn crumb. Peter and I are on the couch, cuddled under a sheep's-wool blanket that Margot sent from Scotland.

From the moment Leo comes on screen in that navy blue suit, I have chest palpitations. He's like an angel, a beautiful, damaged angel.

"What's he so stressed out about?" Peter asks, reaching down and stealing a handful of Kitty's popcorn. "Isn't he a prince or something?"

"He's not a prince," I say. "He's just rich. And his family is very powerful in this town."

"He's my dream guy," Kitty says in a proprietary tone.

"Well, he's all grown up now," I say, not taking my eyes off the screen. "He's practically Daddy's age." Still . . .

"Wait, I thought *I* was your dream guy," Peter says. Not to me, to Kitty. He knows he's not my dream guy. My dream guy is Gilbert Blythe from *Anne of Green Gables*. Handsome, loyal, smart in school.

"Ew," Kitty says. "You're like my brother."

Peter looks genuinely wounded, so I pat him on the shoulder.

JENNY HAN

"Don't you think he's a little scrawny?" Peter presses.

I shush him.

He crosses his arms. "I don't get why you guys get to talk during movies and I get shushed. It's pretty bullshit."

"It's our house," Kitty says.

"Your sister shushes me at my house too!"

We ignore him in unison.

In the play, Romeo and Juliet were only thirteen. In the movie they're more like seventeen or eighteen. Definitely still teens. How did they know they were meant to be? Just one look across a bathroom fish tank was all it took? They knew it was a love worth dying for? Because they do know. They believe. I guess the difference is, in those times people got married so much younger than they do now. Realistically, till death do us part probably only meant, like, fifteen or twenty years, because people didn't live as long back then.

But when their eyes meet across that fish tank . . . when Romeo goes to her balcony and professes his love . . . I can't help it. I believe too. Even though, I know, they barely know each other, and their story is over before it even truly begins, and the real part would have been in the everyday, in the choosing to be with each other despite all the hardships. Still, I think they could have made it work, if they had only lived.

As the credits roll, tears roll down my cheeks and even Peter looks sad; but unsentimental, dry-eyed little Kitty just hops up and says she's taking Jamie Fox-Pickle outside to pee. Off they go, and meanwhile I'm still lost in my emotions on the couch, wiping tears from my eyes. "They had such a good meet-cute," I croak.

"What's a meet-cute?" Peter's lying on his side now, his head propped up on his elbow. He looks so adorable I could pinch his cheeks, but I refrain from saying so. His head is big enough as it is.

"A meet-cute is when the hero and heroine meet for the very first time, and it's always in a charming way. It's how you know they're going to end up together. The cuter the better."

"Like in *Terminator*, when Reese saves Sarah Connor from the Terminator and he says, 'Come with me if you want to live.' Freaking amazing line."

"I mean, sure, I guess that's technically a meet-cute. . . . I was thinking more like *It Happened One Night*. We should add that to our list."

"Is that in color or black-and-white?"

"Black-and-white."

Peter groans and falls back against the couch cushions.

"It's too bad we don't have a meet-cute," I muse.

"You jumped me in the hallway at school. I think that's pretty cute."

"But we already knew each other, so it doesn't really count." I frown. "We don't even remember how we met. How sad."

"I remember meeting you for the first time."

"Nuh-uh. Liar!"

"Hey just because you don't remember something doesn't mean I don't. I remember a lot of things."

"Okay, so how did we meet?" I challenge. I'm sure that whatever comes out of his mouth next will be a lie.

Peter opens his mouth, then snaps it shut. "I'm not telling."

"See! You just can't think of anything."

"No, you don't deserve to know, because you don't believe me."

I roll my eyes. "So full of it."

After I turn off the movie, Peter and I go sit on the front porch, drinking sweet tea I made the night before. It's cool out; there's still enough bite in the air to let you know it isn't quite full-on spring yet, but soon. The dogwood tree in our front yard is just beginning to flower. There is a nice breeze. I think I could sit here all afternoon and watch the branches sway and bow and the leaves dance.

We still have a little time before he has to go help his mom. I would go with him, mind the register while he moves around furniture, but the last time Peter brought me, his mom frowned and said her store was a place of business, not a "teenage hangout." Peter's mom doesn't outwardly dislike me, and I don't even think she inwardly dislikes me—but she still hasn't forgiven me for breaking up with Peter last year. She's kind to me, but there's this distrust, this wariness. It's a let's-wait-and-see kind of feeling—let's wait and see when you hurt my son again. I'd always imagined I would have a great, Ina Garten–type relationship with my first boyfriend's mom. The two of us cooking dinner together, sharing tea and sympathy, playing Scrabble on a rainy afternoon.

"What are you thinking about?" Peter asks me. "You've got that look."

I chew on my lower lip. "I wish your mom liked me better."

"She does like you."

"Peter." I give him a look.

"She does! If she didn't like you, she wouldn't invite you over for dinner."

"She invites me over for dinner because she wants to see you, not me."

"Untrue." I can tell this thought has never occurred to him, but it has the ring of truth and he knows it.

"She wishes we'd break up before we leave for college," I blurt out.

"So does your sister."

I crow, "Ha! So you're admitting your mom wants us to break up!" I don't know what I'm being so triumphant about. The thought is depressing, even if I already suspected it.

"She thinks getting serious when you're young is a bad idea. It has nothing to do with you. I told her, just because it didn't work out with you and Dad, it doesn't mean it'll be like that for us. I'm nothing like my dad. And you're nothing like my mom."

Peter's parents got divorced when he was in sixth grade. His dad lives about thirty minutes away, with his new wife and two young sons. When it comes to his dad, Peter doesn't say much. It's rare for him to even bring him up, but this year, out of the blue, his dad has been trying to reconnect with him—inviting him to a basketball game, over to his house for dinner. So far Peter's been a stone wall.

"Does your dad look like you?" I ask. "I mean, do you look like him?"

Sullenly he says, "Yeah. That's what people always say."

I put my head on his shoulder. "Then he must be very handsome."

"Back in the day, I guess," he concedes. "I'm taller than him now."

This is a thing that Peter and I have in common—he only has a mom and I only have a dad. He thinks I got the better end of the deal, losing a mom who loved me versus a dad who is alive but a dirtbag. His words, not mine. Part of me agrees with him, because I have so many good memories of Mommy, and he has hardly any of his dad.

I loved how after a bath, I would sit cross-legged in front of her and watch TV while she combed the tangles out of my hair. I remember Margot used to hate to sit still for it, but I didn't mind. It's the kind of memory I like best— more of a feeling than an actual remembrance. The hum of a memory, blurry around the edges, soft and nothing particularly special, all kind of blending into one moment. Another memory like that is when we'd drop Margot off at piano lessons, and Mommy and I would have secret ice cream sundaes in the McDonald's parking lot. Caramel and strawberry sauce; she'd give me her peanuts so I had extra. Once I asked her why she didn't like nuts on her sundae, and she said she did like them, but I *loved* them. And she loved me.

But despite all of these good memories, memories I wouldn't trade for anything, I know that even if my mom was a dirtbag, I'd rather have her here with me than not. One day, I hope Peter will feel that way about his dad.

"What are you thinking about now?" Peter asks me.

"My mom," I say.

Peter sets down his glass and stretches out and rests his head in my lap. Looking up at me, he says, "I wish I could've met her."

"She would've really liked you," I say, touching his hair. Hesitantly, I ask, "Do you think I might get to meet your dad some day?"

A cloud passes over his face, and I wish I hadn't brought it up. "You don't want to meet him," he says. "He's not worth it." Then he snuggles closer to me. "Hey, maybe we should go as Romeo and Juliet for Halloween this year. People at UVA go all out for Halloween."

I lean back against the post. He's changing the subject, and I know it but I play along. "So we'd be going as the Leo and Claire version of Romeo and Juliet."

"Yeah." He tugs on my braid. "I'll be your knight in shining armor."

I touch his hair. "Would you be willing to consider growing your hair out a little bit? And maybe . . . dyeing it blond? Otherwise people might think you're just a knight."

Peter is laughing so hard I doubt he hears the rest of my

sentence. "Oh my God, Covey. Why are you so hilarious?"

"I was joking!" Half joking. "But you know I take costuming seriously. Why bother doing something if you're only going to do it halfway?"

"Okay, I would maybe wear a wig, but I'm not promising anything. It'll be our first UVA Halloween."

"I've been to UVA for Halloween before." The first fall Margot got her driver's license, we took Kitty trick-or-treating on the lawn. She was Batman that year. I wonder if she might like to do that again.

"I mean we'll finally be able to go to UVA Halloween parties. Like, legit go to them and not have to sneak in. Sophomore year me and Gabe got kicked out of an SAE party and it was the most embarrassing moment of my life."

I look at him in surprise. "You? You're never embarrassed."

"Well, I was that day. I was trying to talk to this girl who was dressed up in a Cleopatra costume and these older guys were like, 'Get your ass out of here, scrub,' and she and her friends laughed. Jerks."

I lean down and kiss him on both cheeks. "I would never laugh."

"You laugh at me all the time," he says. He lifts his head up and pulls my face closer and we are kissing an upside-down Spider-Man type of kiss.

"You like it when I laugh at you," I say, and, smiling, he shrugs.

4

IT'S THE FIRST DAY OF SENIOR WEEK, AND during Senior Week, every day there's a theme. Today's theme is school spirit, and I'm wearing Peter's lacrosse jersey and pigtails with yarn ribbons in our school colors, light blue and white. Peter has painted his face half blue and half white. When he picked me up this morning, I screamed when I saw him.

The rest of the week goes: Tuesday seventies day, Wednesday pajamas day, Thursday characters day (the day I am truly looking forward to), and Friday we're off on our senior trip. The vote was between New York City and Disney World, and New York won. We're driving up on a charter bus for the three-day weekend. It's perfect timing for a trip like this, because the seniors are going crazy waiting to hear from colleges and we could all use a distraction. Except for those of us who applied early decision and already know where they're going, like Peter, and Lucas Krapf, who's going to Sarah Lawrence. The majority of my class will stay in state. It's like our guidance counselor, Mrs. Duvall, is always saying: What's the point of living in Virginia if not to take advantage of all the great state schools? I think it's nice that so many of us will still be here in Virginia, that we aren't scattering off to the four corners of the earth.

At lunchtime, when Peter and I walk into the cafeteria, the a cappella group is serenading a junior girl with the song "Will You Still Love Me Tomorrow?" but with the words "Will You Go to Prom with Me, Gina?" We stop and listen before we get in line for our food. Prom isn't for another few months, but promposals have already started in earnest. So far the most impressive was last week, when Steve Bledell hacked into the announcements board and replaced the day's events with *Will you go to prom with me, Liz?* and it took two days for the IT department to figure out how to fix it. Just this morning, Darrell filled Pammy's locker with red roses, and he spelled out *PROM?* in petals on the door. The janitor yelled at him for it, but the pictures look amazing on Pammy's Instagram. I don't know what Peter's planning. He's not exactly one for big romantic gestures.

When we're in line for food, Peter reaches for a brownie and I say, "Don't—I brought cookies," and he gets excited.

"Can I have one now?" he asks. I pull my Tupperware out of my bag and Peter grabs one. "Let's not share with anybody else," he says.

"Too late," I say, because our friends have spotted us.

Darrell is singing, "Her cookies bring all the boys to the yard," as we walk up to the table. I set the Tupperware down on the table and the boys wrestle for it, snatching cookies and gobbling them up like trolls.

Pammy manages to snag one and says, "Y'all are beasts."

Darrell throws his head back and makes a beastlike sound, and she giggles.

"These are amazing," Gabe groans, licking chocolate off his fingers.

Modestly I say, "They're all right. Good, but not amazing. Not perfect." I break a piece off of Peter's cookie. "They taste better fresh out of the oven."

"Will you please come over to my house and bake me cookies so I know what they taste like fresh out of the oven?" Gabe bites into another one and closes his eyes in ecstasy.

Peter snags one. "Stop eating all my girlfriend's cookies!" Even a year later, it still gives me a little thrill to hear him say "my girlfriend" and know that I'm her.

"You're gonna get a gut if you don't quit with that shit," Darrell says.

Peter takes a bite of cookie and lifts up his shirt and pats his stomach. "Six-pack, baby."

"You're a lucky girl, Large," Gabe says.

Darrell shakes his head. "Nah, Kavinsky's the lucky one."

Peter catches my eye and winks, and my heart beats quicker.

I have a feeling that when I'm Stormy's age, these everyday moments will be what I remember: Peter's head bent, biting into a chocolate chip cookie; the sun coming through the cafeteria window, bouncing off his brown hair; him looking at me.

After school, Peter has lacrosse practice, and I sit in the stands and do my homework. Of all the guys on the team, Peter is the only one going to a division one school, and Coach White is already crying about what the team will look like when Peter's gone. I don't understand all the ins and outs of the game, but I know when to cheer and when to boo. I just like to watch him play. He thinks every shot he takes will go in, and they usually do.

Daddy and Ms. Rothschild are, officially, a couple, and they have been since last September. Kitty's over the moon; she takes credit for it at every opportunity. "It was all a part of my master plan," she brags. I'll give it to her. The girl does have vision. After all, she got Peter and me back together against all the odds, and now we're in love.

For not having a lot in common, Ms. Rothschild and Daddy are a surprisingly good couple. (Again, not unlike Peter and me.) Proximity really does make all the difference. Two lonely neighbors, Netflix, a couple of dogs, a bottle of white wine. If you ask me, it's lovely. Daddy has way more of a life now that Ms. Rothschild's in it. They're always going places together, doing actual activities. Like on a Saturday morning, before any of us are awake, they'll go hiking and watch the sun rise. I've never known Daddy to hike, but he's taken to it like a fish to water. They go out to dinner; they go to wineries; they meet up with Ms. Rothschild's friends. Sure, he still likes to stay in and watch a documentary, but his world is so much more with her in it—and so much less lonely, which I never knew he was, these eight long years since Mommy died. But he must have been, now that I see him so energized and so out and about. Ms. Rothschild eats with us at least a few times a week, and it's gotten to where it feels strange to not see her sitting there at the kitchen table, with her rich, throaty laugh and her glass of white wine next to Daddy's glass of beer.

After dinner that night, when I bring out cookies and ice cream for dessert, Daddy says, "More cookies?" and he and Ms. Rothschild exchange a meaningful look. Spreading vanilla ice cream on a cookie with a spoon, Daddy says, "You've been doing a lot of baking lately. You must be pretty stressed waiting on those college acceptance letters."

"It has nothing to do with that," I tell them. "I'm only trying to perfect my chocolate chip cookie recipe. Just be grateful, you guys."

Daddy begins, "You know, I read a study that found that baking is actually therapeutic. It's something to do with the repetition of measuring ingredients, and creativity. Psychologists call it behavioral activation."

"Hey, whatever works," Ms. Rothschild says, breaking a piece of cookie off and popping it into her mouth. "I go to SoulCycle; that's where I find my center." If Margot were here, she'd roll her eyes at that. Ms. Rothschild made me go with her once—I kept losing the beat and trying to find it again but to no avail. "Lara Jean, you've got to come with me again. There's a great new instructor who plays all Motown music. You'll love it."

"When can I go with you, Tree?" Kitty asks. That's what Kitty's taken to calling Ms. Rothschild. I still think of her as Ms. Rothschild, and I slip up from time to time, but I try to call her Trina to her face when I remember.

"You can come with me when you're twelve," she says. "Those are the rules of SoulCycle."

It's hard to believe that Kitty is eleven already. Kitty is eleven and I'll be eighteen in May. Time goes by so quickly. I look across the table at Daddy, who is looking at Kitty with a sad kind of smile, and then at me. I know he must be thinking the same thing.

He catches my eye and sings, "Lara Jean, don't you worry 'bout a thing," in his best Stevie Wonder voice, and we all groan. Biting into his makeshift ice cream sandwich, Daddy says, "You've worked hard; everything will turn out the way it's supposed to."

"There's no way in the world that UVA would ever say no to you," Ms. Rothschild says.

"Knock on wood," Kitty says, rapping the kitchen table with her knuckle. To me she says, "You knock too."

Dutifully I knock on the table. "What does knock on wood even mean?"

Daddy perks up. "Actually, it's thought to come from Greek mythology. According to Greek myths, dryads lived in trees, and people would invoke them for protection. Hence knocking on wood: just that added bit of protection so as not to tempt fate."

Now it's Ms. Rothschild, Kitty, and me exchanging a look. Daddy's so square, and Ms. Rothschild seems so young compared to him, even though he's not that much older than her. And yet it works.

★ ★ ★

That night I can't fall asleep, so I lie in bed going over my extracurriculars again. The highlights are Belleview and my internship at the library last summer. My SAT score is higher than the UVA average. Margot got in with just forty more than me. I got a five on the AP US history exam. I've known people to get into UVA with less than that.

Hopefully my essay gave me a bit of shine. I wrote about my mom and my sisters, and all the ways she's shaped us—when she was alive and after she wasn't. Mrs. Duvall said it was the best she'd read in years, but Mrs. Duvall has always had a soft spot for the Song girls, so who knows.

I toss and turn for another few minutes, and finally I just throw off my covers and get out of bed. Then I go downstairs and start measuring out ingredients for chocolate chip cookies.

5

IT'S THURSDAY, CHARACTERS DAY, THE DAY
I've been looking forward to all week. Peter and I spent
hours going back and forth over this. I made a strong case
for Alexander Hamilton and Eliza Schuyler, but had to back
down when I realized how expensive it would be to rent
Colonial costumes on such short notice. I think couples
costumes might be my favorite part of being in a couple.
Besides the kissing, and the free rides, and Peter himself.

He wanted to go as Spider-Man and have me wear a red
wig and be Mary Jane Watson, mostly because he already had
the costume—and because he's really fit from lacrosse, and
why not give the people what they want? His words, not mine.

In the end we decided to go as Tyler Durden and Marla
Singer from *Fight Club*. It was actually my best friend Chris's
idea. She and Kitty and I were watching it at my house, and
Chris said, you and Kavinsky should go as those psychos.
She said it would be good for the shock value—for me, anyway. At first I balked because Marla isn't Asian and I have my
only-Asian-people-costumes policy, but then Peter's mom
found him a red leather jacket at an estate sale, and it just
came together. As for my costume, Ms. Rothschild is loaning
me clothes from her own wardrobe, because she was young
in the nineties.

This morning, Ms. Rothschild comes over before work to help me get ready. I'm sitting at the kitchen table in her black slip dress and a fake mohair jacket and a wig, which Kitty delights in messing up to get that crazy bedhead look. I keep swatting her moussed-up hands away, and she keeps saying, "But this is the look."

"You're lucky I'm a pack rat," Ms. Rothschild says, sipping coffee from her thermos. She reaches into her bag and tosses me a pair of high, high black platform heels. "When I was in my twenties, Halloween was my thing. I was the queen of dressing up. It's your turn to take the crown now, Lara Jean."

"You can still be the queen," I tell her.

"No, dressing up in costumes is a young person's game. If I wore a sexy Sherlock Holmes costume now, I'd just look desperate." She fluffs up my wig. "It's all right. My time has passed." To Kitty she says, "What do you think? A little more gunmetal eye shadow, right?"

"Let's not take it too far," I say. "This is still school."

"The whole point of wearing a costume is taking it too far," Ms. Rothschild says airily. "Take lots of pictures when you get to school. Text them to me so I can show my work friends. They'll get a kick out of it. . . . God, speaking of work, what time is it?"

Ms. Rothschild is always running late, something that drives Daddy crazy because he's always ten minutes early. And yet!

When Peter comes to pick me up, I run outside and open the passenger-side door and scream when I see him. His hair is blond!

"Oh my God!" I shriek, touching his hair. "Did you bleach it?"

He grins a self-satisfied kind of grin. "It's spray. My mom found it for me. I can use it again when we do Romeo and Juliet for Halloween." He's eyeing me in my getup. "I like those shoes. You look sexy."

I can feel my cheeks warm up. "Be quiet."

As he backs out of my driveway, he glances at me again and says, "It's the truth, though."

I give him a shove. "All I'm saying is, people better know who I am."

"I've got you covered," he assures me.

And he does. When we walk down the senior hallway, Peter cues up the Pixies' "Where Is My Mind?" on his phone, loud, and people actually clap for us. Not one person asks if I'm a manga character.

After school, Peter and I are lying on the couch; his feet are hanging off the end. He's still in his costume, but I've changed into my regular clothes. "You always have the cutest socks," he says, lifting up my right foot. These ones are gray with white polka dots and yellow bear faces.

Proudly I say, "My great-aunt sends them from Korea. Korea has the cutest stuff, you know."

"Can you ask her to send me some too? Not bears, but maybe, like, tigers. Tigers are cool."

"Your feet are too big for socks as cute as these. Your toes would pop right out. You know what, I bet I could find you some socks that fit at . . . um, the zoo." Peter sits up and starts tickling me. I gasp out, "I bet the—pandas or gorillas have to—keep their feet warm somehow . . . in the winter. Maybe they have some kind of deodorized sock technology as well." I burst into giggles. "Stop . . . stop tickling me!"

"Then stop being mean about my feet!" I've got my hand burrowed under his arm, and I am tickling him ferociously. But by doing so, I have opened myself up to more attacks.

I yell, "Okay, okay, truce!" He stops, and I pretend to stop, but sneak a tickle under his arm, and he lets out a high-pitched un-Peter-like shriek.

"You said truce!" he accuses. We both nod and lie back down, out of breath. "Do you really think my feet smell?"

I don't. I love the way he smells after a lacrosse game—like sweat and grass and him. But I love to tease, to see that unsure look cross his face for just half a beat. "Well, I mean, on game days . . . ," I say. Then Peter attacks me again, and we're wrestling around, laughing, when Kitty walks in, balancing a tray with a cheese sandwich and a glass of orange juice.

"Take it upstairs," she says, sitting down on the floor. "This is a public area."

Disentangling myself, I give her a glare. "We aren't doing anything private, *Katherine*."

"Your sister says my feet stink," Peter says, pointing his foot in her direction. "She's lying, isn't she?"

She deflects it with a pop of her elbow. "I'm not smelling your foot." She shudders. "You guys are kinky."

I yelp and throw a pillow at her.

JENNY HAN

She gasps. "You're lucky you didn't knock over my juice! Daddy will kill you if you mess up the rug again." Pointedly she says, "Remember the nail-polish-remover incident?"

Peter ruffles my hair. "Clumsy Lara Jean."

I shove him away from me. "I'm not clumsy. You're the one who tripped over his own feet trying to get to the pizza the other night at Gabe's."

Kitty bursts into giggles and Peter throws a pillow at her. "You guys need to stop ganging up on me!" he yells.

"Are you staying for dinner?" she asks when her giggles subside.

"I can't. My mom's making chicken fried steak."

Kitty's eyes bulge. "Lucky. Lara Jean, what are we having?"

"I'm defrosting some chicken breasts as we speak," I say. She makes a face, and I say, "If you don't like it, maybe you could learn to cook. I won't be around to cook your dinners anymore when I'm at college, you know."

"Yeah, right. You'll probably be here every night." She turns to Peter. "Can I come to your house for dinner?"

"Sure," he says. "You can both come."

Kitty starts to cheer, and I shush her. "We can't, because then Daddy will have to eat alone. Ms. Rothschild has Soul-Cycle tonight."

She takes a bite of her cheese sandwich. "I'm making myself another sandwich, then. I don't want to eat old freezer-burn chicken."

I sit up suddenly. "Kitty, I'll make something else if you'll braid my hair tomorrow morning. I want to do something special for New York." I've never been to New York before in my life. For our last family vacation, we took a vote, and I picked New York, but I was voted down in favor of Mexico. Kitty wanted to eat fish tacos and swim in the ocean, and Margot wanted to see Mayan ruins and have a chance to work on her Spanish. In the end, I was happy to be outvoted. Before Mexico, Kitty and I had never even left the country. I've never seen water so blue.

"I'll braid your hair only if I have time left over after I do mine," Kitty says, which is the best I can hope for, I suppose. She's just so good at doing hair.

"Who will braid my hair when I'm at college?" I muse.

"I will," Peter says, all confidence.

"You don't know how," I scoff.

"The kid will teach me. Won't you, kid?"

"For a price," Kitty says.

They negotiate back and forth before finally settling on Peter taking Kitty and her friends to the movies one Saturday afternoon. Which is how I come to be sitting cross-legged on the floor while Peter and Kitty sit on the couch above me, Kitty demonstrating a French braid and Peter recording it on his phone.

"Now you try it," she says.

He keeps losing a piece and getting frustrated. "You have a lot of hair, Lara Jean."

"If you can't get the French, I'll teach you something more basic," Kitty says, and there is no mistaking the contempt in her voice.

JENNY HAN

Peter hears it too. "No, I'm gonna get it. Just give me a second. I'm gonna master it just like I mastered the other kind of French." He winks at me.

Kitty and I both scream at him for that. "Don't talk like that in front of my sister!" I yell, shoving him in the chest.

"I was kidding!"

"Also, you're not *that* good at French kissing." Even though, yeah, he is.

Peter gives me a *Who are you kidding?* look, and I shrug, because who *am* I kidding?

Later, I'm walking Peter to his car when he stops in front of the passenger-side door and asks, "Hey, how many guys have you kissed?"

"Just three. You, John Ambrose McClaren—" I say his name fast, like ripping off a Band-Aid, but Peter still has enough time to scowl. "And Allie Feldman's cousin."

"The kid with the lazy eye?"

"Yeah. His name was Ross. I thought he was cute. It happened at a sleepover at Allie's; I kissed him on a dare. But I wanted to."

He gives me a speculative look. "So me, John, and Allie's cousin."

"Uh-huh."

"You're forgetting one person, Covey."

"Who?"

"Sanderson!"

I wave my hand. "Oh, that doesn't really count."

"Allie Feldman's cousin Ross who you kissed on a dare counts, but not *Josh*, who you technically cheated on me with?" Peter wags his finger at me. "Nuh-uh. I don't think so."

I shove him. "We weren't actually together then and you know it!"

"A technicality, but okay." He gives me a sidelong look. "Your number's higher than mine, you know. I've only ever kissed Gen, Jamila, and you."

"What about the girl you met at Myrtle Beach with your cousins? Angelina?"

A funny look crosses over his face. "Oh yeah. How'd you know about that?"

"You bragged about it to everyone!" It was the summer before seventh grade. I remember it drove Genevieve crazy, that some other girl had kissed Peter before she did. We tried to find Angelina online, but we didn't have much to go on. Just her name. "So that makes it four girls you've kissed, and you did a lot more with them than kiss, Peter."

"Fine!"

I'm on a roll now. "You're the only boy I've ever *kissed* kissed. And you were the first. First kiss, first boyfriend, first everything! You got so many of my firsts, and I didn't get any from you."

Sheepishly he says, "Actually that's not entirely true."

I narrow my eyes. "What do you mean?"

"There was never any girl at the beach. I made the whole thing up."

"There was no Angelina with big boobs?"

"I never said she had big boobs!"

"Yes you did. You told Trevor that."

"Okay, fine! Geez. You're missing the whole point, by the way."

"What's the whole point, Peter?"

He clears his throat. "That day in McClaren's basement. You were my first kiss too."

Abruptly I stop laughing. "I was?"

"Yeah."

I stare at him. "Why didn't you ever tell me?"

"I don't know. I guess I forgot. Also it's embarrassing that I made up a girl. Don't tell anybody!"

I'm filled with a glowy kind of wonder. So I was Peter Kavinsky's first kiss. How perfectly wonderful!

I throw my arms around him and lift my chin expectantly, waiting for my good-night kiss. He nuzzles his face against mine, and I feel gladness for the fact that he has smooth cheeks and barely even needs to shave. I close my eyes, breathe him in, wait for my kiss. And he plants a chaste peck on my forehead. "Good night, Covey."

My eyes fly open. "That's all I get?"

Smugly he says, "You said earlier that I'm not that good at kissing, remember?"

"I was kidding!"

He winks at me as he hops in his car. I watch him drive away. Even after a whole year of being together, it can still feel so new. To love a boy, to have him love you back. It feels miraculous.

I don't go inside right away. Just in case he comes back. Hands on my hips, I wait a full twenty seconds before I turn toward the front steps, which is when his car comes peeling back down our street and stops right in front of our house. Peter sticks his head out the window. "All right then," he calls out. "Let's practice."

I run back to his car, I pull him toward me by his shirt, and angle my face against his—and then I push him away and run backward, laughing, my hair whipping around my face.

"Covey!" he yells.

"That's what you get!" I call back gleefully. "See you on the bus tomorrow!"

That night, when we're in the bathroom brushing our teeth, I ask Kitty, "On a scale of one to ten, how much will you miss me when I go to college? Be honest."

"It's too early for this kind of talk," she says, rinsing her toothbrush.

"Just answer."

"A four."

"A four! You said you missed Margot a six point five!"

Kitty shakes her head at me. "Lara Jean, why do you have to remember every little thing? It's not healthy."

"The least you can do is pretend you'll miss me!" I burst out. "It's the decent thing to do."

"Margot was going all the way across the world. You're

only going fifteen minutes away, so I won't even have a chance to miss you."

"Still."

She clasps her hands to her heart. "Okay. How's this? I'm going to miss you so much I'll cry every night!"

I smile. "That's more like it."

"I'll miss you so much, I'll want to slit my wrists!" She cackles wildly.

"Katherine. Don't talk like that!"

"Then quit fishing for compliments," she says, and she goes off to bed, while I stay behind and pack up my toiletries for the New York trip tomorrow. If I get into UVA, I'll probably just keep a set of my makeup and creams and combs here at home, so I won't have to pack every time. Margot had to be so careful about what she brought with her to Saint Andrews, because Scotland is so far away and she isn't able to make the trip back home very often. I'll probably only pack for fall and winter and leave all my summer things at home, and then just switch them out when the seasons change.

6

IN THE MORNING, DADDY DRIVES ME TO
school to catch the charter bus. "Call me as soon as you're
settled in your room," he says as we wait at the traffic light
by school.

"I will."

"Did you pack the emergency twenty?"

"Yes." Last night, Daddy gave me a twenty-dollar bill to
put in the secret pocket of my jacket, just in case. I have his
credit card, too, for spending money. Ms. Rothschild loaned
me her tiny umbrella and her portable cell phone charger.

Daddy gives me a sidelong look and a sigh. "It's all happening so fast now. First your senior trip, then prom, then
graduation. Only a matter of time before you're out of the
house too."

"You'll still have Kitty," I say. "Though it's true that she
isn't exactly the ray of sunshine that I am." He laughs. "If
I get into UVA, I'll be around all the time, so don't you
worry about a thing." I sing it the way he does, like Stevie
Wonder.

On the bus I sit next to Peter; Chris sits with Lucas. I thought
it might be a tough sell to get Chris to come on the senior
trip, and it would have been, if Disney World had won out.

But she's never been to New York before either, so it ended up being easy peasy.

We're on the road for an hour before Peter engages everybody in a game of Never Have I Ever, which I pretend to be asleep for, because I have not done much of anything, drugs-wise or sex-wise, and that's all anybody cares about. Mercifully, the game dies down pretty fast, I suppose because it's a lot less exciting when there are no red Solo cups involved. Just as I'm opening my eyes and stretching my arms and "waking up," Gabe suggests Truth or Dare, and my stomach takes a nosedive.

Ever since Peter's and my hot tub video scandal last year, I've felt self-conscious about what people might be thinking about what we do or don't do. Sex-wise, I mean. And Truth or Dare is miles worse than Never Have I Ever! *How many people have you had sex with? Have you ever been in a threeway? How many times a day do you jerk off?* Those are the kinds of questions people ask each other, and if anybody ever asked them of me, I would have to say that I'm a virgin, and in some ways, that's even more subversive than any other answer. Usually, I slip away to the kitchen or another room when this game gets started at other parties. But there's nowhere for me to slip away to today, for we are on a bus, and I am well and truly trapped.

Peter gives me an amused look. He knows what I'm thinking. He says he doesn't care what people think, but I know that's not true. Historically, Peter cares very much what other people think of him.

"Truth or dare," Gabe says to Lucas.

Lucas takes a swig of his Vitaminwater. "Truth."

"Have you ever had sex with a dude?"

My whole body goes tight. Lucas is gay, and he's out, but he isn't *out* out. He doesn't want to deal with having to explain himself to people all the time, and why should he have to? It's not like it's anybody else's business.

There's a quick beat before Lucas says, "No. Is that an offer?"

Everybody laughs, and Lucas has a slight smile on his face as he takes another swig of Vitaminwater, but I can see the tension in his neck, his shoulders. It must take a toll, having to be on guard for these kinds of questions, ready to deflect, to smile, to laugh it off. My virginity question is tiny in comparison. But I still don't want to answer.

I pray that Lucas picks me next, because I know he'll go easy on me. But Lucas must not notice the pleading glances I am throwing his way, because instead of picking me, he chooses Genevieve, who is sitting a few rows back, looking at her phone. She's been dating a guy from her church and he goes to a different school, so no one sees her around as much. I heard from Chris that her parents got divorced, and that her dad moved into a new condo with his girlfriend. Chris said Genevieve's mom had a breakdown and had to be hospitalized for a few days, but things are better now, which I'm glad for. Peter sent daffodils to her mom when she came back home, and we labored over what the card should say—we finally decided on just *Be well, Wendy. Love, Peter.* The flowers were my idea, and I chipped in, but of course I didn't put my name on the card. I've just always liked Wendy; she's been nice to me since I was little. I still get that nervous dip in my stomach when I see Genevieve, but not as bad as it used to be. I know we'll never be friends again, and I've made my peace with it.

"Truth or dare, Gen," Lucas calls out.

She looks up. Automatically she says, "Dare." Of course Genevieve picks dare; she's a lot of things, but she's no coward. I'd rather do anything than answer a sex question, so I'll likely be picking dare too.

Lucas dares Genevieve to go sit next to Mr. Jain and put her head on his shoulder. "Make it believable," Lucas says. Everyone howls with laughter. I can tell she really doesn't want to do it, but again, she's not a coward.

We all watch as she makes her way up the aisle and then stops at Mr. Jain's row. Mr. Jain is new this year; he teaches biology. He's on the younger side, handsome; he wears skinny jeans with button-downs to school. Genevieve slides into the seat next to him, and all I can see is the back of her head as she talks. He's smiling. Then she snuggles closer to him and drops her head on his shoulder, and he jumps like a scared cat. Everyone is laughing, and Mr. Jain turns around and shakes his head at us, looking relieved it was a joke.

Genevieve returns to us, triumphant. She takes her seat and looks around the group; our eyes meet for a moment, and my stomach dips. Then she looks away. "Truth or dare, Chrissy."

"This game is so lame," Chris says. Gen just stares at her,

eyebrows raised in challenge, and Chris finally rolls her eyes and says, "Whatever. Truth." When they go head-to-head like this, it's impossible not to notice that they are related—first cousins, on their moms' side.

Genevieve takes her time thinking up her question. Then she lands the whammy. "Did you or did you not play doctor with our cousin Alex when we were in third grade? And don't lie."

Everyone is whooping and hollering, and Chris's face has gone bright red. I give her a sympathetic look. I know the answer to this one. "True," she mutters, and everyone howls.

Luckily for me, this is about when Mr. Jain gets up and puts a DVD in the DVD player, so the game dissolves and my turn never comes. Chris turns around and says to me in a low voice, "You got off so easy."

"Don't I know it," I whisper back, and Peter chuckles. He can chuckle all he wants, but I'm sure he's a little relieved too. Not that he's ever said so, but it's not like he'd want the whole senior class to know that he and his girlfriend of a year—longer, if you count our fake relationship—have never had sex before.

Hardly anybody in our class has been to New York City, so we're all just a little wide-eyed about it. I don't think I've ever been in a place so alive. It's a city that has its own heartbeat. I just can't believe how many people there are, how crowded it is, how sophisticated everyone looks. They all look like—like city people. Except for the tourists like us, of course. Chris tries to act bored and unfazed by it all, but when we get on the subway to go to the Empire State Building, she doesn't hold on to the pole and nearly falls over when we come to a sudden stop. "It's different than in DC," she mutters. That's for sure. DC is the closest big city to Charlottesville, but it's still a sleepy little town compared to New York. There's so much to see, so many stores I wish we could stop in. Everyone is in a hurry; they all have plans and places to be. Peter gets screamed at by an old lady for walking and looking at his cell phone, which makes everyone laugh, and for once, Peter is embarrassed. It's all so overwhelming.

When we get to the Empire State Building, I make Peter take a selfie with me at the elevators. At the top, I feel light-headed, we're so high up. Ms. Davenport tells me to sit with my head between my knees for a minute, which helps. When the nausea passes, I get up and go looking for Peter, who has disappeared during my time of need.

As I turn the corner, I hear Peter calling out, "Wait! Wait! Sir!" He's following a security guard who is approaching a red backpack on the floor.

The security guard bends down and picks it up. "Is this yours?" he demands.

"Uh, yeah—"

"Why did you leave it on the ground?" He unzips the backpack and pulls out a teddy bear.

Peter's eyes dart around. "Can you put that back inside? It's for a promposal for my girlfriend. It's supposed to be a surprise."

The security guard is shaking his head. He mutters to

himself and starts looking in the backpack again.

"Sir, please just squeeze the bear."

"I'm not squeezing the bear," the security guard tells him.

Peter reaches out and squeezes the teddy bear and the bear squeaks out, "Will you go to prom with me, Lara Jean?"

I clap my hands to my mouth in delight.

Sternly the security guard says, "You're in New York City, kid. You can't just leave a backpack on the ground for your proposal."

"It's actually called a *promposal*," Peter corrects, and the security guard gives him a look. "Sorry. Can I just have the bear back?" He spots me then. "Tell him *Sleepless in Seattle* is your favorite movie, Lara Jean!"

I rush over. "Sir, it's my favorite movie. Please don't kick him out."

The security guard is trying not to smile. "I wasn't going to kick him out," he says to me. To Peter he says, "Just be more aware next time. In New York, we're vigilant. If we see something, we say something, do you feel me? This is not whatever little country town you guys are from. This is *New York City*. We do not play around here."

Both Peter and I nod, and the security guard walks away. As soon as he's gone, Peter and I look at each other and break out into giddy laughter. "Somebody reported my book bag!" he says. "My promposal got fucked."

I take the teddy bear out of his bag and hug it to my chest. I'm so happy I don't even tell him not to cuss. "I love it."

"You were going to turn the corner, and see the book bag

right here by the telescopes. Then you were going to pick up the bear, and squeeze it, and—"

"How was I going to know to squeeze it?" I ask.

Peter pulls a crumpled piece of paper out of the bag. It says, *Squeeze Me.* "It fell off when the security guard was manhandling it. See? I thought of everything."

Everything except the ramifications of leaving an unattended bag in a public place in New York City, but still! It's the thought that counts, and the thought is the sweetest. I squeeze the bear, and again he says, "Will you go to prom with me, Lara Jean?" "Yes, I will, Howard." Howard is, of course, the name of the bear from *Sleepless in Seattle.*

"Why are you saying yes to him and not to me?" Peter demands.

"Because he asked." I raise my eyebrows at him and wait.

Rolling his eyes, Peter mumbles, "Lara Jean, will you go to prom with me? God, you really do ask for a lot."

I hold the bear out to him. "I will, but first kiss Howard."

"Covey. No. Hell, no."

"Please!" I give him a pleading look. "It's in the movie, Peter."

And grumbling, he does it, in front of everybody, which is how I know he is utterly and completely mine.

On the bus to our hotel in New Jersey, Peter whispers to me, "What do you think—should we sneak out after bed checks and come back to the city?" He's mostly joking. He knows I'm not the type to sneak out on a school trip.

His eyes go wide when I say, "How would we even get to the city? Do taxis go from New Jersey to New York?" I can't even believe I am considering it. It's so unlike me. Hastily I say, "No, no, never mind. We can't. We'd get lost, or mugged, and then we'd get sent home, and then I'd be so mad we missed out on Central Park and everything."

Peter gives me a skeptical look. "Do you really think Jain and Davenport would send us home?"

"Maybe not, but they might make us stay at the hotel all day long as punishment, which is even worse. Let's not risk it." Then: "What would we do?" I'm playing pretend now, not really planning, but Peter plays along.

"We could go hear some live music, or go to a comedy show. Sometimes famous comedians do surprise sets."

"I wish we could see *Hamilton*." When we drove through Times Square, Lucas and I craned our heads to see if we could get a glimpse of the *Hamilton* marquee, but no such luck.

"Tomorrow I want to get a New York bagel and see how it stacks up against Bodo's." Bodo's Bagels are legendary in Charlottesville; we're very proud of those bagels.

Putting my head on his shoulder, I yawn and say, "I wish we could go to Levain Bakery so I could try their cookie. It's supposed to be like no chocolate chip cookie you've had before. I want to go to Jacques Torres's chocolate shop too. His chocolate chip cookie is the definitive chocolate chip cookie, you know. It's truly legendary. . . ." My eyes drift closed, and Peter pats my hair. I'm starting to fall asleep when I realize he's unraveling the milkmaid braids Kitty pinned on the crown of my head. My eyes fly back open. "Peter!"

"Shh, go back to sleep. I want to practice something."

"You'll never get it back to how she had it."

"Just let me try," he says, collecting bobby pins in the palm of his hand.

When we get to the hotel in New Jersey, despite his best efforts, my braids are lumpy and loose and won't stay pinned. "I'm sending a picture of this to Kitty so she'll see what a bad student you are," I say as I gather up my things.

"No, don't," Peter quickly says, which makes me smile.

The next day is surprisingly springlike for March. The sun is shining and flowers are just beginning to bud. It feels like I'm in *You've Got Mail*, when Kathleen Kelly goes to meet Joe Fox in Riverside Park. I would love to see the exact garden where they kiss at the end of the movie, but our tour guide brings us to Central Park instead. Chris and I are taking pictures of the *Imagine* mosaic in Strawberry Fields when I realize Peter is nowhere in sight. I ask Gabe and Darrell, but no one's seen him. I text him, but he doesn't reply. We're about to move on to Sheep Meadow for a picnic, and I'm starting to panic, because what if Mr. Jain or Ms. Davenport notices he's not here? He comes jogging up just as we're about to go. He's not even out of breath or the least bit concerned he almost got left behind.

"Where were you?" I demand. "We almost left!"

Triumphantly he holds up a brown paper bag. "Open it and see."

I grab the bag from him and look inside. It's a Levain chocolate chip cookie, still warm. "Oh my God, Peter! You're so thoughtful." I get on my tiptoes and hug him, and then turn to Chris. "Isn't he so thoughtful, Chris?" Peter's sweet, but he's never this sweet. This is two romantic things in a row, so I figure I should praise him accordingly, because the boy responds well to positive reinforcement.

She's already got her hand inside the bag, and she stuffs a piece of cookie in her mouth. "Very thoughtful." She reaches for another piece, but Peter snatches the bag away from her.

"Damn, Chris! Let Covey have a bite before you eat the whole thing."

"Well, why'd you only get one?"

"Because it's huge! And it cost, like, five bucks for one."

"I can't believe you ran and got this for me," I say. "You weren't nervous you'd get lost?"

"Nah," he says, all proud. "I just looked at Google Maps and ran for it. I got a little turned around when I got back in the park, but somebody gave me directions. New Yorkers are really friendly. All that stuff about them being rude must be bullshit."

"That's true. Everyone we've met has been really nice. Except for that old lady who screamed at you for walking and looking at your phone," Chris says, snickering at Peter, who scowls at her. I take a big bite of the cookie. The Levain cookie is more like a scone, really dense and doughy. Heavy, too. It really is like no chocolate chip cookie I've ever tasted.

"So?" Peter asks me. "What's the verdict?"

"It's unique. It's in a class of its own." I'm taking another bite when Ms. Davenport comes up and hustles us along, eyeing the cookie in my hand.

Our tour guide has a pointer that looks like the Statue of Liberty's torch, and he holds it up in the air to shepherd us through the park. It's actually pretty embarrassing, and I wish we could just go off by ourselves and explore the city, but no. He has a ponytail and he wears a khaki vest, and I think he's kind of corny, but Ms. Davenport seems to be into him. After Central Park we take the subway downtown and get off to walk across the Brooklyn Bridge. While everyone else is in line for ice cream at Brooklyn Ice Cream Factory, Peter and I run over to Jacques Torres's chocolate shop. It's Peter's idea. Of course I ask Ms. Davenport for permission first. She's busy talking to the tour guide, so she waves us off. I feel so grown up, walking through the streets of New York without any adults.

When we get to the store, I'm so excited, I'm shaking. Finally I get to try Jacques's famous chocolate chip cookie. I bite into it. This cookie is flat, chewy, dense. Chocolate has pooled on top and hardened! The butter and sugar taste almost caramelized. It's heaven.

"Yours are better," Peter says, his mouth rudely full, and I shush him, looking around to make sure the girl at the register didn't hear.

"Stop lying," I say.

"I'm not!"

He is. "I just don't know why mine aren't like his," I say.

"It must be the industrial ovens." It seems I'll just have to accept my not-quite-perfect chocolate chip cookie and be content with good enough.

As we step out the door, I notice a bakery across the street called Almondine and another one on the opposite corner called One Girl Cookies. New York is truly a city of baked goods.

Peter and I walk back to the ice cream shop holding hands. Everyone is out on the pier, sitting on benches, eating their ice cream, and taking selfies with the Manhattan skyline behind them. New York keeps surprising me with how pretty it is.

Peter must be thinking the same thing, because he squeezes my hand and says, "This city is awesome."

"It really is."

I'm sound asleep when there is a knock at the door. I wake up with a start. It's still dark outside. In the bed across the room, Chris doesn't stir.

Then I hear Peter's voice on the other side of the door. "Covey, it's me. Want to go watch the sunrise on the roof?"

I get out of bed and open the door, and there is Peter, in a UVA hoodie, holding a Styrofoam cup of coffee and a cup with a tea bag hanging out the side. "What time is it?"

"Five thirty. Hurry, go get your coat."

"Okay, give me two minutes," I whisper. I run to our bathroom and brush my teeth and then I fumble around in the darkness for my jacket. "I can't find my jacket!"

"You can wear my hoodie," Peter offers from the doorway.

From under her blanket Chris growls, "If you guys don't shut up, I swear to God."

"Sorry," I whisper. "Do you want to watch the sunrise with us?"

Peter shoots me a pouty look, but Chris's head is still under her blanket, so she doesn't see. "No. Just leave!"

"Sorry, sorry," I say, and I scurry out the door.

We take the elevator to the top, and it's still dark outside, but it's beginning to get light. The city is just waking up. Right away Peter shrugs out of his hoodie, and I put my arms up and he slips it over my head. It's warm and smells like the detergent his mother uses.

Peter leans over the edge, looking across the water to the city. "Can't you picture us living here after college? We could live in a skyscraper. With a doorman. And a gym."

"I don't want to live in a skyscraper. I want to live in a brownstone in the West Village. Near a bookstore."

"We'll figure it out," he says.

I lean over the edge too. I never would have pictured myself living in New York City. Before I came here, it seemed like such an intimidating place, for tough people who aren't afraid to get into a fight with someone on the subway, or men in suits who work on Wall Street, or artists who live in SoHo lofts. But now that I'm here, it's not so scary, not with Peter by my side. I steal a look at him. Is this how it goes? You fall in love, and nothing seems truly scary anymore, and life is one big possibility?

7

It's a six-hour trip back to Virginia, and I'm asleep for most of it. It's dark out by the time we pull into the school parking lot, and I see Daddy's car parked up front. We've all had our own cars and been driving ourselves around for so long, but pulling into the school parking lot and seeing all the parents waiting there for us feels like being in elementary school again, like coming back from a field trip. It's a nice feeling. On the way home, we pick up a pizza and Ms. Rothschild comes over and she and Daddy and Kitty and I eat it in front of the TV.

After, I unpack, do the bit of homework I have left, talk to Peter on the phone, and then get ready for bed. But I end up tossing and turning for what feels like eternity. Maybe it's all the sleep I got on the bus, or maybe it's the fact that any day now, I'll hear from UVA. Either way, I can't sleep, so I creep downstairs and start opening drawers.

What could I bake this time of night that wouldn't involve waiting for butter to soften? It's a perpetual question in my life. Ms. Rothschild says we should just leave butter out in a dish like she does, but we aren't a leave-the-butter-out family, we are a butter-in-the-refrigerator family. Besides, it messes with the chemistry if the butter is too soft, and in Virginia in the spring and summertime, butter melts quick.

I suppose I could finally try baking the cinnamon roll brownies I've been playing around with in my head. Katharine Hepburn's brownie recipe plus a dash of cinnamon plus cinnamon cream cheese swirl on top.

I'm melting chocolate in a double boiler and already regretting starting this project so late when Daddy pads into the kitchen in the tartan robe Margot gave him for Christmas this past year. "You can't sleep either, huh?" he says.

"I'm trying out a new recipe. I think I might call them cinnabrownies. Or sin brownies."

"Good luck waking up tomorrow," Daddy says, rubbing the back of his neck.

I yawn. "You know, I was thinking maybe you'd call in for me and I'd sleep in a little and then you and I could have a nice, relaxing father-daughter breakfast together. I could make mushroom omelets."

He laughs. "Nice try." He nudges me toward the stairs. "I'll finish up the sin brownies or whatever they're called. You go to bed."

I yawn again. "Can I trust you to do a cream cheese swirl?" Daddy looks alarmed and I say, "Forget it. I'll finish making the batter and bake them tomorrow."

"I'll help," he says.

"I'm pretty much done."

"I don't mind."

"Okay then. Can you measure me out a quarter cup of flour?"

Daddy nods and gets out the measuring cup.

"That's the liquid measuring cup. We need the dry measuring cups so you can level off the flour." He goes back to the cupboard, and switches them out. I watch as he scoops flour and then carefully takes a butter knife to the top. "Very good."

"I learn from the best," he says.

I cock my head at him. "Why are you still awake, Daddy?"

"Ah. I guess I have a lot on my mind." He puts the top back on the flour canister and then stops and hesitates before asking, "How do you feel about Trina? You like her, right?"

I take the pot of chocolate off the heat. "I like her a lot. I think I might even love her. Do *you* love her?"

This time Daddy doesn't hesitate at all. "I do."

"Well, good," I say. "I'm glad."

He looks relieved. "Good," he says back. Then he says it again. "Good."

Things must be pretty serious if he's asking me such a question. I wonder if he's thinking of asking her to move in. Before I can ask, he says, "No one will ever take the place of your mom. You know that, don't you?"

"Of course I do." I lick the chocolate spoon with the tip of my tongue. It's hot, too hot. It's good that he should love again, that he should have someone, a real partner. He's been alone so long it felt like the normal thing, but this is a better thing. And he's happy, anyone can see it. Now that Ms. Rothschild's here, I can't picture her not here. "I'm glad for you, Daddy."

8

All morning long I've been checking my phone, just like pretty much every senior at my school has been doing all week. Monday came and went with no word from UVA, then Tuesday, then Wednesday. Today is Thursday, and still nothing. The UVA admissions office always send out acceptances before April first, and last year, notices went out the third week of March, so it really could be any day now. The way it goes is, they put the word out on social media to check the Student Info System, and then you log in to the system and learn your fate.

Colleges used to send acceptance letters in the mail. Mrs. Duvall says that sometimes parents would call the school when the mailman came, and the kid would jump in their car and drive home as fast as they could. There's something romantic about waiting for a letter in the mail, waiting for your destiny.

I'm sitting in French class, my last class of the day, when someone shrieks, "UVA just tweeted! Decisions are out!"

Madame Hunt says, *"Calmez-vous, calmez-vous,"* but everyone's getting up and grabbing their phones, not paying attention to her.

This is it. My hands tremble as I log in to the system; my

heart is going a million miles a minute waiting for the website to load.

> The University of Virginia received over
> 30,000 applications this year. The Committee
> on Admission has examined your application
> and carefully considered your academic, personal,
> and extracurricular credentials, and while your
> application was very strong, we are sorry to
> inform you . . .

This can't be real. I'm in a nightmare and any moment I'm going to wake up. Wake up wake up wake up.

Dimly, I can hear people talking all around me; I hear a scream of joy down the hallway. Then the bell rings, and people are jumping out of their seats and running out the door. Madame Hunt murmurs, "They usually don't send out the notices until after school." I look up, and she's looking at me with sad, sympathetic eyes. Mom eyes. Her eyes are what undo me.

Everything is ruined. My chest hurts; it's hard to breathe. All of my plans, everything I was counting on, none of it will come true now. Me coming home for Sunday night dinner, doing laundry on weeknights with Kitty, Peter walking me to class, studying all night at Clemons Library. It's all gone.

Nothing will go like we planned now.

I look back down at my phone, read the words again. *We are sorry to inform you . . .* My eyes start to blur. Then I read it again, from the beginning. I didn't even get wait-listed. I don't even have that.

I stand up, get my bag, and walk out the door. I feel a stillness inside of me, but at the same time this acute awareness of my heart pumping, my ears pounding. It's like all the parts are moving and continuing to function as they do, but I've gone completely numb. I didn't get in. I'm not going to UVA; they don't want me.

I'm walking to my locker, still in a daze, when I nearly run right into Peter, who is turning the corner. He grabs me. "So?" His eyes are bright and eager and expectant.

My voice comes out sounding very far away. "I didn't get in."

His mouth drops. "Wait—what?"

I can feel the lump rising in my throat. "Yeah."

"Not even wait-listed?"

I shake my head.

"Fuck." The word is one long exhale. Peter looks stunned. He lets go of my arm. I can tell he doesn't know what to say.

"I have to go," I say, turning away from him.

"Wait—I'll come with you!"

"No, don't. You have an away game today. You can't miss that."

"Covey, I don't give a shit about that."

"No, I'd rather you didn't. Just—I'll call you later." He reaches for me and I sidestep away from him and hurry down the hallway, and he calls out my name, but I don't stop. I just have to make it to my car, and then I can cry. Not yet. Just a hundred more steps, and then a hundred more than that.

I make it to the parking lot before the tears come. I cry the whole drive home. I cry so hard I can barely see, and I have to pull over at a McDonald's to sit in the parking lot and cry some more. It's starting to sink in, that this isn't a nightmare, this is real, and this fall I won't be going to UVA with Peter. Everyone will be so disappointed. They were all expecting I'd get in. We all thought it was going to happen. I never should have made such a big deal about wanting to go there. I should've just kept it to myself, not let anyone see how much I wanted it. Now they'll all be worried for me, and it'll be worse than Madame Hunt's sad mom eyes.

When I get home, I take my phone and go upstairs to my room. I take off my school clothes, put on my pajamas, and crawl into bed and look at my phone. I've got missed calls from Daddy, from Margot, from Peter. I go on Instagram, and my feed is all people posting their reaction shots to getting into UVA. My cousin Haven got in; she posted a screen grab of her acceptance letter. She won't be going there, though. She's going to Wellesley, her first choice. She doesn't even care about UVA; it was her safety school. I'm sure she'll feign sympathy for me when she finds out I didn't get in, but inside she'll feel secretly superior. Emily Nussbaum got in. She posted a picture of herself in a UVA sweatshirt and baseball cap. Gosh, did everyone get in? I thought my grades were better than hers. I guess not.

A little while later, I hear the front door open and Kitty's footsteps come running up the stairs. She throws open my bedroom door, but I am on my side, eyes closed, pretending to be asleep. "Lara Jean?" she whispers.

I don't reply. I need a little while longer before I have to face her and Daddy and tell them I didn't make it. I make my breathing go heavy and natural, and then I hear Kitty retreat and close the door quietly behind her. Before long, I fall asleep for real.

When I wake up, it's dark outside. It always feels so bleak to fall asleep when it's still light out and then wake up to darkness. My eyes feel swollen and sore. Downstairs, I hear water running in the kitchen sink and the clink of silverware against dishes. I go down the staircase and stop before I make it to the bottom. "I didn't get into UVA," I say.

Daddy turns around; his sleeves are rolled up, his arms soapy, his eyes even sadder than Madame Hunt's. Dad eyes. He turns off the faucet and comes over to the staircase, hoists me up, and draws me into his arms for a hug. His arms are still wet. "I'm so sorry, honey," he says. We're almost the same height, because I am still standing on the stairs. I'm focusing on not crying, but when he finally releases me, he tips up my chin and examines my face worriedly, and it's all I can do to keep it together. "I know how badly you wanted this."

I keep swallowing to keep down the tears. "It still doesn't feel real."

He smooths the hair out of my eyes. "Everything is going to work out. I promise it will."

"I just—I just really didn't want to leave you guys," I cry, and I can't help it, tears are rolling down my face. Daddy's wiping them away as fast as they can fall. He looks like he's going to cry too, which makes me feel worse, because I had planned to put on a brave face, and now look.

Putting his arm around me, he admits, "Selfishly, I was looking forward to having you so close to home. But Lara Jean, you're still going to get into a great school."

"But it won't be UVA," I whisper.

Daddy hugs me to him. "I'm so sorry," he says again.

He's sitting next to me on the staircase, his arm still around me, when Kitty comes back inside from walking Jamie Fox-Pickle. She looks from me to Daddy, and she drops Jamie's leash. "Did you not get in?"

I wipe my face and try to shrug. "No. It's okay. It wasn't meant to be, I guess."

"Sorry you didn't get in," she says, her voice tiny, her eyes sorrowful.

"Come give me a hug at least," I say, and she does. The three of us sit like that on the staircase for quite some time, Daddy's arm around my shoulder, Kitty's hand on my knee.

Daddy makes me a turkey sandwich, which I eat, and then I go back upstairs and get back in bed to look at my phone again, when there's a knock at my window. It's Peter, still in his lacrosse uniform. I jump out of bed and open the window for him. He climbs inside, searches my face, and then says, "Hey, rabbit eyes," which is what he calls me when I've been crying. It makes me laugh, and it feels good to laugh. I reach out to hug him and he says, "You don't want to hug me right now. I didn't shower after the game. I came straight here."

I hug him anyway, and he doesn't smell bad to me at all. "Why didn't you ring the doorbell?" I ask, looking up at him, hooking my arms around his waist.

"I thought your dad might not like me coming over so late. Are you okay?"

"Kind of." I let go of him and sit down on my bed, and he sits at my desk. "Not really."

"Yeah, me too." There's a long pause, and then Peter says, "I feel like I didn't say the right things earlier. I was just bummed. I didn't think this was going to happen."

I stare down at my bedspread. "I know. Me either."

"It just sucks so much. Your grades are way better than mine. Cary got in, and you're better than him!"

"Well, I'm not a lacrosse player or a golfer." I try not to sound bitter-hearted, but it's an effort. A very traitorous, very small thought worms its way into my head—it's not fair that Peter's going and I'm not, when I deserve it more. I worked harder. I got better grades, higher SAT scores.

"Fuck them."

"Peter."

"Sorry. Screw them." He exhales. "This is insane."

Automatically I say, "Well, it's not *insane*. UVA's a really competitive school. I'm not mad at them. I just wish I was going there."

He nods. "Yeah, me too."

Suddenly, we hear the toilet flush from the hallway, and we both freeze. "You'd better go," I whisper.

Peter gives me one more hug before climbing back out my window. I stand there and watch him run down the street to where he parked his car. After he drives away, I check my phone, and there are two missed calls from Margot and then a text from her that says, I'm so sorry.

And that's when I start to cry again, because that's when it finally feels real.

9

WHEN I WAKE UP IN THE MORNING, IT'S THE first thing I think of. How I'm not going to UVA, how I don't even know where I'm going. My whole life I've never had to worry about that. I've always known where my place is, where I belong. Home.

As I lie there in bed, I start a mental tally of all the things I'm going to miss out on, not going to a college just around the corner from home. The moments.

Kitty's first period. My dad's an OB, so it's not like he doesn't have it covered, but I've been waiting for this moment, to give Kitty a speech about womanhood that she'll hate. It might not happen for another year or two. But I got mine when I was twelve and Margot got hers when she was eleven, so who knows? When I got my first period, Margot explained all about tampons and what kind to use for what days, and to sleep on your belly when your cramps are particularly bad. She made me feel like I was joining some secret club, a woman's club. Because of my big sister, the grief I felt about growing up was less acute. Kitty likely won't have either of her big sisters here, but she does have Ms. Rothschild, and she's only just across the street. She's grown so attached to Ms. Rothschild that she'll probably prefer a period talk from her anyway, truth be told. Even if in the future Daddy and Ms.

Rothschild were to break up, I know Ms. Rothschild would never turn her back on Kitty. They're cemented.

I'll miss Kitty's birthday, too. I've never not been at home for her birthday. I'll have to remind Daddy to carry on our birthday-sign tradition.

For the first time ever, all of the Song girls will be living truly apart. We three probably won't ever live in the same house together again. We'll come home for holidays and school breaks, but it won't be the same. It won't be what it was. But I suppose it hasn't been, not since Margot left for college. The thing is, you get used to it. Before you even realize it's happening, you get used to things being different, and it will be that way for Kitty too.

At breakfast I keep stealing glances at her, memorizing every little thing. Her gangly legs, her knobby knees, the way she watches TV with a half smile on her face. She'll only be as young as this for a little while longer. Before I leave, I should do more special things with her, just the two of us.

At the commercial break she eyes me. "Why are you staring at me?"

"No reason. I'm just going to miss you is all."

Kitty slurps the rest of her cereal milk. "Can I have your room?"

"What? No!"

"Yeah, but you won't be living here. Why should your room just sit there and go to waste?"

"Why do you want my room and not Margot's? Hers is bigger."

Practically, she says, "Yours is closer to the bathroom and it's got better light."

I dread change, and Kitty steps right into it. She leans in extra hard. It's her way of coping. "You'll miss me when I'm gone, I know it, so quit pretending you won't," I say.

"I've always wondered what it would be like to be an only child," she says in a singsong voice. When I frown, she hurries to say, "Only kidding!"

I know Kitty's just being Kitty, but I can't help but feel a tiny stab of hurt. Why would anyone want to be an only child? What's so great about having no one to warm your feet up against on a cold winter night?

"You'll miss me," I say, more to myself than to her. She doesn't hear me anyway; her show is back on.

When I get to school, I go straight to Mrs. Duvall's office to tell her the news. As soon as Mrs. Duvall sees the look on my face, she says, "Come sit down," and she gets up from behind her desk and closes the door behind me. She sits in the chair next to mine. "Tell me."

I take a deep breath. "I didn't get into UVA." Now that I've said it a few times, you'd think it would be easier to get the words out, but it's not—it's worse.

She heaves a sigh. "I'm surprised. I'm very, very surprised. Your application was strong, Lara Jean. You're a wonderful student. I did hear that they got a few thousand more applicants this year than in years past. Still, I would've thought you'd be wait-listed at the very least." All I can do is give her a small shrug in response, because I don't trust my voice right now. She leans forward and hugs me. "I heard from a source in the admissions department that William and Mary will be sending out their decisions today, so buck up for that. And there's still UNC, and U of R. Where else did you apply? Tech?"

I shake my head. "JMU."

"All great schools. You'll be fine, Lara Jean. I'm not the least bit worried about you."

I don't say what I'm thinking, which is that we both thought I'd get into UVA, too; instead I just offer a weak smile.

When I walk out, I see Chris at the lockers. I tell her the news about UVA, and she says, "You should come with me and work on a farm in Costa Rica."

Stunned, I lean back against the wall and say, "Wait— what?"

"I told you about this."

"No, I don't think you did." I've known Chris wasn't going away to college, that she was going to go to community college first and then see. She doesn't have the grades, or much inclination, really. But she never said anything about Costa Rica.

"I'm going to take a year off and go work on farms. You work for like five hours, and they give you room and board. It's amazing."

"But what do you know about farming?"

"Nothing! It doesn't matter. You just have to be willing to

work; they'll teach you. I could also work at a surfing school in New Zealand, or learn how to make wine in Italy. Basically, I could go anywhere. Doesn't that sound amazing?"

"It does. . . ." I try to smile but my face feels tight. "Is your mom okay with it?"

Chris picks at her thumbnail. "Whatever, I'm eighteen. She doesn't have a choice."

I give her a dubious look. Chris's mom is tough. I have a hard time picturing her being okay with this plan.

"I told her I'd do this for a year and then come back and go to PVCC, and then transfer to a four-year college," she admits. "But who knows what will happen? A year is a long time. Maybe I'll marry a DJ, or join a band, or start my own bikini line."

"That all sounds so glamorous."

I want to feel excited for her, but I can't seem to muster up the feeling. It's good that Chris has her own thing to look forward to, something that no one else in our class is doing. But it feels like everything all around me is shifting in ways I didn't expect, when all I want is for things to stand still.

"Will you write me?" I ask.

"I'll Snapchat everything."

"I'm not on Snapchat, and besides, that's not the same thing." I nudge her with my foot. "Send me a postcard from every new place you go, please."

"Who knows if I'll even have access to a post office? I don't know how post offices work in Costa Rica."

"Well, you can try."

"I'll try," she agrees.

I haven't seen as much of Chris this year. She got a job hostessing at Applebee's, and she's become very close with her work friends. They're all older, some of them have kids, and they pay their own bills. I'm pretty sure Chris hasn't told any of them she still lives at home and pays exactly no bills. When I visited her there last month, one of the servers said something about hoping to make enough that night for rent, and she looked at Chris and said, "You know how it is," and Chris nodded like she did. When I gave her a questioning look, she pretended not to see.

The warning bell rings, and we start walking to our first-period classes. "Kavinsky must be freaking out that you didn't get into UVA," Chris says, checking her reflection in a glass door we walk past. "So I guess you guys will do long-distance?"

"Yeah." My chest gets tight. "I guess."

"You should definitely get people in place to keep an eye on the situation," she says. "You know, like spies? I think I heard Gillian McDougal got in. She'd spy for you."

I give her a look. "Chris, I trust Peter."

"I know—I'm not talking about him! I'm talking about random girls on his floor. Dropping by his room. You should give him a picture of you to keep him company, if you know what I mean." She frowns at me. "Do you know what I mean?"

"Like, a sexy picture? No way!" I start backing away from her. "Look, I've gotta go to class." The last thing I want to do is think about Peter and random girls. I'm still trying to get used to the idea that we won't be together at UVA this fall.

JENNY HAN

Chris rolls her eyes. "Calm down. I'm not talking about a nudie. I would never suggest that for you of all people. What I'm talking about is a pinup-girl shot, but not, like, cheesy. Sexy. Something Kavinsky can hang up in his dorm room."

"Why would I want him to hang up a sexy picture of me in his dorm room for all the world to see?"

Chris reaches out and flicks me on the forehead.

"Ow!" I shove her away from me and rub the spot where she flicked me. "That hurt!"

"You deserved it for asking such a dumb question." She sighs. "I'm talking about preventative measures. A picture of you on his wall is a way for you to mark your territory. Kavinsky's hot. And he's an athlete. Do you think other girls will respect the fact that he's in a long-distance relationship?" She lowers her voice and adds, "With a Virgin Mary girlfriend?"

I gasp and then look around to see if anyone heard. "Chris!" I hiss. "Can you please not?"

"I'm just trying to help you! You have to protect what's yours, Lara Jean. If I met some hot guy in Costa Rica with a long-distance gf who he wasn't even *sleeping* with? I don't think I'd take it very seriously." She gives me a shrug and a sorry-not-sorry look. "You should definitely frame the picture too, so people know you're not someone to mess with. A frame says permanence. A picture taped on a wall says here today, gone tomorrow."

I chew on my bottom lip thoughtfully. "So maybe a picture of me baking, in an apron—"

"With nothing underneath?" Chris cackles, and I flick her forehead lightning quick.

"Ow!"

"Get serious then!"

The bell rings again, and we go our separate ways. I can't see myself giving Peter a sexy picture of me, but it does give me an idea—I could give him a scrapbook instead. All of our greatest hits. That way when he's missing me at UVA, he can look at it. And keep it on his desk, for any "random girl" who might happen by. Of course I won't mention this idea to Chris—she'd just laugh and call me Grandma Lara Jean. But I know Peter will love it.

10

I'M ON PINS AND NEEDLES ALL DAY, WAIT-
ing to hear the news from William and Mary. My entire
focus is on my phone, waiting for it to buzz, waiting for that
e-mail. In AP English class, Mr. O'Bryan has to ask me three
times about the slave narrative tradition in *Beloved.*

When it does buzz, it's just Margot asking me if I've heard
anything yet, and then it buzzes again, and it's Peter asking
me if I've heard anything yet. But nothing from William and
Mary.

Then, when I'm in the girls' room in between classes, it
finally does buzz, and I scramble to zip up my jeans so I can
check my phone. It's an e-mail from University of North
Carolina at Chapel Hill, telling me my application has been
updated. I stand there in the bathroom stall, and even though
I truly don't expect to get in, my heart is pounding like
crazy as I click on the link and wait.

Wait-listed.

I should be happy about it, because UNC is so competitive and the wait list is better than nothing, and I would be
happy . . . if I had already gotten into UVA. Instead it's like
another punch in the stomach. What if I don't get in anywhere? What will I do then? I can see my Aunt Carrie and
Uncle Victor now: *Poor Lara Jean, she didn't get into UVA or*

UNC. She's so different from her sister; Margot's such a go-getter.

When I get to the lunch table, Peter is waiting for me with an eager look on his face. "Did you hear anything?"

I sit down in the seat next to him. "I got wait-listed at UNC."

"Aw, shit. Well, it's impossible to get in there out of state unless you're a basketball player. Honestly, even getting on the wait list is impressive."

"I guess so," I say.

"Screw them," he says. "Who wants to go there anyway?"

"A lot of people." I unwrap my sandwich, but I can't bear to take a bite, because my stomach's tied up in knots.

Peter gives a begrudging shrug. I know he's just trying to make me feel better, but UNC is a great school and he knows it and I know it, and there's no use pretending it's not.

All through lunch I'm listlessly sipping on my Cherry Coke and listening to the guys go on about the game they've got coming up in a few days. Peter looks over at me at one point and squeezes my thigh in a reassuring way, but I can't even muster up a smile in return.

When the guys get up to go to the weight room, it's just Peter and me left at the table, and he asks me worriedly, "Aren't you going to eat something?"

"I'm not hungry," I say.

Then he sighs and says, "It should be you going to UVA and not me," and just like that, poof, the traitorous little thought I had last night about me deserving it more than him disappears like perfume mist into the air. I know how hard

Peter worked at lacrosse. He earned his spot. He shouldn't be thinking those kinds of thoughts. It's not right.

"Don't ever say that. You earned it. You deserve to go to UVA."

His head down, he says, "So do you, though." Then his head snaps up, his eyes alight. "Do you remember Toney Lewis?" I shake my head. "He was a senior when we were freshmen. He went to PVCC for two years and then he transferred to UVA his junior year! I bet you could do that too, but you'd be able to do it even sooner, since you're going to a regular four-year college. Getting in as a transfer is a million times easier!"

"I guess that's true. . . ." Transferring hadn't occurred to me. I'm still getting used to the idea that I won't be going to UVA.

"Right? Okay, so this fall you'll go to William and Mary or U of R or wherever you get in, and we'll visit each other all the time, and you'll apply to transfer for next year, and then you'll be with me at UVA! Where you belong!"

Hope flares inside of me. "Do you really think it'll be that easy for me to get in?"

"Yeah! You should've gotten in in the first place! Trust me, Covey."

Slowly, I nod. "Yeah! Okay. Okay."

Peter breathes a sigh of relief. "Good. So we have a plan."

I steal a french fry off his plate. I can already feel my appetite coming back to me. I'm stealing another fry when my phone vibrates. I snatch it up and check—it's an e-mail from the office of admissions at William and Mary. Peter looks over my shoulder and back at me, his eyes wide. His leg bounces up and down against mine as we wait for the page to load.

> *It is with great pleasure that I offer you admission to the College of William and Mary . . .*

Relief floods over me. Thank God.

Peter jumps out of his seat and picks me up and swings me around. "Lara Jean just got into William and Mary!" he shouts to the table and anyone who is listening. Everyone at our table cheers.

"See?" Peter crows, hugging me. "I told you everything would work out."

I hug him back tightly. More than anything else, I feel relieved. Relieved to be in, relieved to have a plan.

"We'll make it work until you're here," he says in a soft voice, burrowing his face in my neck. "It's two hours away— that's nothing. I bet your dad would let you take the car. It's not like Kitty needs it yet. And I'll do the trip with you a few times to get you comfortable with it. It's gonna be all good, Covey."

I'm nodding.

When I sit back down, I send a group text to Margot, Kitty, Ms. Rothschild, and my dad.

I got into W&M!!!

I throw in those exclamation marks for good measure, to show how excited I am, to make sure they know they shouldn't feel sorry for me anymore, that everything is great now.

My dad sends back a string of emojis. Ms. Rothschild writes, You go girl!!!!! Margot writes, YAYYYYYYY! We will celebrate IRL next week!

After lunch, I stop by Mrs. Duvall's office to tell her the good news, and she is thrilled. "I know it's your second choice, but in some ways it might be an even better fit than UVA was. It's smaller. I think a girl like you could really shine there, Lara Jean."

I smile at her, receive her hug, but inside I'm thinking, *I guess she didn't think a girl like me could really shine at UVA.*

By the end of the week, I get into James Madison and University of Richmond, too, which I'm happy about, but I'm still set on William and Mary. I've been to Williamsburg plenty of times with my family, and I can picture myself there. It's a small campus, a pretty one. And it really isn't far from home. It's less than two hours away. So I'll go, I'll study hard, and then after a year I'll transfer to UVA, and everything will be exactly the way we planned.

11

I'M THE ONE WHO GOES TO THE AIRPORT to pick up Margot and Ravi, while Daddy puts finishing touches on dinner and Kitty does her homework. I put the address into the GPS, just in case, and I make it there without incident, thank God. Our airport is small, so I just circle around while I wait for the two of them to come out.

When I pull up to the curb, Margot and Ravi are waiting, sitting on their suitcases. I park and then jump out and run over to Margot and throw my arms around her. Her hair is freshly bobbed around her chin, she's wearing a sweatshirt and leggings, and as I squeeze her tight, I think *Oh, how I've missed my sister!*

I let go, and then I take a good look at Ravi, who is taller than I realized. He is tall and skinny with dark skin and dark hair and dark eyes and long lashes. He looks so unlike Josh, but so like a boy that Margot would date. He has one dimple, on his right cheek. "It's nice to meet you in real life, Lara Jean," he says, and right away I'm bowled over by his accent. My name sounds so much fancier all dressed up in an English accent.

I'm feeling nervous, and then I see that his T-shirt says DUMBLEDORE'S ARMY, and I relax. He's a Potter person, like us. "It's nice to meet you, too. So what house are you?"

He grabs both Margot's and his suitcases and loads them into the trunk. "Let's see if you can guess. Your sister got it wrong."

"Only because you were trying to impress me for the first month I knew you," she protests. Ravi laughs and climbs into the backseat. I think it's a good sign of his character that he doesn't automatically go for shotgun. Margot looks at me. "Do you want me to drive?"

I'm tempted to say yes, because I always like it better when Margot drives, but I shake my head, jingle my keys high. "I've got it."

She raises her eyebrows like she's impressed. "Good for you."

She goes to the passenger side, and I get in the front seat. I look at Ravi in my rearview mirror. "Ravi, by the time you leave our house, I will have figured out *your* house."

When we get home, Daddy and Kitty and Ms. Rothschild are waiting for us in the living room. Margot looks startled to see her there sitting on the couch with Daddy, her bare feet in his lap. I've grown so used to it, to her being around, that it feels to me like Ms. Rothschild is part of the family now. It hadn't occurred to me how jarring it would be for Margot. But the truth is, Ms. Rothschild and Margot haven't spent a lot of time together because she's been away at school; she wasn't around when Ms. Rothschild and Daddy first started dating and she's only been home once since, for Christmas.

As soon as Ms. Rothschild sees Margot, she jumps up to

give her a big hug and compliments her on her hair. She hugs Ravi, too. "God, you're a tall drink of water!" she quips, and he laughs, but Margot just has a stiff smile on her face.

Until she sees Kitty, who she wraps up in a bear hug and then, seconds later, squeals, "Oh my God, Kitty! Are you wearing a bra now?" Kitty gasps and glares at her, her cheeks a dull angry red.

Abashed, Margot mouths, *Sorry.*

Ravi hurries to step forward and shake Daddy's hand. "Hello, Dr. Covey, I'm Ravi. Thank you for inviting me."

"Oh, we're glad to have you, Ravi," Daddy says.

Then Ravi smiles at Kitty and lifts his hand in greeting and says, a tad awkwardly, "Hi, Kitty."

Kitty nods at him without making eye contact. "Hello."

Margot is still staring at Kitty in disbelief. I've been here all along, so it's harder for me to see how much Kitty has grown in the past year, but it's true, she has. Not so much in the chest department—the bra is merely ornamental at this point—but in other ways.

"Ravi, can I get you something to drink?" Ms. Rothschild chirps. "We have juice, Fresca, Diet Coke, water?"

"What's a Fresca?" Ravi asks, his brow furrowed.

Her eyes light up. "It's a delicious grapefruity soda. Zero calories! You have to try it!" Margot watches as Ms. Rothschild goes to the kitchen and opens up the cabinet where we keep our cups. Filling a glass with ice, she calls out, "Margot, what about you? Can I get you something?"

"I'm fine," Margot answers in a pleasant enough tone, but

I can tell she doesn't appreciate being offered a drink in her own home by someone who doesn't live there.

When Ms. Rothschild returns with Ravi's Fresca, she presents it to him with a flourish. He thanks her and takes a sip. "Very refreshing," Ravi says, and she beams.

Daddy claps his hands together. "Should we take the bags upstairs? Give you guys a chance to freshen up before dinner? We've got the guest room all set up." He gives me a fond look before saying, "Lara Jean put in a new pair of slippers and a robe for you, Ravi."

Before Ravi can reply, Margot says, "Oh, that's so nice. But actually, I think Ravi's just going to stay with me in my room."

It's as if Margot has dropped a stink bomb in the middle of our living room. Kitty and I are looking at each other with huge *OMG* eyes; Daddy just looks stunned and at a complete loss for words. When I made up the guest room for Ravi, folded a set of towels for him on the side of the bed, and put out the robe and slippers, it never occurred to me that he'd be staying in Margot's room. Clearly, the thought never occurred to Daddy either.

Daddy's face is growing redder by the second. "Oh, um . . . I don't know if . . ."

Margot purses her lips nervously as she waits for Daddy to finish his sentence. We're all waiting, but he can't seem to figure out what to say next. His eyes dart over to Ms. Rothschild for help, and she puts her hand on the small of his back in support.

Poor Ravi looks supremely uncomfortable. My first thought was that he was a Ravenclaw like Margot; now I'm thinking he's a Hufflepuff like me. In a soft voice he says, "I truly don't mind staying in the guest room. I'd hate to make things awkward."

Daddy starts to answer him, but Margot gets there first. "No, it's totally fine," she assures Ravi. "Let's go get the rest of our stuff out of the car."

The second they leave, Kitty and I turn to each other. At the same time we say, "Oh my God."

Kitty ponders, "Why do they need to stay in the same room together? Do they have to have sex that bad?"

"Enough, Kitty," Daddy says, his tone sharper than I've heard him use with her. He turns and leaves, and I hear the sound of his office door closing. His office is where he goes when he is really mad. Ms. Rothschild gives her a stern look and follows after him.

Kitty and I look at each other again. "Yikes," I say.

"He didn't have to snap," Kitty says sullenly. "I'm not the one whose boyfriend is staying in my bed."

"He didn't mean it." I tuck her against me, wrapping my arms around her bony shoulders. "Gogo has a lot of nerve, huh?" She's very impressive, my sister. I just feel sorry for Daddy. This isn't a fight he's used to having—or any kind of fight at all, really.

Of course I text Peter right away and tell all. He sends back a lot of wide-eyed emojis. And: Do you think your dad would let us stay in the same room?? Which I ignore.

★ ★ ★

When Ravi goes upstairs to wash up and change, Ms. Rothschild says she has dinner out with the girls, so she'd better get going. I can tell Margot is relieved. After Ms. Rothschild leaves, Kitty takes Jamie Fox-Pickle for a walk, and Margot and I head to the kitchen to fix a salad to go with the chicken Daddy's roasting. I'm eager to have a moment alone with her so we can talk about the whole sleeping-arrangements situation, but I don't get a chance to ask, because as soon we step into the kitchen, Margot hisses at me, "Why didn't you tell me Daddy and Ms. Rothschild are so serious?"

"I told you she's over here for dinner almost every night!" I whisper back. I start rinsing a basket of cherry tomatoes so the sound of the water running will give us cover.

"She was walking around like she lives here! And since when do we have Fresca? We've never been a Fresca-drinking family."

I start slicing the tomatoes in half. "She loves it, so I always make sure to buy a case when I go to the store. It's actually very refreshing. Ravi seemed to like it."

"That's not the point!"

"What's your problem with Ms. Rothschild all of a sudden? You guys got along great when you were home for Christmas—" I break off as Daddy walks into the kitchen.

"Margot, can I talk to you for a minute?"

Margot pretends to be busy counting out silverware. "Sure, what's up, Daddy?"

Daddy glances at me, and I look back down at the tomatoes.

I am staying for moral support. "I would prefer if Ravi stayed in the guest room."

Margot bites her lip. "Why?"

There's an awkward silence before Daddy says, "I'm just not comfortable—"

"But Daddy, we're in college. . . . You do realize we've shared a bed before, right?"

Wryly he says, "I had my suspicions, but thank you for that confirmation."

"I'm almost twenty years old. I've been living away from home, thousands of miles away, for nearly two years." Margot glances over at me and I shrink down. I should've left when I had the chance. "Lara Jean and I aren't little kids anymore—"

"Hey, don't bring me into this," I say, as jokingly as I can.

Daddy sighs. "Margot, if you're set on this, I'm not going to stop you. But I would just remind you that this is still my house."

"I thought it was *our* house." She knows she's won this battle, so she keeps her voice light as meringue.

"Well, you freeloaders don't pay the mortgage on it, I do, so that should make it my house slightly more." With that final dad joke, he puts on oven mitts and takes the sizzling chicken out of the oven.

When we sit down to eat, Daddy stands at the head of the table and carves the chicken with the fancy new electric carving knife Ms. Rothschild got him for his birthday. "Ravi, can I offer you dark meat or white?"

Ravi clears his throat. "Um, I'm so sorry, but I actually don't eat meat."

Daddy gives Margot a horrified look. "Margot, you didn't tell me Ravi was a vegetarian!"

"Sorry," she says, grimacing. "I totally forgot. But Ravi loves salad!"

"I truly do," he assures Daddy.

"I'll take Ravi's portion," I offer. "I'll take two thighs."

Daddy saws off two thighs for me. "Ravi, tomorrow morning I'm making you a mean breakfast enchilada. No meat!"

Smiling, Margot says, "We're going to DC early tomorrow morning. Maybe the day he leaves?"

"Done," Daddy says.

Kitty is unnaturally subdued. I'm not sure if it's nervousness from having a boy she doesn't know sit at her dining room table, or if it's just because she's getting older, and she's less a kid in the way she interacts with new people. Though I suppose a twenty-one-year-old boy is really more of a young man.

Ravi has such nice manners—probably because he is English, and isn't it a fact that English people have better manners than Americans? He says sorry a lot. "Sorry, can I just . . ." "Sorry?" His accent is charming, I keep saying pardon so he'll speak again.

For my part, I try to lighten the mood with questions about England. I ask him why English people call private school public school, if his public school was anything like Hogwarts, if he's ever met the royal family. His answers are: because they are open to the paying public; they had head boys and head girls and prefects but no Quidditch; and he once saw Prince William at Wimbledon, but only the back of his head.

After dinner, the plan is for Ravi, Margot, Peter, and me to go to the movies. Margot invites Kitty to come along, but she demurs, citing her homework as the reason. I think she's just nervous around Ravi.

I get ready in my room, dab a little perfume, a little lip balm, put on a sweatshirt over my cami and jeans because the theater gets cold. I'm ready fast, but Margot's door is closed, and I can hear them talking quietly yet intensely. It's a strange thing to see her door closed. I feel like a little spy standing outside the door, but it's awkward, because who knows if Ravi has a shirt on, or what? It's so adult, that closed door, those hushed voices.

Through the door I clear my throat and say, "Are you guys ready? I told Peter we'd meet him at eight."

Margot opens the door. "Ready," she says, and she doesn't look happy.

Ravi steps out behind her, carrying his suitcase. "I'm just going to drop this off in the guest room, and then I'm all set," he says.

As soon as he's gone, I whisper to Margot, "Did something happen?"

"Ravi didn't want to make a bad impression on Daddy by us staying in the same room. I told him it was fine, but he doesn't feel comfortable."

"That's very considerate of him." I wouldn't say so to

JENNY HAN

Margot, but it was totally the right move. Ravi just keeps rising in my estimation.

Reluctantly she says, "He's a very considerate guy."

"Really handsome, too."

A smile spreads across her face. "And there's that."

Peter's already at the movie theater when we arrive, I'm sure because of Margot. He has no problem being late for me, but he would never dare be late for my big sister. Ravi buys all four of our tickets, which Peter is really impressed by. "Such a classy move," he whispers to me as we sit down. Peter deftly maneuvers it so we're sitting me, Peter, Ravi, Margot, so he can keep talking to him about soccer. Or football, as Ravi says. Margot gives me an amused look over their heads, and I can tell all the unpleasantness from before is forgotten.

After the movie, Peter suggests we go for frozen custards. "Have you ever had frozen custard before?" he asks Ravi.

"Never," Ravi says.

"It's the best, Rav," he says. "They make it homemade."

"Brilliant," Ravi says.

When the boys are in line, Margot says to me, "I think Peter's in love—with my boyfriend," and we both giggle.

We're still laughing when they get back to our table. Peter hands me my pralines and cream. "What's so funny?"

I just shake my head and dip my spoon into the custard.

Margot says, "Wait, we have to cheers my sister getting into William and Mary!"

My smile feels frozen as everyone clinks their custard cups against mine. Ravi says, "Well done, Lara Jean. Didn't Jon Stewart go there?"

Surprised, I say, "Why yes, yes he did. That's a pretty random fact to know."

"Ravi's specialty is random facts," Margot says, licking her spoon. "Don't get him started on the mating habits of bonobos."

"Two words," Ravi says. Then he looks from Peter to me and whispers, "Penis fencing."

Margot's so lit up around Ravi. I once thought she and Josh were meant for each other, but now I'm not so sure. When they talk about politics, they're both equally passionate, and they go back and forth, challenging each other but also conceding points. They're like two flints sparking. If they were on a TV show, I could see them as rival residents at a hospital who first grudgingly respect each other and then fall madly in love. Or two political aides at the White House, or two journalists. Ravi is studying bioengineering, which has not a lot to do with Margot's anthropology, but they sure make a great team.

The next day, Margot takes Ravi to Washington, DC, and they visit a few of the museums on the Mall and the Lincoln Memorial and the White House. They invited Kitty and me to go along, but I said no on behalf of both of us because I was pretty sure they would want some time alone and because I wanted to be cozy at home and work on my scrapbook for Peter. When they get back that night, I ask Ravi what his favorite thing to do in DC was, and he says the National Museum of African American History and Culture by far, which makes me regret my decision not to go, because I haven't been there yet.

We turn on a BBC show on Netflix that Margot has been raving about, and it was filmed near where Ravi grew up, so he points out landmark places like his first job and his first date. We eat ice cream right out of the cartons, and I can tell that Daddy likes Ravi by the way he keeps urging him to have more. I'm sure he noticed that Ravi is staying in the guest room, and I'm sure he appreciates the gesture. I hope Ravi and Margot keep dating, because I could see him in our family forever. Or at least stay together long enough for Margot and me to take a trip to London and stay at his house!

Ravi has to leave for Texas the next afternoon, and while I'm sad to see him go, I'm also a little bit glad, because then we get to have Margot all to ourselves before she leaves again.

When we say good-bye, I point at him and say, "Hufflepuff."

He grins. "You got it in one." Then he points at me. "Hufflepuff?"

I grin back. "You got it in one."

That night we're in my bedroom watching TV on my laptop when Margot brings up college—which is how I know that on some level she was waiting for Ravi to go too, so she could talk to me about real things. Before we load the next episode, she looks over at me and says, "Can we talk about UVA? How are you feeling about it now?"

"I was sad, but it's all right. I'm still going to go there." Margot gives me a quizzical look, and I explain, "I'm going to transfer after freshman year. I talked to Mrs. Duvall, and she said if I got good grades at William and Mary, I would definitely get in as a transfer."

Her forehead wrinkles up. "Why are you talking about transferring from William and Mary when you aren't even there yet?" When I don't answer right away, she says, "Is this because of Peter?"

"No! I mean, it is, in part, but not completely." I hesitate before saying the thing I haven't said out loud. "You know that feeling, like you're meant to be somewhere? When I visited William and Mary, I didn't get that feeling. Not like with UVA."

"It might be that no school gives you the exact feeling you have with UVA," Margot says.

"Maybe so—which is why I'm going to transfer after a year."

She sighs. "I just don't want you to live a half life at William and Mary because the whole time you're wishing you were with Peter at UVA. The freshman-year experience is so important. You should at least give it a fair chance, Lara Jean. You might really love it there." She gives me a look heavy with meaning. "Remember what Mommy said about college and boyfriends?"

How could I forget?

JENNY HAN

Don't be the girl who goes to college with a boyfriend.

"I remember," I say.

Margot takes my laptop and goes on the William and Mary website. "This campus is so pretty. Look at this weather vane! It all looks like something out of an English village."

I perk up. "Yeah, it kind of does." Is it as pretty as UVA's campus? No, not to me, but then I don't think anywhere is as pretty as Charlottesville.

"And look, William and Mary has a guacamole club. And a storm-watchers club. And oh my God! Something called a wizards-and-muggles club! It's the largest Harry Potter club at any US university."

"Wow! That *is* pretty neat. Do they have a baking club?"

She checks. "No. But you could start one!"

"Maybe . . . That would be fun. . . ." Maybe I *should* join a club or two.

She beams at me. "See? There's a lot to be excited about. And don't forget the Cheese Shop."

The Cheese Shop is a specialty food store right by campus, and they sell cheese, obviously, but also fancy jams and bread and wine and gourmet pastas. They make really great roast beef sandwiches with a house dressing—a mayonnaisey mustard that I have tried to duplicate at home, but nothing tastes as good as in the shop, on their fresh bread. Daddy loves to stop at the Cheese Shop for new mustards and a sandwich. He'd be happy to have an excuse to go there. And Kitty, she loves the Williamsburg outlet mall. They sell kettle corn there, and it's really addictive. They pop it right in front of you, and the popcorn is so hot, it melts the bag a little.

"Maybe I could get a job in Colonial Williamsburg," I say, trying to get into the spirit. "I could churn butter. Wear period garb. Like, a calico dress with an apron or whatever they wore in Colonial times. I've heard they're not allowed to speak to each other in modern-day language, and kids are always trying to trip them up. That could be fun. The only thing is, I'm not sure if they hire Asian people because of historical accuracy. . . ."

"Lara Jean, we live in the time of *Hamilton*! Phillipa Soo is half-Chinese, remember? If she can play Eliza Hamilton, you can churn butter. And if they refuse to hire you, we'll put it on social media and make them." Margot tilts her head and looks at me. "See! There's so much to be excited about, if you let yourself be." She puts her hands on my shoulders.

"I'm trying," I say. "I really am."

"Just give William and Mary a chance. Don't dismiss it before you even get there. Okay?"

I nod. "Okay."

12

THE NEXT MORNING IS GRAY AND RAINY OUT and it's just us three girls, because Daddy's left a note for us on the refrigerator saying he got called into the hospital, and he'll see us for dinner that night. Margot's still jet-lagged, so she got up early and fixed scrambled eggs and bacon. I'm luxuriously spreading eggs on buttered toast and listening to the rain tap on the roof, when I say, "What if I didn't go to school today, and we did something fun?"

Kitty brightens. "Like what?"

"Not you. You still have to go to school. I'm basically done. No one cares if I go anymore."

"I think Daddy probably cares," Margot says.

"But if we could do anything . . . what would we do?"

"Anything?" Margot bites into her bacon. "We'd take the train to New York City and enter the *Hamilton* lottery, and we'd win."

"You guys can't go without me," Kitty says.

"Be quiet, And Peggy," I say, giggling.

She glares at me. "Don't call me And Peggy."

"You don't even know what we're talking about, so calm down."

"I know you're cackling about it like a witch. Also, I do so know about *Hamilton*, because you play the soundtrack all day long." She sings, "Talk less; smile more."

"For your information, it's a cast recording, not a sound-track," I say, and she makes a big show of rolling her eyes.

In truth, if Kitty's anyone, she's a Jefferson. Wily, stylish, quick with a comeback. Margot's an Angelica, no question. She's been sailing her own ship since she was a little girl. She's always known who she was and what she wanted. I suppose I'm an Eliza, though I'd much rather be an Angelica. In truth *I'm* probably And Peggy. But I don't want to be the And Peggy of my own story. I want to be the Hamilton.

It rains all day, so as soon as we get home from school, the first thing Kitty and I do is get back into our pajamas. Margot never got out of hers. She's wearing her glasses, her hair in a knot at the top of her head (it's too short to stay put), Kitty is in a big tee, and I'm happy it's cold enough to wear my red flannels. Daddy is the only one still in his day clothes.

We order two large pizzas for dinner that night, plain cheese (for Kitty) and a supreme with the works. We're on the living room couch, shoving oozy slices of pizza into our mouths, when Daddy suddenly says, "Girls, there's something I'd like to talk to you about." He clears his throat like he does when he's nervous. Kitty and I exchange a curious look, and then he blurts out, "I'd like to ask Trina to marry me."

I clap my hands to my mouth. "Oh my God!"

Kitty's eyes bulge, her mouth goes slack, and then she flings her pizza aside and lets out a shriek so loud that Jamie Fox-

Pickle jumps. She catapults herself at Daddy, who laughs. I jump up and hug his back.

I can't stop smiling. Until I look at Margot, whose face is completely blank. Daddy's looking at her too, eyes hopeful and nervous. "Margot? You still there? What do you think, honey?"

"I think it's fantastic."

"You do?"

She nods. "Absolutely. I think Trina's great. And Kitty, you adore her, don't you?" Kitty's too busy squealing and flopping around on the couch with Jamie to answer. Softly, Margot says, "I'm happy for you, Daddy. I really am."

The *absolutely* is what gives her away. Daddy's too busy being relieved to notice, but I do. Of course it's weird for her. She's still getting used to seeing Ms. Rothschild in our kitchen. She hasn't gotten to see all the ways Ms. Rothschild and Daddy make sense. To Margot, she's still just our neighbor who used to wear terry-cloth booty shorts and a bikini top to mow the lawn.

"I'll need your guys's help with the proposal," Daddy says. "Lara Jean, I'm sure you'll have some ideas for me, right?"

Confidently I say, "Oh, yeah. People have been doing promposals, so I have lots of inspiration."

Margot turns to me and laughs, and it almost sounds real. "I'm sure Daddy will want something more dignified than 'Will You Marry Me' written in shaving cream on the hood of somebody's car, Lara Jean."

"Promposals have gotten way more sophisticated than in your day, Gogo," I say. I'm playing along, teasing her so she can feel normal again after the bomb Daddy just dropped.

"*My* day? I'm only two years ahead of you." She tries to sound light, but I can hear the strain in her voice.

"Two years is like dog years when it comes to high school. Isn't that right, Kitty?" I pull her toward me and hug her tight to my chest. She squirms away.

"Yeah, both of you guys are ancient beings," Kitty says. "Can I be a part of the proposal too, Daddy?"

"Of course. I can't get married without you guys." He looks teary. "We're a team, aren't we?"

Kitty is hopping up and down like a little kid. "Yeah!" she cheers. She's over the moon, and Margot sees it too, how important this is to her.

"When are you going to propose?" Margot asks.

"Tonight!" Kitty pipes up.

I glare at her. "No! That's not enough time to think up the perfect way. We need a week at least. Plus you don't even have a ring. Wait a minute, do you?"

Daddy takes off his glasses and wipes his eyes. "Of course not. I wanted to wait and talk to you girls first. I want all three of you to be here for the proposal, so I'll do it when you come back for the summer, Margot."

"That's too far away," Kitty objects.

"Yes, don't wait that long, Daddy," Margot says.

"Well, you'll have to help me pick out the ring at least," Daddy says.

"Lara Jean has a better eye for that kind of thing," Margot says serenely. "Besides, I barely know Ms. Rothschild. I haven't a clue what kind of ring she'd like."

A shadow crosses over Daddy's face. It's the *I barely know Ms. Rothschild* that put it there.

I rush to put on my best Hermione voice. "You 'haven't a clue'?" I tease. "P.S., did you know you're still American, Gogo? We don't talk as classy as that in America."

She laughs; we all do. Then, because I think she saw that brief shadow too, she says, "Make sure to take tons of pictures so I can see."

Gratefully Daddy says, "We will. We'll videotape it, whatever it is. God, I hope she says yes!"

"She'll say yes, of course she'll say yes," we all chorus.

Margot and I are wrapping slices of pizza in plastic and then double wrapping in foil. "I told you guys two pizzas would be too much," she says.

"Kitty will eat it for her after-school snack," I say. "So will Peter." I glance toward the living room, where Kitty and Daddy are snuggled up on the couch, watching TV. Then I whisper, "So how do you really feel about Daddy asking Ms. Rothschild to marry him?"

"I think it's completely bonkers," she whispers back. "She lives across the street, for pity's sake. They can just date like two grown-ups. What's the point of getting *married*?"

"Maybe they just want it to be official. Or maybe it's for Kitty."

"They haven't even been dating that long! How long has it been, six months?"

"A little longer than that. But Gogo, they've known each other for years."

She stacks up the slices of foiled pizza and says, "Can you imagine how weird it'll be to have her living here?"

Her question gives me pause. Ms. Rothschild *is* at the house a lot, but that's not the same as living here. She has her own ways of doing things, and so do we. Like, she wears shoes at her house, but we don't wear them here, so she takes them off when she comes over. And, now that I think about it, she's never slept over here before; she always goes back home at the end of the night. So that might feel a little weird. Also, she stores bread in the refrigerator, which I hate, and to be quite honest, her dog Simone sheds a lot and has been known to pee on the carpet. But the thing is, since I'm not going to UVA, I won't be around much longer—I'll be away at college. "Neither of us will be living here full-time though," I say at last. "Just Kitty, and Kitty's thrilled to death."

Margot doesn't respond right away. "Yes, they do seem really close." She goes to the freezer and makes space for the pizza, and with her back facing me she says, "Don't forget, we have to go prom-dress shopping before I leave."

"Ooh, okay!" It feels like two seconds ago that we were shopping for Margot's prom dress, and now it's my turn.

Daddy, who I didn't realize had walked into the kitchen, pipes up with, "Hey, maybe Trina could go too?" He casts a hopeful look my way. I'm not the one he should be looking at. I already love Ms. Rothschild. It's Margot she has to win over.

I look over at Margot, who is giving me wide panic eyes.

"Um . . . ," I say. "I think it should just be a Song girls thing this time."

Daddy nods like he understands. "Ah. Got it." Then he says to Margot, "Can the two of us spend a little daughter-dad time together before you leave? Maybe take our bikes on a trail?"

"Sounds good," she says.

When his back is turned, Margot mouths, *Thank you*. I feel disloyal to Ms. Rothschild, but Margot is my sister. I have to be on her side.

I think maybe Margot's feeling guilty about cutting Ms. Rothschild out of the dress shopping expedition, because she keeps trying to make it more of a thing. When we go to the mall the next day after school, she announces that we'll each pick two dresses, and I have to try all of them on no matter what, and then we'll rate them. She even printed out thumbs-up and thumbs-down emojis and made paddles for us to use.

It's cramped in the dressing room, and there are dresses everywhere. Margot gives Kitty the job of rehanging and organizing, but Kitty's already given it up in favor of playing Candy Crush on Margot's phone.

Margot hands me one of her picks first—it's a flowy black dress with fluttery cap sleeves. "You could do your hair up for this one."

Without looking up, Kitty says, "I would go with beachy waves."

Margot makes a face at her in the mirror.

"Is black really me, though?" I wonder.

"You should try wearing black more often," Margot says. "It really suits you."

Kitty picks at a scab on her leg. "When I go to prom, I'm going to wear a tight leather dress," she says.

"It can get hot in Virginia in May," I say, as Margot zips me up. "You could wear a leather dress to homecoming though, since it's in October."

We study my reflection in the mirror. The dress is too big in the bodice, and the black makes me look like a witch, but a witch in an ill-fitting dress.

"I think you need bigger boobs for that dress," Kitty says. She holds up the thumbs-down paddle.

I frown at her in the mirror. She's right, though. "Yeah, I think you're right."

"Did Mommy have big boobs?" Kitty asks suddenly.

"Hmm. I think they were on the small side," Margot says. "Like an A?"

"What size do you wear?" she asks.

"A B."

Eyeing me, Kitty says, "And Lara Jean's small like Mommy."

"Hey, I'm practically a B!" I protest. "I'm a large A. An almost B. Somebody unzip me."

"Tree has big boobs," Kitty says.

"Are they real?" Margot asks as she pulls down my zipper.

I step out of the dress and hand it over to Kitty to hang. "I think so."

"They're real. I've seen her in a bikini, and hers spread when she's lying down, and that's how you know. The fake ones stay in place like scoops of ice cream." Kitty picks up Margot's phone again. "Also, I asked her."

"If they were fake, I doubt she'd tell you that," Margot says.

Kitty frowns at her. "Tree doesn't lie to me."

"I'm not saying she'd lie; I'm saying she might be private about plastic surgery! Which is her right!" Kitty just shrugs coolly.

I quickly put on the next dress to get off the subject of Ms. Rothschild's boobs. "What do you guys think of this one?"

They both shake their heads and reach for the thumbs-down paddle at the same time. At least they are united in their dislike of my dress.

"Where's my pick? Try mine on next." Kitty's pick is a skin-tight, white, off-the-shoulder bandage dress I would never in a million years wear, and she knows it. "I just want to see it on you."

I try it on to appease her, and Kitty insists it's the best dress of all the dresses, because she wants to have the winning pick. In the end, none of the dresses are my style, but I'm not bothered by it. Prom is still more than a month away, and I want to scour vintage shops before I commit to anything from a regular store. I like the idea of a lived-in dress, a dress that has gone places, seen things, a dress that a girl like Stormy might've worn to a dance.

When Margot leaves for Scotland the next morning, she makes me promise to send pictures of potential dresses so she can weigh in. She doesn't say another word about Ms. Rothschild, but then, she wouldn't, because that's not her style.

13

LUCAS SAYS, "I THINK PROM IS A LOT LIKE New Year's Eve." He and Chris and I are hanging out in the nurse's office, because she is out to lunch, and she doesn't care if we lie on her couch. Since we're so far into senior year, all the teachers are in a pretty generous mood.

"New Year's Eve is for basics," Chris sneers, picking at her nails.

"Will you let me finish?" Lucas sighs and begins again. "As I was *saying*, prom buckles under the weight of all the expectations you put on it. One perfect high school night that every American teenager is supposed to have. You spend all this time and money and you feel obligated—no, *owed* an epic night. What can possibly live up to that amount of pressure?"

I think the perfect high school night will end up being some random little nothing moment that you didn't plan or expect; it just happened. I think I've already had like twelve perfect high school nights, with Peter, so I don't need prom to be epic. When I picture my prom night, I picture Peter in a tux, being polite to my dad, putting a corsage on Kitty. All of us taking a picture by the mantel. I make a mental note to ask Peter to get an extra little corsage for her.

"So does that mean you aren't going?" I ask Lucas.

He sighs again. "I don't know. There's no one here I would even want to go with."

"If I wasn't going with Peter, I would ask you," I say. Then I look from Lucas to Chris. "Hey, why don't you guys go together?"

"I'm not going to prom," Chris says. "I'll probably go clubbing in DC with my Applebee's people."

"Chris, you can't not go to prom. You can go clubbing with your Applebee's friends anytime. We only get one senior prom."

My birthday's the day after prom and I'm a little hurt that Chris seems to have forgotten. If she goes clubbing in DC, she'll probably stay all weekend and I won't even see her on my actual birthday.

"Prom's going to be lame. No offense. I mean, I'm sure you'll have fun, Lara Jean; you're going with the prom king. And what's that girl's name you're friends with now? Tammy?"

"Pammy," I say. "But it won't be fun if you're not there."

She puts her arm around me. "Aww."

"We always said we'd go to prom together and watch the sun rise over the elementary school playground!"

"You can watch it with Kavinsky."

"That's not the same!"

"Calm down," Chris says. "You're probably going to lose your V that night anyway, so I'll be the last thing you'll be thinking about."

"I wasn't planning on having sex on prom night!" I hiss.

My eyes dart over at Lucas, who is looking at me, bug-eyed.

"Lara Jean . . . you and Kavinsky haven't had sex yet?"

I look to make sure no one's in the hallway listening. "No, but please don't tell anybody. Not that I'm ashamed of it or anything. I just don't want everyone knowing my business."

"I get it, obviously, but wow," he says, still sounding shocked. "That's . . . wow."

"Why is it so wow?" I ask him, and I can feel my cheeks warming.

"He's so . . . hot."

I laugh. "That's true."

"There's a reason why having sex on prom night is a thing," Chris says. "I mean, yes, it's tradition, but also, everybody's dressed up, you get to stay out all night . . . Most of these people will never look as good as they do on prom night, grooming-wise, and that's sad. All these lemmings getting their manis and their pedis and their blowouts. So basic."

"Don't you get blowouts?" Lucas says.

Chris rolls her eyes. "Of course."

I say, "Then why are you judging other people for—"

"Look, that's not my point here. My point is . . ." She frowns. "Wait, what were we talking about?"

"Blowouts, manis, lemmings?" Lucas says.

"Before that."

"Sex?" I suggest.

"Right! My point is, losing your virginity on prom night

is a cliché, but clichés are clichés for a reason. There's a practicality to it. You get to stay out all night, you look great, et cetera, et cetera. It just makes sense."

"I'm not having sex for the first time because it's convenient and my hair looks good, Chris."

"Fair enough."

I don't know for sure, but I imagine my first time will probably be at college, in my own room, as an adult. It's hard to imagine it happening now, at home, when I'm Lara Jean the sister and the daughter. At college, I'll just be Lara Jean.

14

IT'S DECIDED THAT DADDY WILL PROPOSE to Ms. Rothschild on Saturday, after hiking on one of their favorite trails. He's going to do it right by a waterfall. The plan is for Peter and Kitty and me to hide behind trees and record the whole thing, then pop out with a romantic picnic basket. Daddy was nervous about the video part, in case Ms. Rothschild doesn't say yes, but Kitty begged. "It's for Margot," she kept saying, when really she's just nosy and wants to see it go down. Of course I do too. Peter's along for the ride, literally. He's giving us a ride.

That morning, before he leaves to pick up Ms. Rothschild, Daddy says, "Guys, if it doesn't look like it's going to be a yes, can you stop videotaping?"

I'm carefully wrapping roast beef sandwiches in wax paper. I look up to say, "She's going to say yes."

"Just promise me you'll quietly slip away," he says. He gives Kitty a pointed look.

"You got it, Dr. Covey," Peter says, lifting his hand for a high five.

As they slap hands, I say, "Daddy, did you pack the ring?"

"Yup!" Then he frowns. "Wait, did I?" He pats his pockets and unzips the inside compartment of his windbreaker. "Damn, I forgot it!" Then he runs upstairs.

Peter and I exchange a look. "I've never seen your dad so stressed out," he says, popping a grape in his mouth. "He's usually a cool customer."

I slap Peter's hand away from the grapes.

Kitty steals a grape and says, "He's been like this all week."

Daddy runs back downstairs with the engagement ring. Kitty and I helped him pick it out. It's a white-gold princess cut with a diamond halo. I was certain about the princess cut and Kitty was certain about the halo.

Daddy heads off to pick up Ms. Rothschild, and I finish putting together the picnic basket. I'm glad to have an excuse to bring it out. I bought it from a yard sale ages ago, and I haven't used it once. I pack a bottle of champagne, a perfect cluster of grapes, the sandwiches, a wedge of Brie, crackers.

"Pack a bottle of water, too," Peter says. "They'll be dehydrated from the hike."

"And probably from all the crying after she says yes," Kitty says.

"Should we play some music for them, when he gets down on one knee?" Peter suggests.

"We didn't discuss that part of the plan, and Daddy's nervous enough as it is," I say. "He can't be thinking about how we're hiding in the bushes waiting to cue up music for them. It'll make him self-conscious."

"Besides, we can add the music in post," Kitty says. "We need to be able to hear the dialogue."

I give her a look. "Katherine, this isn't a movie. This is real life."

I leave them to go to the downstairs bathroom, and after I wash my hands, I'm turning off the faucet when I hear Kitty say, "Peter, when Lara Jean's gone, will you still come visit me sometimes?"

"Course I will."

"Even if you guys break up?"

There's a pause. "We're not breaking up."

"But if you do?" she presses.

"We won't."

She ignores this. "Because we never see Josh anymore, and he said he'd visit too."

Peter scoffs. "Are you kidding me? You think I'm the same as Sanderson? *Me?* I'm a completely different league than him. I'm insulted you would even compare us."

Kitty lets out a relieved kind of laugh, the kind that sounds more like a sigh. "Yeah, you're right."

"Trust me, kid. You and I have our own thing."

I love him so much for that I could cry. He'll look after Kitty for me, I know he will.

Daddy told us they'd get to the waterfall around noon, so we should be there by eleven forty-five to get into position. We end up going a little earlier than that, just to be on the safe side, at Kitty's insistence.

We pick a hiding spot far enough away that Ms. Rothschild won't spot us, but close enough to see. Kitty and I hide behind a tree, and Peter crouches behind one close by, phone in his hand, ready to record. Kitty wanted to be the one to do it, but I make the executive decision that it should be Peter, because he isn't as emotionally invested in this moment and will have a steady hand.

Just after twelve, they come up the trail. Ms. Rothschild is laughing about something, and Daddy is laughing robotically with that same nervous look on his face. It's funny to watch them interact when she doesn't know we're watching. Kitty was right; it is a bit like a movie. He looks somehow younger next to her—maybe it's because he's in love. They walk over to the waterfall, and Ms. Rothschild sighs with happiness. "God, it's gorgeous up here," she says.

"I can barely hear anything," Kitty whispers to me. "The waterfall is too loud."

"Shh. You're the one being loud."

"Let's take a picture," Daddy says, fishing around in his windbreaker pocket.

"I thought you were morally opposed to selfies!" She laughs. "Hold on, let me try and fix my hair for this momentous occasion." She pulls her hair out of its ponytail holder and tries to fluff it up. Then she pops what looks like a cough drop or a piece of candy in her mouth.

Daddy's taking so long that for a second I'm afraid he's lost the ring or his nerve, but then he gets down on one knee. Daddy clears his throat. It's happening. I grab Kitty's hand and squeeze it. Her eyes are shining. My heart is bursting.

"Trina, I never expected to fall in love again. I thought I got my shot, and I was okay with that, because I had my girls. I didn't realize anything was missing. Then came you."

Ms. Rothschild's hands are covering her mouth. She has tears in her eyes.

"I want to spend the rest of my life with you, Trina." Ms. Rothschild starts choking on her candy, and Daddy leaps up off his knee and starts pounding her on the back. She's coughing like crazy.

From his tree Peter whispers, "Should I go do the Heimlich on her? I know how to do it."

"Peter, my dad's a doctor!" I whisper back. "He's got it."

As her coughing subsides, she stands up straight and wipes her eyes. "Wait. Were you asking me to marry you?"

"I was trying to," Daddy says. "Are you all right?"

"Yes!" She claps her hands to her cheeks.

"Yes, you're all right, or yes, you'll marry me?" Daddy asks her, and he's only half kidding.

"Yes, I'll marry you!" she screams, and Daddy reaches for her, and they kiss.

"This feels private," I whisper to Kitty.

"It's all part of the show," she whispers back.

Daddy hands Ms. Rothschild the ring box. I can't quite make out what he says next, but whatever it was, it makes her double over laughing.

"What's he saying?" Kitty asks me, just as Peter says, "What did he say?"

"I can't hear! Both of you be quiet! You're ruining the video!"

Which is when Ms. Rothschild looks over in our direction. Shoot.

We all pop back behind our respective trees, and then I hear Daddy's wry voice call out, "You can come out, guys. She said yes!"

We run out from behind the trees; Kitty launches herself into Ms. Rothschild's arms. They fall over onto the grass, and Ms. Rothschild is laughing breathlessly, her laughter echoing through the woods. I hug Daddy, and meanwhile Peter's still playing videographer, recording the moment for posterity like the good boyfriend he is.

"Are you happy?" I ask, looking up at my dad.

His eyes brimming with tears, he nods and hugs me tighter.

And just like that, our little family grows bigger.

15

IT'S THE FIRST NIGHT WE'VE ALL BEEN together for dinner since the engagement, and Daddy's in the kitchen making a salad. Us girls are sitting in the living room just hanging out. Kitty is doing her homework; Ms. Rothschild is sipping on a glass of white wine. It's all very mellow—perfect timing for me to bring up wedding business. I've spent the last week working on a mood board for Daddy and Ms. Rothschild's wedding: *Pride and Prejudice* the movie, a whole wall of roses for the photo-booth area, *The Virgin Suicides*, wine-bottle floral centerpieces as a nod to Charlottesville wineries.

When I present it to Ms. Rothschild on my laptop, she looks vaguely alarmed. She sets down her wine glass and looks closer at the screen. "This is beautiful, Lara Jean. Really lovely. You've put a lot of time into this!"

So much time, in fact, that I skipped Peter's lacrosse game this week, plus a movie night at Pammy's. But this is important. Of course I don't say any of this out loud; I just smile a beatific smile. "Does this vision feel in line with what you were thinking?

"Well . . . to be honest, I think we were thinking we'd just go to the justice of the peace. Selling my house and figuring out how I'm going to fit all my junk in here is enough of a headache already."

Daddy comes out with the wooden salad bowl in his hands. Dryly he says, "So you're saying marrying me is a headache?"

She rolls her eyes. "You know what I'm saying, Dan! It's not like you have the time to plan a big wedding either." She takes a sip of wine and turns to me. "Your dad and I have both been married before, so neither of us feels like making a big fuss. I'll probably just wear a dress I already have."

"Of *course* we should make a big fuss. Do you know how many years it took Daddy to find someone who'd eat his cooking and watch his documentaries?" I shake my head. "Ms. Rothschild, you're a miracle. For that we *have* to celebrate." I call out to my dad, who's disappeared back into the kitchen. "Did you hear that, Daddy? Ms. Rothschild wants to go to *city hall*. Please disabuse her of this notion."

"Will you please stop calling me Ms. Rothschild? Now that I'm going to be your wicked stepmother, you should at least call me Trina. Or Tree. Whatever feels right to you."

"How about Stepmother?" I suggest, all innocence. "That feels pretty right."

She swats at me. "Girl! I will cut you."

Giggling, I dart away from her. "Let's get back to the wedding. I don't know if this is a sensitive issue or not, but did you keep your old wedding photos? I want to see what your bridal style was."

Ms. Rothschild pulls a terrible face. "I think I threw out everything. I might have a picture tucked in an album somewhere. Thank God I got married before social media was a thing. Can you imagine, getting divorced and having to take down all your wedding pictures?"

"Isn't it bad luck to talk about divorce when you're planning your wedding?"

She laughs. "Well then, we're already doomed." I must look alarmed because she says, "I'm kidding! I'll hunt around for a wedding picture to show you if you want, but honestly, I'm not real proud of it. Smoky eye was the thing back then, and I took it a little too far. Plus I did that early two thousands thing with the chocolate lip liner and the frosted lip."

I try to keep my face neutral. "Right, okay. What about your dress?"

"One-shoulder, with a mermaid style skirt. It made my butt look amazing."

"I see."

"Quit judging me!"

Daddy puts his hand on Ms. Rothschild's shoulder. "What if we did it here at the house?"

"Like in the backyard?" She considers this. "I think that could be nice. A little barbecue, just family and a few friends?"

"Daddy doesn't have any friends," Kitty says from across the living room, her math book in her lap.

Daddy frowns at her. "I do too have friends. I have Dr. Kang from the hospital, and there's Marjorie, and Aunt D. But er, yes, it would be a small group on my side."

"Plus Nana," Kitty says, and both Daddy and Ms. Rothschild look nervous at the mention of Nana. Daddy's mother isn't the friendliest person.

"Don't forget Grandma," I throw in.

Grandma and Ms. Rothschild met at Thanksgiving, and while Daddy didn't explicitly introduce her as his girlfriend, Grandma is shrewd and she doesn't miss a thing. She gave Ms. Rothschild the third degree, asking if she had any kids of her own, how long she'd been divorced, if she had any student-loan debt. Ms. Rothschild held up pretty well, and when I walked Grandma out to the car to say good-bye, she said Ms. Rothschild was "not bad." She said she dressed young for her age, but she also said that Ms. Rothschild had a lot of energy and a brightness to her.

"I've already done the big wedding thing," Ms. Rothschild says. "It'll be small on my side too. A few friends from college, Shelly from work. My sister Jeanie, my SoulCycle friends."

"Can we be your bridesmaids?" Kitty asks, and Ms. Rothschild laughs.

"Kitty! You can't just ask that." But I turn to Ms. Rothschild, waiting to hear what she will say.

"Sure," she says. "Lara Jean, would you be okay with that?"

"I would be honored," I say.

"So you three girls, and my friend Kristen, because she'll kill me if I don't ask her."

I clap my hands together. "Now that that's settled, let's get back to the dress. If it's going to be a backyard wedding, I feel like your dress should reflect that."

"As long as it has sleeves so my bat wings don't flap around," she says.

"Ms. Roth—I mean, Trina, you don't have bat wings," I say. She's very in shape from all her Pilates and SoulCycle.

Kitty's eyes light up. "What are bat wings? That sounds gross."

"Come here, and I'll show you." Kitty obeys, and Ms. Rothschild lifts her arm and stretches it out; then at the last second she grabs Kitty and tickles her. Kitty's dying laughing, and so is Ms. Rothschild.

Breathlessly she says, "Gross? That'll teach you to call your wicked stepmother-to-be gross!"

Daddy looks as happy as I've ever seen him.

Later that night in our bathroom, Kitty's brushing her teeth, and I'm scrubbing my face with a new exfoliant I ordered off a Korean beauty site. It's walnut shells and blueberry. "Mason jars and gingham—but elegant," I muse.

"Mason jars are played out," Kitty says. "Look on Pinterest. Literally everybody does Mason jars."

Her words do have the ring of truth. "Well, I'm definitely wearing a flower crown on my head. I don't care if you say it's played out."

Flatly she says, "You can't wear a flower crown."

"Why not?"

She spits out toothpaste. "You're too old. That's for flower girls."

"No, you aren't envisioning it correctly. I wasn't thinking baby's breath. I was thinking little pink and peach roses, with a lot of greenery. Pale green greenery, you know that kind?"

She shakes her head, resolute. "We aren't fairies in a forest. It's too cutesy. And I know Gogo's going to agree with me."

I have a sinking feeling she will too. I decide to put this argument aside for now. It won't be won today. "For dresses, I was thinking we could wear vintage. Not off-white, but tea-stained white. Sort of nightgown-style. Very ethereal— not fairy, more like celestial being."

"I'm wearing a tuxedo."

I nearly choke. "A what!"

"A tuxedo. With matching Converse."

"Over my dead body!"

Kitty shrugs.

"Kitty, this wedding isn't black tie. A tuxedo isn't going to look right at a backyard wedding! The three of us should match, like a set! The Song girls!"

"I've already told Tree and Daddy, and they both love the idea of me in a tux, so get over it." She's got that look on her face, the obstinate look she gets when she's really digging her heels in. Like a bull.

"At the very least you should wear a seersucker suit, then. It will be too hot for a tuxedo, and seersucker breathes." I feel like I've made a concession here, so she should too, but no.

"You don't get to decide everything, Lara Jean. It's not your wedding."

"I know that!"

"Well, just keep it in mind."

I reach out to shake her, but she flounces off before I can. Over her shoulder, she calls out, "Worry about your own life!"

16

*IT'S AN EARLY-RELEASE DAY AND I'M HURRY-*ing down the hallway to meet Peter at his locker when Mrs. Duvall stops me. "Lara Jean! Are you coming to the mixer this evening?"

"Um . . ." I don't remember hearing anything about a mixer.

She tsks me. "I sent you a reminder e-mail last week! It's a little get-together for local students who were accepted to William and Mary. There'll be a few of you from our school, but lots of other schools too. It's a nice opportunity for you to meet some people before you get there."

"Oh . . ." I did see that e-mail, but I forgot all about it. "I would love to go, but I can't because I have a . . . um, family obligation."

Which is, technically, true. Peter and I are going to an estate sale in Richmond—he has to pick up end tables for his mom's antiques store, and I'm looking for a cake table for Daddy and Trina's wedding.

Mrs. Duvall gives me a lingering look and says, "Well, I'm sure there'll be another one. A lot of people would kill to be in your spot, Lara Jean, but I'm sure you already know that."

"I do," I assure her, and then I scuttle off to meet Peter.

The estate sale turns out to be a bust—for me, anyway.

Peter picks up the end tables, but I don't see anything appropriate for an ethereal backyard wedding. There's one chest of drawers that is a possibility, if I painted it, maybe, or stenciled some rosebuds on it, but it costs three hundred dollars, and I have a feeling Daddy and Trina would balk at the price. I take a picture of it just in case.

Peter and I go to a place I read about on the Internet called Croaker's Spot, where we get fried fish and buttery cornbread dripping in sweet sauce. "Richmond's cool," he says, wiping sauce off his chin. "Too bad William and Mary isn't in Richmond. It's closer to UVA, too."

"Just by thirty minutes," I say. "Anyway I was thinking about it, and it won't even be a full year until I'm at UVA." I start counting the months off my fingers. "It's really like nine months. And I'll be home for winter break, and then we have spring break."

"Exactly," he says.

When I get home, it's dark out, and Daddy, Trina, and Kitty are at the kitchen table finishing up dinner. Daddy starts to get up when I walk in. "Sit down, I'll fix you a plate," he says. With a wink he says, "Trina made her lemon chicken."

Trina's lemon chicken is just chicken breasts with lemon seasoning cooked in Pam, but it's her specialty and it's pretty good. Sliding into a seat, I say, "No thanks, I just ate a ton of food."

"Did they serve dinner at the mixer?" Daddy asks, sitting back down. "How was it?"

"How did you know about the mixer?" I ask him, leaning down to pet Trina's dog Simone, who followed me into the kitchen and is now sitting at my feet, hoping for a crumb.

"They sent an invitation in the mail. I put it on the fridge!"

"Oh, whoops. I didn't go. I went to Richmond with Peter to look for a cake table for the wedding."

Daddy frowns. "You went all the way to Richmond on a school night? For a cake table?"

Uh-oh. I quickly pull out my phone to show them. "It's a little expensive, but we could have the drawers kind of half-open, bursting with roses. Even if we didn't get this exact one, if you like it, I'm sure I could find something similar to it."

Daddy leans in to look. "Drawers of roses bursting out? That sounds very expensive and not exactly ecologically responsible."

"Well I suppose we could do daisies, but it doesn't really have the same effect." I cast a look over at Kitty before continuing. "I want to circle back on the bridesmaid dresses."

"Wait a minute, I want to circle back on you skipping out on your college mixer to go to Richmond," Daddy interjects.

"Don't worry, Daddy, I'm sure there will be a million of them before fall," I tell him. "Kitty, about the bridesmaid dresses—"

Without even looking up, Kitty says, "You just wear the nightgown outfit on your own."

I choose to ignore the fact that she called it a nightgown outfit and say, "It won't look right if it's just me. The beauty of it is the set. All of us matching, very ethereal, like angels.

Then it becomes a look, a moment. If I wear it on my own it won't work. It needs to be all three of us." I don't know how many more times I have to say the word "ethereal" to make people understand what the vibe of this wedding is.

Kitty says, "If you want to be a set, you're welcome to wear a tux too. I would be fine with that."

I take a deep breath to keep from screaming at her. "Well, let's just see what Margot says about all this."

"Margot won't care either way."

Kitty gets up to put her plate in the sink, and when her back is turned, I raise my hands like I'm going to strangle her. "Saw that," she says. I swear, she has eyes in the back of her head.

"Trina, what do you think?" I ask.

"Honestly, I could care less what you guys wear, but you're going to have to run it by Margot and Kristen. They might have their own ideas."

Delicately I say, "Just FYI, it's 'I couldn't care less,' not 'I could care less.' Because if you could, then you are technically caring."

Trina rolls her eyes, and Kitty slides back into her chair and says, "Why are you like this, Lara Jean?"

I shove her in the side. To Trina I say, "Kristen is a grown woman, so I'm sure she'll be fine with whatever us kids do. She's an adult."

Trina doesn't look so sure. "She won't want anything that shows her arms. She'll try to convince you to put a matching cardigan on top."

"Um, no."

Trina puts her hands up. "You have to take it up with Kristen. Like I said, I could care less." She crosses her eyes at me, and I laugh and so does Kitty.

"Wait a minute, can we talk more about this mixer you didn't go to?" Daddy asks, his brow furrowed. "That sounded like a really nice event."

"I'll go to the next one," I promise him. Of course, I don't mean it.

There's no point in me going to mixers and getting attached to people when I'm only going to be there nine months.

After I make myself a bowl of ice cream, I go upstairs and text Margot to see if she is awake. She is, so I immediately call her to shore up support on the dress situation, and Kitty's right—Margot doesn't care either way.

"I'll do whatever you guys want to do," she says.

"The hottest places in hell are reserved for people who maintain neutrality in times of crisis," I say, licking my spoon.

She laughs. "I thought the hottest places in hell were reserved for women who don't help other women."

"Well, I suppose hell has a lot of rooms. Honestly, don't you think Kitty will look silly in a tuxedo? It's a backyard wedding. The feel is supposed to be ethereal!"

"I don't think she'll look any sillier than you'll look in a flower crown all by yourself. Just let her wear it, and you wear your flower crown, and I'll be neutral. Honestly, I don't even see the point in me being a bridesmaid when Ms. Rothschild and I barely know each other. I mean, I know she's doing it to be nice, but it's so not necessary. It's all a bit much."

Now I'm regretting stirring the waters and pushing the whole tuxedo-versus-flower-crown issue. The last thing I want is for Margot to get any ideas about dropping out of the wedding. She's lukewarm on Trina at best. Hastily I say, "Well, we don't have to wear flower crowns. You and I could wear plain dresses and Kitty could wear her tux, and that would look fine."

"How was that William and Mary mixer today? Did you meet any cool people?"

"How does everybody but me know about the mixer!"

"It was on the fridge."

"Oh. I didn't go."

There's a pause. "Lara Jean, have you sent in your William and Mary deposit yet?"

"I'm about to! It's not due until May first."

"Are you thinking about changing your mind?"

"No! I just haven't gotten around to it yet. Things have been crazy around here, with all the wedding planning and everything."

"It sounds like the wedding is getting really big. I thought they just wanted to do a simple thing."

"We're weighing our options. It'll still be simple. I just think the day should be really special, something we'll always remember."

After we get off the phone, I go downstairs to put my ice cream bowl in the sink, and on the way back, I stop in the living room, where Mommy and Daddy's wedding portrait hangs above the fireplace. Her dress is lace, with cap sleeves and a flowy skirt. Her hair is up, in a side bun, with a few tendrils that slip out. She's wearing diamond earrings I never saw her wear in real life. She hardly ever wore jewelry, or much makeup, either. Daddy's in a gray suit, but no gray in his hair yet; his cheeks are apple smooth, no stubble. She looks the way I remember her, but he looks so much younger.

It hits me that we'll have to move the picture. It would just be too awkward for Trina to have to look at it every day. She doesn't seem bothered by it now, but after she's living here, after they're married, she's bound to feel differently. I could hang it in my room, though Margot might want it too. I guess I'll ask her when she's back.

Trina's friend Kristen comes over after dinner later that week, armed with a bottle of rosé and a stack of bridal magazines. The way Trina talks about Kristen, I was picturing someone really intimidating and tall, but Kristen is my height. She has brown hair cut in a short bob, tan skin. I'm impressed by her collection of *Martha Stewart Weddings*—it goes back years and years. "Please just don't crease the corners," she says, which makes me frown. As if I would ever.

"I think we should discuss the bridal shower first," she says. She's petting Jamie Fox-Pickle; his sandy head is in her lap. I've never seen him take to a stranger so quickly, which I take to be a good sign.

I say, "I thought a tea party could be fun. I'd make little

JENNY HAN

sandwiches with the crusts cut off, and little bite-sized scones, and clotted cream . . ."

"I was thinking a SoulCycle party," Kristen says. "I'd have matching neon tank tops made that say 'Team Trina.' We could rent out the whole class!"

I try not to look disappointed, and just nod like, *Hmm*.

"Guys, both of those ideas sound so great, but I'm thinking no bridal shower," Trina interjects. Kristen gasps and I do too. With an apologetic smile she explains, "We have too much stuff as it is. The whole point of a bridal shower is to shower the bride with everything she'll need for her house, and I can't think of one thing we'd need."

"We don't have an ice cream maker," I say. I've been wanting to experiment with ice creams for a while now, but the one I want is more than four hundred dollars. "And Daddy's always talking about a pasta machine."

"We can buy those things for ourselves. We're grown-ups, after all." Kristen opens her mouth to argue, but Trina says, "Kris, I'm firm on this. No bridal shower. I'm in my forties, for Pete's sake. I've been to this rodeo before."

Stiffly Kristen says, "I don't see what that has to do with anything. The point of a bridal shower is to make the bride feel special and loved. But fine. If it's that important to you, we won't do one."

"Thank you," Trina says. She leans over and puts her arm around Kristen, who gives her a stern look.

"But where I will not negotiate is a bachelorette. You've gotta have a bach. Period."

Smiling, Trina says, "I will not fight you on that. Maybe we can do your SoulCycle idea for my bachelorette."

"No way. We gotta go big. So, Vegas, am I right? You love Vegas. I'm gonna e-mail the girls tonight so Sarah's husband can get us a suite at the Bellagio—"

"It's gonna be a no on Vegas," Trina says. "The bachelorette has to be local and PG so the girls can come."

"What girls?" Kristen demands.

Trina points to me. "My girls." She smiles at me shyly and I smile back, feeling warm inside.

"What if we did karaoke?" I suggest, and Trina claps her hands in delight.

Kristen's mouth drops. "No offense, Lara Jean, but what the hell is going on here, Trina! You can't have your future stepchildren at your bach. It's just not right. We're not gonna be able to celebrate the way you're supposed to celebrate a bach. Like the old days—aka get naked wasted so you can live up your last moments as a single woman."

Trina looks at me and shakes her head. "For the record, we never got 'naked wasted.'" To Kristen she says, "Kris, I don't think of them as my future stepchildren. They're just . . . the girls. But don't worry. We'll have fun. Margot's in college, and Lara Jean's practically in college. They can be exposed to a little sangria and chardonnay."

"You do love your white wine," I say, and Trina swats at my shoulder.

Kristen exhales loudly. "Well, what about the little one?"

"Kitty's very mature for her age," Trina says.

Kristen crosses her arms. "I'm putting my foot down. You can't bring a child on a bachelorette. It isn't right."

"Kris!"

At this I feel like I have to speak up. "I'm going to side with Kristen on this one. We won't be able to bring Kitty to karaoke. She's too young. They won't let an eleven-year-old in."

"She'll be so disappointed, though."

"She'll live," I say.

Kristen sips on her rosé and says, "Disappointment is good for kids; it prepares them for the real world, where it's not all about them and their feelings."

Trina rolls her eyes. "If you're putting your foot down on having Kitty at the bachelorette, I'm putting my foot down on penises. I mean it, Kris. No penis cake, no penis straws, no penis pasta. No penises, period."

I blush. There's such a thing as penis pasta?

"Fine." Kristen pushes out her lower lip.

"All right, then. Can we move on to the actual wedding, please?"

I run and get my laptop and pull up my vision board, which is when Kitty decides to grace us with her presence. She's been in the living room watching TV. "Where are we in the planning?" she wants to know.

Kristen eyes her before saying, "Let's talk food."

"What about food trucks?" I suggest. "Like, a waffle truck?"

Kristen purses her lips. "I was thinking barbecue. Trina loves barbecue."

"Hmm," I say. "But a lot of people do barbecue, don't they? It's kind of . . ."

"Played out?" Kitty suggests.

"I was going to say common." But yeah.

"But Trina loves barbecue!"

"Can y'all please stop talking about me like I'm not here?" Trina says. "I do love barbecue. And can we do Mason jars?"

I'm expecting Kitty to denigrate Mason jars again, but she doesn't say anything of the sort. She says, "What do we think about edible flowers in the drinks?" I'm pretty sure that was one of my ideas that she just stole.

Trina does a shimmy in her seat. "Yes! I love it!"

I'm quick to add, "We could do a nice punch bowl and float some flowers on top."

Kristen gives me an approving look.

Bolstered, I grandly say, "And as for the cakes, we'll need a wedding cake and a groom's cake."

"Do we really need two cakes?" Trina asks, chewing on her nail. "There won't be that many people there."

"This is the South; we have to have a groom's cake. For yours I was thinking yellow cake with vanilla buttercream frosting." Trina beams at me. That's her favorite kind of cake, just plain. Not exactly exciting to bake, but it's her favorite. "For Daddy's, I was thinking . . . a Thin Mint cake! Chocolate cake with mint frosting, but with Thin Mints crumbled on top." I have such a vision for this cake.

This time Kitty's the one to give me an approving nod. I feel more in my element then I have in weeks.

17

KITTY'S MIXING NAIL-POLISH COLORS ON
a paper plate while I'm looking up "celebrity updos" for
Trina's wedding hair. I'm lying on the couch, with pillows propped up behind me, and she is on the floor, with
nail-polish bottles all around her. Suddenly she asks me,
"Have you ever thought about, like, what if Daddy and
Trina have a baby and it looks like Daddy?"

Kitty thinks of all sorts of things that would never have
occurred to me. I hadn't once thought of that—that they
might have a baby or that this pretend baby wouldn't look
like us. The baby would be all Daddy and Trina. No one
would have to wonder whose child he was or calculate who
belongs to who. They'd just assume.

"But they're both so old," I say.

"Trina's forty-three. You can get pregnant at forty-three.
Maddie's mom just had a baby and she's forty-three."

"True . . ."

"What if it's a boy?"

Daddy with a son. It's a startling thought. He's not exactly
sporty, not in a traditional male sense. I mean, he likes to go
biking and he plays doubles tennis in the spring. But I'm sure
there are things he'd want to do with a son that he doesn't do
with us because no one's interested. Fishing, maybe? Football

he doesn't care about. Trina cares more than he does.

When my mom was pregnant with Kitty, Margot wanted another sister but I wanted a boy. The Song girls and their baby brother. It would be nice to get that baby brother after all. Especially since I won't be at home and have to hear it crying in the middle of the night. I'll just get to buy the baby little shearling booties and sweaters with red foxes or bunnies.

"If they named him Tate, we could call him Tater Tot," I muse.

Two red blotches appear on Kitty's cheeks, and just like that, she looks as young as I always picture her in my head: a little kid. "I don't want them to have another baby. If they have a baby, I'll be in the middle. I'll be nothing."

"Hey!" I object. "I'm in the middle now!"

"Margot's oldest and smartest, and you're the prettiest." *I'm the prettiest?? Kitty thinks I'm the prettiest?* I try not to look too happy, because she's still talking. "I'm only the youngest. If they have a baby, I won't even be that."

I put down my computer. "Kitty, you're a lot more than the youngest Song girl. You're the wild Song girl. The mean one. The spiky one." Kitty's pursing her lips, trying not to smile at this. I add, "And no matter what, Trina loves you; she'll always love you, even if she did have a baby which I don't think she will." I stop. "Wait, did you mean it when you said I was the prettiest?"

"No, I take it back. I'll probably be the prettiest by the time I get to high school. You can be the nicest." I leap off the couch and grab her by the shoulders like I'm going to shake her, and she giggles.

"I don't want to be the nicest," I say.

"You are, though." She says it not like an insult, but not exactly like a compliment. "What do you wish you had of mine?"

"Your nerve."

"What else?"

"Your nose. You have a little nubbin of a nose." I tap it. "What about me?"

Kitty shrugs. "I don't know." Then she cracks up, and I shake her by the shoulders.

I'm still thinking about it later that evening. I hadn't thought of Daddy and Trina having a baby. But Trina doesn't have any children, just her "fur baby" golden retriever Simone. She might want a baby of her own. And Daddy's never said so, but is there a chance he'd want to try one more time for a son? The baby would be eighteen years younger than me. What a strange thought. And even stranger still: I'm old enough to have a baby of my own.

What would Peter and I do if I got pregnant? I can't even picture what would happen. All I can see is the look on Daddy's face when I tell him the news, and that's about as far as I get.

The next morning, on the way to school in Peter's car, I steal a look at his profile. "I like how you're so smooth," I say. "Like a baby."

"I could grow a beard if I wanted to," he says, touching his chin. "A thick one."

Fondly I say, "No, you couldn't. But maybe one day, when you're a man."

He frowns. "I *am* a man. I'm eighteen!"

I scoff, "You don't even pack your own lunches. Do you even know how to do laundry?"

"I'm a man in all the ways that count," he boasts, and I roll my eyes.

"What would you do if you were drafted to go to war?" I ask.

"Uh . . . aren't college kids given a pass on that? Does the draft even still exist?"

I don't know the answers to either of these questions, so I barrel forward. "What would you do if I got pregnant right now?"

"Lara Jean, we're not even having sex. That would be the immaculate conception."

"If we were?" I press.

He groans. "You and your questions! I don't know. How could I know what I would do?"

"What do you *think* you would do?"

Peter doesn't hesitate. "Whatever you wanted to do."

"Wouldn't you want to decide together?" I'm testing him—for what, I don't know.

"I'm not the one who has to carry it. It's your body, not mine."

His answer pleases me, but still I keep going. "What if I said . . . let's have the baby and get married?"

Again Peter doesn't hesitate. "I'd say sure. Yeah!"

Now I'm the one frowning. "'Sure'? Just like that? The

biggest decision of your life and you just say sure?"

"Yeah. Because I *am* sure."

I lean over to him and put my palms on his smooth cheeks. "That's how I know you're still a boy. Because you're so sure."

He frowns back at me. "Why are you saying it like it's a bad thing?"

I let go. "You're always so sure of everything about yourself. You've never been not sure."

"Well, I'm sure of this one thing," he says, staring straight ahead. "I'm sure I'd never be the kind of dad my dad is, no matter how old I am."

I go quiet, feeling guilty for teasing him and bringing up bad feelings. I want to ask if his dad is still reaching out to make amends, but the closed-up look on Peter's face stops me. I just wish he and his dad could fix things between them before he goes to college. Because right now, Peter *is* still a boy, and deep down, I think all boys want to know their dads, no matter what kind of men they are.

After school, we go through the drive-thru, and Peter's already tearing into his sandwich before we're out of the parking lot. Between bites of fried chicken sandwich, he says, "Did you mean it when you said before that you couldn't picture marrying me?"

"I didn't say that!"

"I mean, you kind of said that. You said I'm still a boy and you couldn't marry a boy."

Now I've gone and hurt his feelings. "I didn't mean it like that. I meant I couldn't picture marrying anybody right now. We're both still babies. How could we *have* a baby?" Without thinking, I say, "Anyway, my dad gave me a whole birth-control kit for college, so we don't even have to worry about it."

Peter nearly chokes on his sandwich. "A birth-control kit?"

"Sure. Condoms and . . ." Dental dams. "Peter, do you know what a dental dam is?"

"A what? Is that what dentists use to keep your mouth open when they clean it?"

I giggle. "No. It's for oral sex. And here I thought you were this big expert and *you* were going to be the one to teach *me* everything at college!"

My heart speeds up as I wait for him to make a joke about the two of us finally having sex at college, but he doesn't. He frowns and says, "I don't like the thought of your dad thinking we're doing it when we're not."

"He just wants us to be careful is all. He's a professional, remember?" I pat him on the knee. "Either way, I'm not getting pregnant, so it's fine."

He crumples up his napkin and tosses it in the paper bag, his eyes still on the road. "Your parents met in college, didn't they?"

I'm surprised he remembers. I don't remember telling him that. "Yeah."

"So how old were they? Eighteen? Nineteen?" Peter's headed somewhere with this line of questioning.

"Twenty, I think."

His face dims but just slightly. "Okay, twenty. I'm eighteen and you'll be eighteen next month. Twenty is just two years older. So what difference does two years make in the grand scheme of things?" He beams a smile at me. "Your parents met at twenty; we met at—"

"Twelve," I supply.

Peter frowns, annoyed that I've messed up his argument. "Okay, so we met when were kids, but we didn't get together until we were seventeen—"

"I was sixteen."

"We didn't get together *for real* until we were both basically seventeen. Which is basically the same thing as eighteen, which is basically the same thing as twenty." He has the self-satisfied look of a lawyer who has just delivered a winning closing statement.

"That's a very long and twisty line of logic," I say. "Have you ever thought about being a lawyer?"

"No, but now I'm thinking maybe?"

"UVA has a great law school," I say, and I get a sudden pang, because college is one thing, but law school? That's so far away, and who knows what will happen between now and then? By then we'll be such different people. Thinking of Peter in his twenties, I feel a sense of yearning for the man I may never get to meet. Right now, today, he's still a boy, and I know him better than anybody, but what if it isn't always this way? Already our paths are diverging, a little more every day, the closer we get to August.

18

TRINA PUT HER HOUSE ON THE MARKET
a couple of weeks after she and Daddy got engaged. Kristen's
a real estate agent, and she told her that now was the time
to sell, because everybody likes to buy in the springtime. It
turns out she was right; a couple made an offer on it the very
same week—sooner than any of us could have imagined.
Daddy and Trina thought the house would sit on the market
for at least a month, but now movers are unloading boxes at
our house and everything's careening forward at lightning
speed.

There was never any big discussion about who was moving in with who—it was just understood that Trina was
coming here. For one, our house is bigger, but also, it's easier
to move one person than four. You would think. For one
person, Trina has a lot of stuff. Boxes and boxes of clothes
and shoes, her exercise equipment, random pieces of furniture, a huge velvet upholstered headboard that I know my
dad is horrified by.

"If it was me, I wouldn't want to move into another
woman's house," Chris says. She's standing at my window,
watching Trina direct the movers. She stopped by on her
way to work to borrow a pair of my shoes.

"What other woman?" I ask her.

"Your mom! I would always feel like it was her house. Like, she picked the furniture, the wallpaper."

"Actually Margot and I picked a lot of it," I say. "I picked the dining room wallpaper; she picked the upstairs bathroom color." I remember that Margot and Mommy and I sat down on the living room floor with all the wallpaper books and carpet samples and paint chips spread around us. We spent the whole afternoon going over every book with a fine-tooth comb, with Margot and me battling over which blue was the right blue for the upstairs bathroom we'd share. I thought robin's-egg blue, and Margot thought sky blue. Mommy finally had us do rock, paper, scissors for it, and Margot won. I sulked over it until I beat her out with my wallpaper choice.

"I'm just saying. I feel like if I was Trina, I would want a fresh start," Chris says.

"Well, that's kind of impossible when her husband-to-be already has three kids."

"You know what I mean. As fresh as possible."

"They're getting a new bed, at least. It's coming tomorrow."

Chris perks up at this. Flopping on my bed, she says, "Ew, is it weird to think about your dad having sex?"

I slap her on the leg. "I don't think about that! So please don't bring it up."

Picking at the strings on her cutoffs, she says, "Trina does have a great body."

"I'm not kidding, Chris!"

"I'm just saying, I would kill to have her body at her age."

"She's not that old."

"Still." Chris preens at me prettily. "If I open the window, can I smoke in here?"

"I think you know the answer to that question, Christina."

She pouts, but it's just for show because she knew I wasn't going to say yes. "Ugh. America is so annoying about smoking. So basic."

Now that Chris is going to Costa Rica, she relishes looking down on everything American. I still can't believe she's leaving. "Are you really not going to prom?" I ask.

"I'm really not."

"You're going to regret not going," I warn her. "When you're working on the farm in Costa Rica, you'll suddenly remember how you didn't go to prom, and you will feel abject regret, and you'll have no one to blame but yourself."

With a laugh, she says, "I highly doubt it!"

After Chris leaves for work, I'm on my computer in the kitchen looking for bridesmaid dresses and/or prom dresses, and Daddy and Trina walk in from being outside with the movers. I try to look busy, like I'm studying, in case they ask for help. Shrewd little Kitty has made herself scarce these past couple of days, and I'm regretting not following her lead.

Daddy pours himself a glass of water, wiping sweat from his brow. "Do you really need to bring that treadmill?" he asks Trina. "It doesn't even work properly."

"It works fine."

Gulping the rest of his water, he says, "I've never seen you use it."

She frowns at him. "That doesn't mean I don't use it. It means I don't use it in front of *you*."

"All right. When's the last time you used it?"

Her eyes narrow. "None of your business."

"Trina!"

"Dan!"

This is a new side to Daddy—bickering, losing his patience just barely. Trina brings it out of him, and I know it sounds strange, but I'm glad for it. It's something I never realized was gone in him. There's making do, living a pleasant life, no big ups or downs, and there's all the friction and fire that come with being in love with someone. She takes forever to get ready, which drives him crazy, and she makes fun of his hobbies, like bird-watching and documentaries. But they just fit.

19

THERE'S A LACROSSE GAME TONIGHT, AND
Pammy can't go because she has to work, and of course
Chris would never deign to go to a lacrosse game, so I bring
Kitty with me. She pretends to mull it over, musing aloud
that it might be boring, but when I say, "Never mind, then,"
she quickly agrees to come.

In the stands we run into Peter's mom and his younger
brother, Owen, so we sit with them. He and Kitty proceed
to each pretend the other doesn't exist—he plays games on
his phone and she plays games on hers. Owen is tall, but he
sits hunched, with his hair in his eyes.

We chat about my dad and Trina's engagement for a bit
and I tell her some of my ideas for the wedding. She's nodding along and then she suddenly says, "I hear congratulations are in order for you, too."

Confused, I say, "What for?"

"William and Mary!"

"Oh! Thank you."

"I know you were hoping to go to UVA, but this might
be for the best anyway." She gives me a sympathetic smile.

I smile back, unsure. Unsure of what, exactly, "for the
best" means. Is she glad I'm not going to UVA with Peter?
Does she think this means we're breaking up now? So all I

say is, "Williamsburg isn't really that far from Charlottesville anyway."

Her response is, "Hmm, yes, that's true." Then Peter scores a point, and we both stand up and cheer.

When I sit back down again, Kitty asks me, "Can we get popcorn?"

"Sure," I say, glad to have an excuse to get up. To Peter's mom and brother I ask, "Do you guys want anything?"

Without looking up, Owen says, "Popcorn."

"You guys can share," Peter's mom says.

I make my way down the bleachers, and I'm heading for the snack bar when I notice a man, standing off to the side, his arms crossed, watching the game. He is tall; he has nut-brown hair. Handsome. When he turns his head and I see his profile, I know who he is, because I know that face. I know that chin, those eyes. He's Peter's dad. It's like seeing the Ghost of Christmas Future, and I'm frozen in place, transfixed.

He catches me staring at him, and offers a friendly smile. I feel like I have no choice but to take a step forward and ask, "Excuse me . . . but are you Peter's dad?"

Surprised, he nods. "Are you a friend of his?"

"I'm Lara Jean Covey. His, um, girlfriend." He looks startled, but then he recovers and extends his hand. I shake it firmly, to give a good impression. "Wow, you look just like him."

He laughs, and I'm struck anew by how much of him is in Peter. "He looks just like me, you mean."

I laugh too. "Right. You were here first."

There is an awkward silence, and then he clears his throat and asks me, "How is he?"

"Oh, he's good. He's great. Did you hear he's going to UVA on a lacrosse scholarship?"

He nods, smiling. "I heard that from his mom. I'm proud of him. Not that I can take any credit for it—but still. I'm really proud of the kid." His eyes flicker back to the field, to Peter. "I just wanted to see him play again. I've missed it." He hesitates before saying, "Please don't mention to Peter that I was here."

I'm so taken by surprise, all I can say is, "Oh . . . okay."

"Thank you, I appreciate it. It was nice to meet you, Lara Jean."

"It was nice to meet you, too, Mr. Kavinsky."

With that, I go back to the bleachers, and only when I'm halfway up there do I remember I forgot the popcorn, so I have to go back down. When I get back to the snack bar, Peter's dad is gone.

Our team ends up losing, but Peter scores three points and it's a good game for him. I'm glad his dad got to see him play, but I really wish I didn't agree to keeping it a secret from Peter. The thought makes my stomach hurt.

In the car I'm still thinking about his dad, but then Kitty says, "That was weird what Peter's mom said about it being a good thing you weren't going to UVA."

"I know, right! You took it that way too?"

"There really wasn't any other way to take it," Kitty says.

I check my side-view mirrors before turning left out of the school parking lot. "I don't think she meant it in a *mean* way, exactly. She just doesn't want to see Peter get hurt, that's all." And neither do I, so maybe it's for the best that I don't say anything to Peter about seeing his dad tonight. What if he gets excited about his dad coming, and then his dad hurts him again? Abruptly I say, "Do you wanna stop and get frozen yogurts?" and of course Kitty says yes.

Peter comes to the house after he showers up, and as soon as I see how happy he is, my mind is made up not to say anything.

We're lying on the living room floor doing face sheet masks. If the kids at school could see him now! Through gritted teeth he asks, "What's this one supposed to do?"

"Brighten dull skin."

He twists toward me and croaks, "Hello, Clarice."

"What are you talking about?"

"It's from *Silence of the Lambs*!"

"Oh, I never saw that. It looked too scary."

Peter sits upright. He's terrible at sitting still. "We have to watch it right now. This is ridiculous. I can't be with someone who's never seen *Silence of the Lambs*."

"Um, I'm pretty sure it's my turn to pick."

"Covey, come on! It's a classic," Peter says, just as his phone buzzes. He answers it, and I hear his mom's voice on the other line. "Hey Mom . . . I'm at Lara Jean's. I'll be home soon. . . . I love you too."

When he gets off the phone, I say, "Hey, I forgot to tell you this earlier, but at the game tonight, your mom said that maybe it was for the best that I didn't get into UVA."

"What?" He sits up and pulls off his face mask.

"Well, she didn't say it exactly like that, but I think that's how she meant it."

"What were her exact words?"

I peel off my mask too. "She congratulated me on getting into William and Mary, and then I think she said, 'I know you were hoping to go to UVA, but this might be for the best anyway.'"

Peter relaxes. "Oh, she always talks like that. She looks for the bright side in things. She's like you."

It didn't seem that way to me, but I don't push it, because Peter's very protective of his mom. I guess he's had to be, since it's just the three of them. But what if it didn't have to be? What if Peter has a real chance of having a relationship with his dad? What if tonight is proof? Casually, I ask him, "Hey, how many graduation announcements did you sign up for?"

"Ten. My family's small. Why?"

"Just wondering. I signed up for fifty, so my grandma could send some to family in Korea." I hesitate before asking, "Do you think you'll send your dad one?"

He frowns. "No. Why would I?" He picks up his phone. "Let's see what movies we have left. If *Silence of the Lambs* is off the table, we could watch *Trainspotting*, or *Die Hard*."

I don't say anything for a moment, and then I snatch his

phone out of his hands. "It's my turn to pick! And I pick . . .
Amélie!"

For someone who once put up such a fuss about not watching rom coms or foreign films, Peter sure loves *Amélie*. It's
about a French girl who is afraid to live in the world, so she
concocts these whimsical fantasies in her head, with lamps
that talk and paintings that move, and crepes that look like
records. It makes me want to live in Paris.

"I wonder what you'd look like with bangs," Peter muses.
"Cute, I bet." At the end of the movie, when she bakes a
plum cake, he turns to me and says, "Do you know how to
bake a plum cake? That sounds delicious."

"You know, mini plum cakes could be good for the dessert table." I start researching recipes on my phone.

"Just make sure you call me when you do your trial run,"
Peter says, yawning.

20

TRINA AND I ARE ON THE COUCH DRINKING
tea. I'm showing her pictures of floral arrangements when
Daddy walks through the front door and collapses on the
couch with us. "Long day?" Trina asks him.

"The longest," he says, closing his eyes.

"Question," I say.

His eyes flutter open. "Yes, my middle-born?"

"What are you guys thinking for the first dance?"

He groans. "I'm too tired to think about dancing right now."

"Please. It's your wedding! Be present, Daddy."

Trina laughs and pokes him in the side with her foot. "Be
present, Dan!"

"Okay, okay. Well, Trina's a big Shania Twain fan." They grin
at each other. "So—what about 'From This Moment On'?"

"Aww," she says. "You really do know me."

"Shania Twain?" I repeat. "Doesn't she sing that song 'Man!
I Feel Like a Woman'?"

Trina holds her mug like it's a microphone and tilts her
head. "From this moment, I will love you," she sings, off-key.

"I don't think I know that song," I say, trying to sound
neutral.

"Play it for her on your phone," she says to Daddy.

"Don't judge," he warns me, and then he plays it.

It's the most un-him song I've ever heard. But he's got a goofy smile on his face the entire time, and it only gets bigger when Trina puts her arm around his shoulder and makes him sway with her to the beat. "It's perfect," I say, and suddenly I feel like crying. I clear my throat. "So now that the song is picked out, we can start ticking other stuff off the list. I've been going back and forth with Tilly's Treats about doing mini banana puddings in little canning jars, and they say they can't do them for less than seven dollars apiece."

Worry lines cross Daddy's forehead. "That seems pricy, no?"

"Don't worry, I've got a call in to a bakery in Richmond, and if the delivery price isn't too bad, that might be the way to go." I flip through my binder. "I've been so busy with desserts, I haven't had a chance to go meet with the band I've been in touch with. They're playing in Keswick this weekend, so I might try and go see them play."

Daddy looks at me with concern in his eyes. "Honey, it seems like maybe you've replaced baking with wedding planning as your stress relief. This is all a little much."

"The band isn't exactly a *band*," I quickly say. "It's a singer and a guy with a guitar. They're just starting out, so it's all very reasonable. I'll know more when I see them in person."

"Don't they have videos you can watch?" Trina asks.

"Sure, but it's not the same as seeing them live."

"I don't think we need a band," Daddy says, exchanging a look with Trina. "I think we'd be fine with just playing music off the computer."

"That's fine, but we'd need to rent sound equipment." I

start flipping through my binder, and Trina reaches out and puts her hand on my arm.

"Sweetie, I love that you want to help us with this, and I'm so grateful. But honestly, I'd rather you didn't stress yourself out. Your dad and I don't really care about any of the details. We just want to get married. We don't need a food truck, or mini banana puddings. We'd truly be just as happy ordering a bunch of barbecue from BBQ Exchange." I start to speak, and she stops me. "You only get one senior year of high school, and I want you to enjoy it. You have a hot boyfriend and you got into a great school. Your birthday is coming up soon. This is the time to just be young and celebrate and enjoy each other!"

"Yes, within reason, of course," Daddy says hastily.

"But guys, I'm not stressed out," I protest. "Focusing on the wedding gives me a sense of peace! It's very calming for me."

"And you've been a big help, but I think there are other things you could be focusing on that are more worthy of your time. Like finishing out your senior year, and preparing for college." Daddy has that firm, immovable look on his face, the one I see so seldom.

I frown. "So you don't want me to help out with the wedding anymore?"

Trina says, "I still want you to be in charge of the bridesmaid dresses, and I'd love for you to bake our wedding cake—"

"And the groom's cake?" I interrupt.

"Sure. But the rest of it we'll take care of. I swear I'm only saying this to you for your own good, Lara Jean. No more haggling over prices with vendors."

"No more impromptu road trips to Richmond for cake tables," Daddy adds.

I sigh a reluctant kind of sigh. "If you're sure . . ."

She nods. "Just go be young. Focus on your prom dress. Have you started looking yet?"

"Sort of." It's hitting me now that we are less than a month away from prom and I still don't have a dress. "If you're really sure . . ."

"We're sure," Daddy says, and Trina nods.

As I head up the stairs, I hear Daddy whisper to her, "Why in the world are you encouraging her to go enjoy her hot boyfriend?"

I almost laugh out loud.

"That's not what I meant!" Trina says.

He makes a harrumph sound. "It sure sounded like it."

"Oh my God, don't take everything so literally, Dan. Besides, her boyfriend *is* hot."

I look at prom dresses on my computer, and I laugh out loud every time I think about Daddy calling Peter my "hot boyfriend." An hour into searching, I'm fairly certain I've found my dress. It's ballerina style, with a metallic lattice bodice and a tulle skirt—the website calls the color dusty pink. Stormy will be pleased.

With that done, I go on the William and Mary website and pay the enrollment deposit like I should've done weeks ago.

★ ★ ★

Later that week, on the ride to school, Peter says he got out of doing a delivery for his mom, and he can go with me to see the band play in Keswick.

Glumly I say, "It turns out Daddy and Trina don't want a band after all. Or much of anything, for that matter. They want this wedding to be very low maintenance. They're just going to borrow some speakers and play music off a computer. Guess what song they picked for their first dance."

"What song?"

"'From This Moment On' by Shania Twain."

He frowns. "I never heard of that before."

"It's really cheesy, but they love it, apparently. Do you realize that we don't have a song? Like, a song that's ours."

"Okay, then let's pick one."

"It doesn't work like that. You don't just *pick* your song. The song picks you. Like the Sorting Hat."

Peter nods sagely. He finally finished reading all seven Harry Potter books and he's always eager to prove that he gets my references. "Got it."

"It has to just . . . happen. A moment. And the song transcends the moment, you know? My mom and dad's song was 'Wonderful Tonight' by Eric Clapton. They danced to it at their wedding."

"So how did it become their song, then?"

"It was the first song they ever slow danced to in college. It was at a dance, not long after they first started dating. I've seen pictures from that night. Daddy's wearing a suit that was too big on him and my mom's hair is in a French twist."

"How about whatever song comes on next, that's our song. It'll be fate."

"We can't just make our own fate."

"Sure we can." Peter reaches over to turn on the radio.

"Wait! Just any radio station? What if it's not a slow song?"

"Okay so we'll put on Lite 101." Peter hits the button.

"Winnie the Pooh doesn't know what to do, got a honey jar stuck on his nose," a woman croons.

Peter says, "What the hell?" as I say, "This can't be our song."

"Best out of three?" he suggests.

"Let's not force it. We'll know it when we hear it, I think."

"Maybe we'll hear it at the prom," Peter offers. "Oh, that reminds me. What color is your dress? My mom's going to ask her florist friend to make your corsage."

"It's dusty pink." It came in the mail yesterday, and when I tried it on for everybody, Trina said it was "the most Lara Jean" dress she'd ever seen. I texted a picture to Stormy, who wrote back, "Ooh-la-la," with a dancing woman emoji.

"What the heck is dusty pink?" Peter wants to know.

"It's like a rose gold color." Peter still looks confused, so I sigh and say, "Just tell your mom. She'll know. And do you think you could bring a little corsage for Kitty, too, and act like it was your idea?"

"Sure, but I could've had that idea on my own, you know," he grumbles. "You should at least give me a chance to have ideas."

I pat him on the knee. "Just please don't forget."

21

IT'S LATE. I'M IN MY BED LOOKING THROUGH my welcome packet from William and Mary. It turns out William and Mary doesn't allow freshmen to have cars on campus, and I'm about to call Peter to tell him, when I get a text from John Ambrose McClaren. When I first see his name on my phone, I feel a jolt of surprise, because it's been so long since we last talked. Then I read the text.

> Stormy died in her sleep last night. The funeral is in Rhode Island on Wednesday. I just thought you'd want to know.

I just sit there for a moment, stunned. How can this be? When I last saw her, she was fine. She was great. She was Stormy. She can't be gone. Not my Stormy. Stormy, who was larger than life, who taught me how to apply red lipstick "so it lasts even after a night of kisses and champagne," she said.

I start to cry and I can't stop. I can't get air in my lungs. I can barely see for crying. My tears keep falling on my phone, and I keep wiping it with the back of my hand. What do I say to John? She was his grandmother, and he was her favorite grandson. They were very close.

First I type, I'm so sorry. Is there anything I can

do? Then I delete it, because what could I possibly do to help?

> I'm so sorry. She had the most spirit of anyone I ever met. I'll miss her dearly.

> Thank you. I know she loved you too.

His text brings fresh tears to my eyes.

Stormy was always saying that she still felt like she was in her twenties. That sometimes she'd dream she was a girl again, and she'd see her ex-husbands and they'd be old but she'd still be Stormy. She said when she woke up in the morning, she'd be surprised to be in her old body with her old bones. "I've still got the gams, though," she said. And she did.

It's almost a relief that the funeral is in Rhode Island, too far away for me to go. I haven't been to a funeral since my mom died. I was nine, Margot was eleven, Kitty just two. The clearest memory I have of that day is sitting beside my dad, Kitty in his arms, feeling his body shake next to mine as he cried silently. Kitty's cheeks were wet with his tears. She didn't understand anything except that he was sad. She kept saying, "Don't cry, Daddy," and he would try to smile for her, but his smile looked like it was melting. I'd never felt that way before—like nothing was safe anymore, or would be ever again.

And now I'm crying again, for Stormy, for my mom, for everything.

She wanted me to transcribe her memoirs for her. *Stormy Weather*, she wanted to call it. We never did get around to doing that. How will people know her story now?

Peter calls, but I'm too sad to talk so I just let it go to voice-mail. I feel like I should call John, but I don't really have the right. Stormy was his grandma, and I was just a girl who volunteered at her nursing home. The one person I want to talk to is my sister, because she knew Stormy too, and because she always makes me feel better, but it's the middle of the night in Scotland.

I call Margot the next day, as soon as I wake up. I cry again as I tell her the news, and she cries with me. It's Margot who has the idea to have a memorial service for her at Belleview. "You could say a few words, serve some cookies, and people could share memories of her? I'm sure her friends would like that, since they won't be able to make it to the funeral."

I blow my nose. "I'm sure Stormy would like it too."

"I wish I could be there for it."

"I wish so too," I say, and my voice quivers. I always feel stronger with Margot beside me.

"Peter will be there, though," she says.

Before I leave for school, I call my old boss Janette over at Belleview and tell her the idea about the memorial service. She agrees right away, and says we could have it this Thursday afternoon, before bingo.

When I get to school and tell Peter about Stormy's memorial service, his face falls. "Shit. I have to go to that

Days on the Lawn thing with my mom." Days on the Lawn is an open house for incoming first-years at UVA. You go with your parents; you sit in on classes, tour the dorms. It's a big deal. I was really looking forward to it, when I thought I might be going.

He offers, "I could skip it, though."

"You can't. Your mom would kill you. You have to go."

"I don't mind," he says, and I believe him.

"It's really okay. You didn't know Stormy."

"I know. I just want to be there for you."

"The offer is what counts," I tell him.

Instead of wearing black, I choose a sundress that Stormy once said she liked me in. It's white, with cornflower-blue forget-me-nots embroidered on the skirt, short puffy sleeves that go a little off the shoulder, and a nipped-in waist. Because I bought it at the end of summer, I've only had the chance to wear it once. I stopped by Belleview on my way to meet Peter at the movies, and Stormy said I looked like a girl in an Italian movie. So I wear that dress, and the white sandals I bought for graduation, and a little pair of lacy white gloves that I just know she'd appreciate. I found them at a vintage store in Richmond called Bygones, and when I put them on, I can almost imagine Stormy wearing them at one of her cotillions or Saturday night dances. I don't wear her pink diamond ring. I want the first time I wear it to be at my prom, the way Stormy would have wanted.

I bring out the punch bowl, a crystal bowl of peanuts, a stack of cocktail napkins embroidered with cherries that I found at an estate sale, the tablecloth we use for Thanksgiving. I put a few roses on the piano, where Stormy used to sit. I make a punch with ginger ale and frozen fruit juice—no alcohol, which I know Stormy would have balked at, but not all of the residents can have it, because of their medications. I do put out a bottle of champagne next to the punch bowl, for anyone who wants to top off their punch with a little something extra. Lastly, I turn on Frank Sinatra, who Stormy always said should've been her second husband, if only.

John said he'd come if he made it back from Rhode Island in time, and I'm feeling a little nervous for that, because I haven't seen him since almost exactly a year ago, on my birthday. We were never a thing, not really, but we almost were, and to me, that's something.

A few people file in. One of the nurses wheels in Mrs. Armbruster, who has fallen to dementia but used to be pretty friendly with Stormy. Mr. Perelli, Alicia, Shanice the receptionist, Janette. It's a good little group. The truth is, there are fewer and fewer people that I know at Belleview. Some of them have moved in with their children; a few have passed away. Not as many familiar faces in the staff, either. The place changed while I wasn't looking.

I'm standing at the front of the room, and my heart is pounding out of my chest. I'm so nervous to make my speech. I'm afraid of stumbling over my words and not doing her justice. I want to do a good job on it; I want to make Stormy proud. Everyone's looking at me with expectant eyes, except for Mrs. Armbruster, who is knitting and staring off into space. My knees shake under my skirt. I take a deep breath, and I'm about to speak when John Ambrose McClaren walks in, wearing a pressed button-down shirt and khakis. He takes a seat on the couch next to Alicia. I give him a wave, and in return, John gives me an encouraging smile.

I take a deep breath. "The year was 1952." I clear my throat and look down at my paper. "It was summer, and Frank Sinatra was on the radio. Lana Turner and Ava Gardner were the starlets of the day. Stormy was eighteen. She was in the marching band, she was voted Best Legs, and she always had a date on Saturday night. On this particular night, she was on a date with a boy named Walt. On a dare, she went skinny-dipping in the town lake. Stormy never could turn down a dare."

Mr. Perelli laughs and says, "That's right, she never could." Other people murmur in agreement, "She never could."

"A farmer called the police, and when they shined their lights on the lake, Stormy told them to turn around before she would come out. She got a ride home in a police car that night."

"Not the first time or the last," someone calls out, and everyone laughs, and I can feel my shoulders start to relax.

"Stormy lived more life in one night than most people do their whole lives. She was a force of nature. She taught me that love—" My eyes well up and I start over. "Stormy taught me that love is about making brave choices every day. That's what Stormy did. She always picked love; she always picked adventure. To her they were one and the same. And now she's off on a new adventure, and we wish her well."

From his seat on the couch, John wipes his eyes with his sleeve.

I give Janette a nod, and she gets up and presses play on the stereo, and "Stormy Weather" fills the room. "Don't know why there's no sun up in the sky . . ."

After, John shoulders his way over to me, holding two plastic cups of fruit punch. Ruefully he says, "I'm sure she'd tell us to spike it, but . . ." He hands me a cup, and we clink. "To Edith Sinclair McClaren Sheehan, better known as Stormy."

"Stormy's real name was Edith? It's so serious. It sounds like someone who wears wool skirts and heavy stockings, and drinks chamomile tea at night. Stormy drank cocktails!"

John laughs. "I know, right?"

"So then where did the name Stormy come from? Why not Edie?"

"Who knows?" John says, a wry smile on his lips. "She'd have loved your speech." He gives me a warm, appreciative sort of look. "You're such a nice girl, Lara Jean." I'm embarrassed, I don't know what to say. Even though we never dated, seeing John again is what I imagine seeing an old boyfriend feels like. A wistful sort of feeling. Familiar, but just a little bit awkward, because there's so much left unsaid between us.

Then he says, "Stormy kept asking me to bring my girl-friend to visit her, and I never got around to it. I feel bad about that now."

As casually as I can, I say, "Oh, are you dating someone?"

He hesitates for just a split-second and then nods. "Her name is Dipti. We met at a Model UN convention at UVA. She beat me out for the gavel for our committee."

"Wow," I say.

"Yeah, she's awesome."

We both start to speak at the same time.

"Do you know where you're going to school?"

"Have you decided—?

We laugh, and a sort of understanding passes between us. He says, "I haven't decided. It's between College Park and William and Mary. College Park has a good business school, and it's really close to DC. William and Mary's ranked higher, but Williamsburg is in the boonies. So I don't know yet. My dad's bummed, because he really wanted me to go to UNC, but I didn't get in."

"I'm sorry." I decide not to mention that I got wait-listed at UNC.

John shrugs. "I might try and transfer there sophomore year. We'll see. What about you? Are you going to UVA?"

"I didn't get in," I confess.

"Aw man! I hear they were insanely selective this year. My school's salutatorian didn't get in, and her application was killer. I'm sure yours was too."

Shyly, I say, "Thanks, John."

"So where are you gonna go if not UVA?"

"William and Mary."

His face breaks into a smile. "Seriously? That's awesome! Where's Kavinsky going?"

"UVA."

He nods. "For lacrosse, right."

"What about . . . Dipti?" I say it like I don't remember her name, even though I do, I mean, I just heard him say it not two minutes ago. "Where's she going?"

"She got in early to Michigan."

"Wow, that's so far."

"A whole lot farther than UVA and William and Mary, that's for sure."

"So are you guys going to . . . stay together?"

"That's the plan," John says. "We're going to at least give the long-distance thing a try. What about you and Peter?"

"That's our plan too, for the first year. I'm going to try to transfer to UVA for the second year."

John clinks his cup against mine. "Good luck, Lara Jean."

"You too, John Ambrose McClaren."

"If I end up going to William and Mary, I'm going to call you."

"You better," I say.

I stay at Belleview a lot longer than I expected. Someone brings out their old records and then people start dancing, and Mr. Perelli insists on teaching me how to rumba, in spite of his bad hip. When Janette puts on Glenn Miller's song "In the Mood," my eyes meet John's, and we share a secret smile, both of us remembering the USO party. It was like something out of a movie. It feels like a long time ago now.

It's strange to feel happy at a memorial for someone you loved, but that's how I feel. I'm happy that the day has gone well, that we've sent Stormy off in style. It feels good to say a proper good-bye, to have the chance.

When I get back from Belleview, Peter's sitting on my front steps with a Starbucks cup. "Is nobody home?" I ask, hurrying up the walk. "Did you have to wait long?"

"Nah." Still sitting, he reaches out his arms and pulls me in for a hug around my waist. "Come sit and talk to me for a minute before we go inside," he says, burying his face in my stomach. I sit down next to him. He asks, "How was Stormy's memorial? How'd your speech go?"

"Good, but first tell me about Days on the Lawn." I grab his Starbucks cup out of his hands and take a sip of coffee, which is cold.

"Eh. I sat in on a class. Met some people. Not that exciting." Then he takes my right hand in his, traces his finger over the lace of my gloves. "These are cool."

There's something bothering him, something he isn't saying. "What's wrong? Did something happen?"

He looks away. "My dad showed up this morning and wanted to come with us."

My eyes widen. "So . . . did you let him come?"

"Nope." Peter doesn't elaborate. Just, nope.

Hesitantly, I say, "It seems like he's trying to have a relationship with you, Peter."

"He had plenty of chances and now it's too late. That ship has fucking sailed. I'm not a kid anymore." He lifts his chin. "I'm a man, and he didn't have anything to do with it. He just wants the credit. He wants to brag to his golf buddies that his son is playing lacrosse for UVA."

I hesitate. Then I think of how his dad looked when he was watching Peter out on the lacrosse field. There was such pride in his eyes—and love. "Peter . . . what if—what if you gave him a chance?"

Peter's shaking his head. "Lara Jean, you don't get it. And you're lucky not to get it. Your dad's freaking awesome. He'd do anything for you guys. My dad's not like that. He's just in it for himself. If I let him back in, he'll just fuck up again. It's not worth it."

"But maybe it is worth it. You never know how long you have with people." Peter flinches. I've never said something like that to him before, brought my mom up like that, but after losing Stormy, I can't help it. I have to say it because it's true and because I'll regret it if I don't. "It's not about your dad. It's about you. It's about not having regrets later. Don't hurt yourself just to spite him."

"I don't want to talk about him anymore. I came over here to make you feel better, not to talk about my dad."

"Okay. But first, promise me you'll think about inviting him to graduation." He starts to speak, and I interrupt him. "Just think about it. That's all. It's a whole month away. You don't have to decide anything right now, so don't say yes or no."

Peter sighs, and I'm sure he's going to tell me no, but instead he asks, "How'd your speech go?"

"I think it went okay. I think Stormy would've liked it. I talked about the time she got caught skinny-dipping and the police came and she had to ride home in a squad car. Oh, and John made it back in time."

Peter nods in a diplomatic sort of way. I'd told him John might be coming today, and all he said was "Cool, cool," because of course he couldn't say anything different. John was Stormy's grandson, after all. "So where's McClaren going to school?"

"He hasn't decided yet. It's between Maryland and William and Mary."

Peter's eyebrows fly up. "*Really*. Well, that's awesome." He says it in a way that makes it clear he doesn't think it's awesome at all.

I give him a funny look. "What?"

"Nothing. Did he hear that you're going there?"

"No, I just told him today. Not that one thing has anything to do with the other. You're being really weird right now, Peter."

"Well, how would you feel if I told you Gen was going to UVA?"

"I don't know. Not that bothered?" I mean that sincerely. All of my bad feelings about Peter and Genevieve feel like such a long time ago. Peter and I have come so far since then. "Besides, it's completely different. John and I never even dated. We haven't spoken in months. Also, he has a girlfriend. Also, he hasn't even decided if he's going there or not."

"So where's his girlfriend going then?"

"Ann Arbor."

He makes a dismissive sound. "That ain't gonna last."

Softly I say, "Maybe people will look at you and me and think the same thing."

"It's literally not the same thing at all. We're only going to be a couple of hours apart, and then you're transferring. That's one year tops. I'll drive down on weekends. It's literally not a big deal."

"You just said literally twice," I say, to make him smile. When he doesn't, I say, "You'll have practice and games. You won't want to be at William and Mary every weekend." It's the first time I've had this thought.

For just a moment Peter looks stung, but then he shrugs and says, "Fine, or you'll come up here. We'll get you used to the drive. It's basically all just I-64."

"William and Mary doesn't let freshmen have cars. Neither does UVA. I checked."

Peter brushes this off. "So I'll get my mom to drop my car off when I want to come see you. It's not like it's far. And you can take the bus. We'll make it work. I'm not worried about us."

I am, a little, but I don't say so, because Peter doesn't seem to want to talk about practicalities. I guess I don't either.

Scooting closer to me, he asks, "Want me to stay over

tonight? I can come back after my mom goes to bed. I can distract you if you get sad."

"Nice try," I tell him, pinching his cheek.

"Did Josh ever spend the night? With your sister, I mean."

I ponder this. "Not that I know of. I mean, I really doubt it. We're talking about my sister and Josh, after all."

"That's them," Peter says, dipping his head low and rubbing his cheek against mine. He loves how soft my cheeks are; he's always saying that. "We're nothing like them."

"You're the one who brought them up," I start to say, but then he is kissing me, and I can't even finish a thought, much less a sentence.

22

THE MORNING OF PROM, KITTY COMES IN my room as I'm painting my toes. "What do you think about this color with my dress?" I ask her.

"It looks like you dipped your toenails in Pepto-Bismol."

I peer down at my feet. It kind of does look like that. Maybe I should do a beige color instead.

The consensus is that the dress requires an updo. "To show off your collarbone," Trina says. I've never thought of my collarbone as something to be shown off; in fact I've never thought of my collarbone at all.

After lunch Kitty goes with me to the hair salon, to supervise. She tells the stylist, "Don't make it too *done*, do you know what I mean?"

The stylist gives me a nervous look in the mirror. "I think so? You want it to look natural?" She's talking to Kitty, not me, because it's obvious who is in charge. "Like a natural chignon?"

"But not too natural. Think Grace Kelly." Kitty pulls up a picture on her phone and shows it to her. "See, like this, but we want the bun to the side."

"Just please don't use too much hairspray," I say meekly, as the stylist coils my hair into a knot at the nape of my neck and shows Kitty.

"That's great," Kitty says to her. To me she says, "Lara Jean, she has to use hairspray if you want it to stay up."

Suddenly I'm having second thoughts about an updo. "Are we sure about the updo?"

"Yes," Kitty says. To the stylist she says, "We're doing the updo."

The updo is more "done" than I'm used to. My hair is in a side bun; the top is smooth like a ballerina. It's pretty, but when I look in the mirror, I don't recognize myself. It's an older, sophisticated version of me who's going to the opera, or the symphony.

After all the time the woman at the salon spent putting my hair up, I end up taking it down when I get home. Kitty yells at me as she brushes my hair out, but I bear it. Tonight I want to feel like me.

"How are we doing your grand entrance?" Kitty asks me as she sweeps the brush through my hair one last time.

"Grand entrance?" I repeat.

"When Peter gets here. How are you going to enter the room?"

Trina, who is lying on my bed eating a Popsicle, pipes up with, "When I went to prom, we did a thing where the dads walked the girls down the stairs and then somebody would announce you."

I look at them both like they are nuts. "Trina, I'm not getting married. I'm going to prom."

"We could turn off all the lights and put on music, and

then you walk out and do a pose at the top of the stairs—"

"I don't want to do that," I interrupt.

Her forehead creases. "What part?"

"All of it."

"But you need a moment where everybody looks at you and only you," Kitty says.

"It's called a first look," Trina explains. "Don't worry, I'll get the whole thing on video."

"If we'd thought about this earlier, we could've really done it up, and maybe it would've gone viral." Kitty shakes her head at me in a disgusted way, as if this is somehow my fault.

"The last thing I need is to go viral again," I tell her. Pointedly I say, "Remember my hot tub video?"

She at least looks a little abashed, for a second. "Let's not linger on the past," she says, fluffing up my hair.

"Hey, birthday girl," Trina says to me. "Is the plan still to go for barbecue tomorrow night?"

"Yup," I say. With Stormy passing away and prom and the wedding and everything else, I haven't given my birthday much thought. Trina wanted to throw me a big party, but I told her I'd rather just have a family dinner out, and cake and ice cream back at the house. Trina and Kitty are baking the cake while I'm at prom, so we'll see how that goes!

When Peter and his mom arrive, I'm still running around doing last minute things.

"Guys, Peter and his mom are here," my dad calls up the stairs.

"Perfume!" I screech to Kitty, who sprays me. "Where's my clutch?"

Trina tosses it to me. "Did you pack a lipstick?"

I open it to check. "Yes! Where are my shoes?"

"Over here," Kitty says, picking them up off the floor. "Hurry up and get strapped in. I'll go downstairs and tell them you're coming."

"I'll open up a bottle of champagne for the grown-ups," Trina says, following her out.

I don't know why I'm so nervous. It's only Peter. I guess prom really is its own kind of magic. The last thing I do is put on Stormy's ring, and I think of how she must be looking down on me right now, happy I'm wearing her ring on prom night, in honor of her and all the dances she went to.

When I come down the stairs, Peter is sitting on the couch with his mom. He is shaking his knee up and down, which is how I know he's nervous too. As soon as he sees me, he stands up.

He raises his eyebrows. "You look—wow." For the past week, he's been asking for details on what my dress looks like, and I held him at bay for the surprise, which I'm glad I did, because it was worth it to see the look on his face.

"You look wow too." His tux fits him so nicely, you'd think it was custom, but it's not; it's a rental from After Hours Formal Wear. I wonder if Mrs. Kavinsky made a few sly adjustments. She's a marvel with a needle and thread. I wish guys could wear tuxedos more often, though I suppose that would take some of the thrill away.

Peter slides my corsage on my wrist; it is white ranunculus and baby's breath, and it's the exact corsage I would have picked for myself. I'm already thinking of how I'll hang it over my bed so it dries just so.

Kitty is dressed up too; she has on her favorite dress, so she can be in the pictures. When Peter pins a daisy corsage on her, her face goes pink with pleasure, and he winks at me. We take a picture of me and her, one of me and Peter and her, and then she says in her bossy way, "Now just one of me and Peter," and I'm pushed off to the side with Trina, who laughs.

"The boys her age are in for it," she says to me and Peter's mom, who is smiling too.

"Why am I not in any of these pictures?" Daddy wonders, so of course we do a round with him too, and a few with Trina and Mrs. Kavinsky.

Then we take pictures outside, by the dogwood tree, by Peter's car, on the front steps, until Peter says, "Enough pictures! We're going to miss the whole thing." When we go to his car, he opens the door for me gallantly.

On the way over, he keeps looking at me. I keep my eyes trained straight ahead, but I can see him in my periphery. I've never felt so admired. This must be how Stormy felt all the time.

As soon as we get to prom, I tell Peter we have to get in line to take our official prom picture with the professional photographer. He says we should just wait till the line dies down, but I insist. I want a good one for my scrapbook, before my hair goes flat. We do the requisite prom pose, with Peter standing behind me, his hands on my hips. The photographer lets us take a look at our picture, and Peter insists on taking another one because he doesn't like the way his hair looks.

After we take our picture, we find all of our friends on the dance floor. Darrell has matched his tie to Pammy's dress—lavender. Chris is wearing a tight black bandage dress—not unlike the one Kitty picked out for me to wear when she and Margot and I went shopping. Lucas looks like an English dandy in his suit, which is tailored to his body just beautifully. I finally convinced the two of them to come, by suggesting they just "stop by." Chris said she was still going clubbing with her work friends, but from the looks of it, she isn't going anywhere anytime soon. She's getting so much attention in her bandage dress.

"Style" comes on and we all go crazy, screaming in each other's faces and jumping up and down. Peter goes craziest of all. He keeps asking me if I'm having fun. He only asks out loud once, but with his eyes he asks me again and again. They are bright and hopeful, alight with expectation. With my eyes I tell him, *Yes yes yes I am having fun.*

We're starting to get the hang of slow dancing, too. Maybe we should take a ballroom-dancing class when I get to UVA so we can actually get good at it.

I tell him this, and fondly he says, "You always want to take things to the next level. Next-level chocolate chip cookies."

"I gave up on those."

"Next-level Halloween costumes."

"I like for things to feel special." At this, Peter smiles down at me and I say, "It's just too bad we'll never dance cheek to cheek."

"Maybe we could order you some dancing stilts."

"Oh, you mean high heels?"

He snickers. "I don't think there's such a thing as ten-inch heels."

I ignore him. "And it's too bad your noodle arms aren't strong enough to pick me up."

Peter lets out a roar like an injured lion and swoops me up and swings me around, just like I knew he would. It's a rare thing, to know someone so well, whether they'll pivot left or right. Outside of my family, I think he might be the person I know best of all.

Of course Peter wins prom king. Prom queen is Ashanti Dickson. I'm just relieved it isn't Genevieve up there, slow dancing with him with a tiara on her head. Ashanti is nearly Peter's height, so the two of them actually can dance cheek to cheek, though they don't. Peter looks out at me and winks. I'm standing off to the side with Marshawn Hopkins, Ashanti's date. He leans over to me and says, "When they come back, we should ignore them and just dance away," which makes me laugh.

I'm proud of Peter out there, at how he dances so tall,

with his back so straight. At a pivotal moment in the song, Peter dips Ashanti, and everyone hoots and hollers and stomps their feet, and I'm proud of that, too. People are so sincere in their affection for him; they can all celebrate Peter because he is nice, and he makes everyone feel good. He just gives the night a little extra shine, and they are glad for it, and so am I. I'm happy he gets this send-off.

One last dance.

We're both quiet. It's not over yet. We still have the whole summer ahead. But high school, the two of us here together, Lara Jean and Peter as we are today, that part is done. We'll never be here exactly like this again.

I'm wondering if he's feeling sad too, and then he whispers, "Check out Gabe over there trying to casually rest his hand on Keisha's butt."

He turns me slightly so I can see. Gabe's hand is indeed hovering at Keisha Wood's lower back/butt area, like an indecisive butterfly looking for a landing spot. I giggle. This is why I like Peter so much. He sees things I don't see.

"I know what our song should be," he says.

"What?"

And then, like magic, Al Green's voice fills the hotel ballroom. "Let's Stay Together."

"You made them play this," I accuse. I'm tearing up a little bit.

He grins. "It's fate."

Whatever you want to do . . . is all right with me-ee-ee.

Peter takes my hand and puts it on his heart. "Let's, let's stay together," he sings. His voice is clear and true, everything I love about him.

On the way to after-prom, Peter says he's hungry, and can we stop at the diner first.

"I think there's going to be pizza at after-prom," I say. "Why don't we just eat there?"

"But I want pancakes," he whines.

We pull into the diner parking lot, and after we park, he gets out of the car and runs around to the passenger side to open my door. "So gentlemanly tonight," I say, which makes him grin.

We walk up to the diner, and he opens the door for me grandly.

"I could get used to this royal treatment," I say.

"Hey, I open doors for you," he protests.

We walk inside, and I stop short. Our booth, the one we always sit in, has pale pink balloons tied around it. There's a round cake in the center of the table, tons of candles, pink frosting with sprinkles and *Happy Birthday, Lara Jean* scrawled in white frosting. Suddenly I see people's heads pop up from under the booths and from behind menus—all of our friends, still in their prom finery: Lucas, Gabe, Gabe's date Keisha, Darrell, Pammy, Chris. "Surprise!" everyone screams.

I spin around. "Oh my God, Peter!"

He's still grinning. He looks at his watch. "It's midnight. Happy birthday, Lara Jean."

I leap up and hug him. "This is just exactly what I wanted to do on my prom night birthday and I didn't even know it." Then I let go of him and run over to the booth.

Everyone gets out and hugs me. "I didn't even know people knew it was my birthday tomorrow! I mean today!" I say.

"Of course we knew it was your birthday," Lucas says.

Darrell says, "My boy's been planning this for weeks."

"It was so endearing," Pammy says. "He called me to ask what kind of pan he should use for the cake."

Chris says, "He called me, too. I was like, how the hell should I know?"

"And you!" I hit Chris on the arm. "I thought you were leaving to go clubbing!"

"I still might after I steal some fries. My night's just getting started, babe." She pulls me in for a hug and gives me a kiss on the cheek. "Happy birthday, girl."

I turn to Peter and say, "I can't believe you did this."

"I baked that cake myself," he brags. "Box, but still." He takes off his jacket and pulls a lighter out of his jacket pocket and starts lighting the candles. Gabe pulls out a lit candle and helps him. Then Peter hops his butt on the table and sits down, his legs hanging off the edge. "Come on."

I look around. "Um . . ."

That's when I hear the opening notes of "If You Were Here" by the Thompson Twins. My hands fly to my cheeks. I can't believe it. Peter's recreating the end scene from *Sixteen Candles*, when Molly Ringwald and Jake Ryan sit on a table with a birthday cake in between them. When we watched the movie a few months ago, I said it was the most romantic thing I'd ever seen. And now he's doing it for me.

"Hurry up and get up there before all the candles melt, Lara Jean," Chris calls out.

Darrell and Gabe help hoist me onto the table, careful not to set my dress on fire. Peter says, "Okay, now you look at me adoringly, and I lean forward like this."

Chris comes forward and puffs out my skirt a bit. "Roll up your sleeve a little higher," she instructs Peter, looking from her phone to us. Peter obeys, and she nods. "Looks good, looks good." Then she runs back to her spot and starts to snap. It takes no effort on my part at all to look at Peter adoringly tonight.

When I blow out the candles and make my wish, I wish that I will always feel for Peter the way I do right now.

23

THE NEIGHBORHOOD POOL ALWAYS OPENS
up on Memorial Day weekend. When we were little, Margot
and I would count down the days. Our mom would pack
ham and cheese sandwiches wrapped in wax paper, carrot
sticks, and a big jug of apple water. Apple water was watered
down sugar-free apple juice, but mostly water. I begged for
soda out of the machine, or fruit punch, but no. Mommy
would slather us up with sunscreen the same way she slath-
ered butter on a turkey. Kitty used to scream her head off;
she was too impatient for the rubdown. Kitty's always been
impatient; she's always wanted more, now. It's funny how
much of who we are as babies is who we are as we get older.
I'd never have known it if it weren't for Kitty. She still makes
the same screwy faces.

Kitty isn't doing swim team this year; she says it isn't fun
anymore now that none of her friends are doing it. When
she didn't know I was watching, I saw her looking at the
meet schedule on the community board with wistfulness in
her eyes. I guess that's part of growing up, too—saying good-
bye to the things you used to love.

Everyone's lawns are freshly cut, and the air smells of clo-
vers and green. The first crickets of summer are chirping.
This is the soundtrack of my summer and every summer.

Peter and I have staked our claim on the lounge chairs farthest away from the kiddie pool, because it's less noisy. I'm studying for my French final, or trying to, at least.

"Come over here so I can get your shoulders first," I call out to Kitty, who is standing by the pool with her friend Brielle.

"You know I don't burn," she calls back, and it's true; her shoulders are already tanned like golden brioche. By the end of summer they'll be dark as the crust on whole wheat bread. Kitty's hair is slicked back, a towel around her shoulders. She's all arms and legs now.

"Just come over here," I say.

Kitty trots over to the lounge chairs Peter and I are sitting on, her flip-flops clacking against the pavement.

I spray her with the sunscreen and rub it into her shoulders. "It doesn't matter if you don't burn. Protect your skin so you don't end up looking like an old leather bag." That's what Stormy used to tell me.

Kitty giggles at "old leather bag." "Like Mrs. Letty. Her skin is hot dog–colored."

"Well, I wasn't talking about any one person in particular. But yeah. She should've worn sunscreen in her younger days. Let that be a lesson to you, my sister." Mrs. Letty is our neighbor, and her skin hangs on her like crepe.

Peter puts on his sunglasses. "You guys are mean."

"Says the guy who once toilet-papered her lawn!"

Kitty giggles and steals a sip of my Coke. "You did that?"

"All lies and propaganda," Peter says blithely.

As the day heats up, Peter convinces me to put down my French book and jump in the pool with him. The pool is crowded with little kids, no one as old as us. Steve Bledell has a pool at his house, but I wanted to come here, for old times' sake.

"Don't you dare dunk me," I warn. Peter starts circling me like a shark, coming closer and closer. "I'm serious!"

He makes a dive for me and grabs me by the waist, but he doesn't dunk me; he kisses me. His skin is cool and smooth against mine; so are his lips.

I push him away and whisper, "Don't kiss me—there are kids around!"

"So?"

"So nobody wants to see teenagers kissing in the pool where kids are trying to play. It isn't right." I know I sound like a priss, but I don't care. When I was little, and there were teenagers horsing around in the pool, I always felt nervous to go in, because it was like the pool was theirs.

Peter bursts out laughing. "You're funny, Covey." Swimming sideways, he says, "'It isn't right,'" and then starts laughing again.

The lifeguard blows the whistle for adult swim, and all the kids get out, including Peter and me. We go back to the lounge chairs, and Peter pushes them closer together.

I turn on my side and, squinting up at the sun, I ask him, "How old do you think you have to be to stay in the pool for adult swim? Eighteen or twenty-one?"

"I don't know. Twenty-one?" He's scrolling on his phone.

"Maybe it's eighteen. We should ask." I put on my sunglasses and start to sing "Sixteen Going on Seventeen" from *The Sound of Music*. "You need someone older and wiser, telling you what to do." I tap him on the nose for emphasis.

"Hey, I'm older than you," he objects.

I run my hand along Peter's cheek and sing, "I am seventeen going on eighteen, I-I-I'll take care of you."

"Promise?" he says.

"Sing it just once for me," I prompt. Peter gives me a look. "Please? I love it when you sing. Your voice is so clean."

He can't help but smile. Peter never met a compliment he didn't smile at. "I don't know the words," he protests.

"Yes you do." I pretend to wave a wand in his face. "*Imperio!* Wait—do you know what that means?"

"It's . . . an unforgivable curse?"

"Yes. Very impressive, Peter K. And what does it do?"

"It makes you do things you don't want to do."

"Very good, young wizard. There's hope for you yet. Now sing!"

"You little witch." He looks around to see if anyone is listening, and then he softly sings, "I need someone older and wiser telling me what to do. . . . You are seventeen going on eighteen . . . I'll depend on you."

I clap my hands in delight. Is there anything more intoxicating than making a boy bend to your will? I roll closer to him and throw my arms around his neck.

"Now you're the one making PDAs!" he says.

"You really do have a pretty voice, Peter. You never should've quit chorus."

"The only reason I ever took chorus is because all the girls were in chorus."

"Well, then forget about joining a chorus at UVA. No a cappella groups either." I mean it to be a joke, truly, but Peter looks bothered. "I'm kidding! Join all the a cappella groups you want! The Hullabahoos are all guys, anyway."

"I don't want to join an a cappella group. And I'm not planning on looking at other girls, either."

Oh. "Of course you'll look at other girls. You have eyes, don't you? I swear, that's just as silly as when people say they don't see color. Everyone sees everyone. You can't help but see."

"That's not what I meant!"

"I know, I know." I sit up and put my French book back in my lap. "Are you really not going to study at all for your US history final on Wednesday?"

"All I need to do at this point is pass," he reminds me.

"It must be nice, it must be nice," I sing.

"Hey, it's not like William and Mary is taking away your spot if you get a C in French," Peter says.

"I'm not worried about French. I'm worried about my calculus exam on Friday."

"Okay, well, it's not like they'll kick you out for getting a C in calculus, either."

"I guess so, but I still want to finish well," I say. The countdown is really on, now that May is nearly over. Just one more week left of school. I stretch out my arms and legs and squint up into the sun and let out a happy sigh. "Let's come here every day next weekend."

"I can't. I'm going on that training weekend, remember?"

"Already?"

"Yeah. It's weird that the season is over and we won't be playing any more games together."

Our school's lacrosse team didn't make it to state championships. They knew it was a long shot, because as Peter likes to say, "There's only one of me." Ha! Next weekend he is off to a training camp with his new team at UVA.

"Are you excited to meet your teammates?" I ask him.

"I already know a few of the guys, but yeah. It'll be cool." He reaches over and starts braiding a section of my hair. "I think I'm getting better at this."

"You have the whole summer to practice," I say, leaning forward so he can reach more of my hair. He doesn't say anything.

24

THE END OF SCHOOL ALWAYS HAS A PAR-
ticular feeling to it. It's the same every year, but this year
the feeling is amplified, because there won't be a next year.
There's an air of things closing down. Teachers wear shorts
and T-shirts to class. They show movies while they clean out
their desks. Nobody has the energy to care anymore. We're
all just counting down, passing time. Everyone knows where
they're going, and the right now already feels like it's in the
rearview. Suddenly life feels fast and slow at the same time.
It's like being in two places at once.

Finals go well; even calculus isn't as bad as I thought. And
just like that, my high school career is coming to an end.
Peter's gone away on his training weekend. It's only been
one day and I'm already longing for him the way I long for
Christmas in July. Peter is my cocoa in a cup, my red mittens,
my Christmas morning feeling.

He said he'd call as soon as he gets back from the gym, so
I keep my phone by my side, with the volume up. Earlier this
morning he called when I was in the shower, and by the time
I saw it, he was gone again. Is this what the future looks like?
It'll be different when I have classes and a schedule of my own,
but for now it feels like I am standing on top of a lighthouse,
waiting for my love's ship to come in. For a romantic kind

of person, it's not an altogether unpleasant feeling, not for now, anyway. It'll be different when it's not so novel anymore, when not seeing him every day is the new normal, but for now, just for now, longing is its own kind of perverse delight.

Late afternoon, I go downstairs in my long white nightgown that Margot says makes me look like *Little House on the Prairie* and Kitty says makes me look like a ghost. I sit at the counter with one leg up and open a can of cling peaches and eat them with a fork, right out of the can. There's something so satisfying about biting into the skin of a syrupy cling peach.

I let out a sigh, and Kitty looks up from her computer and says, "What are you sighing about so loudly?"

"I miss . . . Christmas." I bite into another slice of peach.

She brightens. "So do I! I think we should get a few deer to go in our front yard this year. Not the cheap kind, the classy wire kind that come covered in lights."

I sigh again and set down the can. "Sure." The syrup is starting to feel heavy in my stomach.

"Quit sighing!"

"Why does sighing feel so good?" I muse.

Kitty heaves a big sigh. "Well, it's basically the same thing as breathing. And it feels good to breathe. Air is delicious."

"It is, isn't it?" I spear another slice of peach. "I wonder where you buy those kinds of deer. Target will probably sell them."

"We should go to that store the Christmas Mouse. We can stock up on a bunch of stuff. Don't they have one in Williamsburg?"

"Yeah, on the way to the outlet malls. You know, we could

use a new wreath, too. And if they have lavender lights, that could be cool. It would give it a winter-fairyland kind of feeling. Maybe the whole tree could be in pastels."

Dryly she says, "Let's not get carried away."

I ignore her. "Don't forget that Trina has a lot of her own holiday stuff. She has a whole Christmas village, remember? It's all packed away in those boxes in the garage." Trina's village isn't just a little nativity scene. It has a barber shop and a bakery and a toy store; it's intense. "I don't even know where we'll put it."

She shrugs. "We'll probably have to throw away some of our old stuff." God, Kitty doesn't have an ounce of sentimentality in her! In that same practical tone she adds, "Not everything we have is so great anyway. Our tree skirt is scraggly and chewed-up-looking. Why keep something just because it's old? New is almost always better than old, you know."

I look away. Our mom bought that tree skirt at a Christmas fair the elementary school had. One of the PTA moms was a knitter. Margot and I fought over which to pick; she liked the red with tartan trim, and I liked the white because I thought it would look like our tree was standing in snow. Mommy went with the red, because she said the white would get dirty fast. The red has held up well, but Kitty's right; it's probably time to retire it. I'll never let her throw it away though, and neither will Margot. At the very least, I'll cut off a square and put it in my hat box for safekeeping.

"Trina has a nice tree skirt," I say. "It's white fur. Jamie Fox-Pickle will love to snuggle with it."

My phone buzzes, and I jump to see if it's Peter, but it's only Daddy saying he's picking up Thai food for dinner, and do we want pad thai or pad see yew? I sigh again.

"I swear, Lara Jean, if you sigh one more time!" Kitty threatens. Eyeing me, she says, "I know it's not really Christmas you're missing. Peter's been gone for like one day and you're acting like he went off to war or something."

I ignore her and type back pad see yew out of pure spite, because I know Kitty prefers pad thai.

That's when I get the e-mail notification. It's from UNC admissions. My application has been updated. I click on the link. *Congratulations* . . .

I'm off the wait list.

What in the *what*?

I sit there, stunned, reading it over and over. I, Lara Jean Song Covey, was accepted to the University of North Carolina at Chapel Hill. I can't believe it. I never thought I'd get in. But I'm in.

"Lara Jean? Hello?"

Startled, I look up.

"I just asked you a question three times. What's up with you?"

"Um . . . I think I just got in to UNC Chapel Hill."

Kitty's jaw drops. "Whoa!"

"Weird, right?" I shake my head in wonder. Who'd have ever thought it? Not me. I'd all but forgotten about UNC after I got wait-listed.

"UNC is a really hard school to get into, Lara Jean!"

"I know." I'm still in a daze. After I didn't get into UVA, I felt so low, like I wasn't good enough to be there. But UNC! It's even harder to get into UNC out of state than it is UVA in state.

Kitty's smile fades a little. "But aren't you going to William and Mary? Didn't you already send in your deposit? And aren't you transferring to UVA next year anyway?"

UVA. For those few seconds, I forgot about transferring to UVA and I was just happy about UNC. "That's the plan," I say. My phone buzzes, and my heart jumps, thinking it's Peter, but's it's not. It's a text from Chris.

Wanna go to Starb

I write back, GUESS WHAT. I got into UNC!

OMG!
I'm calling you

A second later my phone rings and Chris screams, "Holy shit!"

"Thank you! I mean, wow. I just . . . it's such a great school. I figured—"

"So what are you going to do?" she demands.

"Oh." I glance over at Kitty, who is watching with eagle eyes. "Nothing. I'm still going to William and Mary."

"But isn't UNC a better school?"

"It's higher ranked. I don't know. I've never been there."

"Let's go," she says.

"To visit? When?"

"Right now! Spontaneous road trip!"

"Are you crazy? It's four hours away!"

"No it's not. It's only three hours and twenty-five minutes. I just looked it up."

"By the time we get there, it'll be—"

"Six o'clock. Big deal. We'll walk around, get dinner, and then drive back. Why not! We're young. And you need to know what you're saying no to." Before I can protest again, she says, "I'm picking you up in ten minutes. Pack some snacks for the road." Then she hangs up.

Kitty is eyeing me. "You're going to North Carolina? Right now?"

I'm feeling pretty euphoric at the moment. I laugh and say, "I guess!"

"Does that mean you're going there instead of William and Mary?"

"No, it's just—I'm just going to visit. Nothing's changed. Don't tell Daddy, though."

"Why not?"

"Just—because. You can tell him I'm with Chris, and that I won't be at dinner, but don't mention anything about UNC."

And then I'm getting dressed and flying around the house like a banshee, throwing things into a tote. Dried wasabi peas, Pocky sticks, bottled water. Chris and I have never gone on a road trip together before; I've always wanted to do that with her. And what would it hurt to just look at Chapel Hill, just to see? I won't be going there, but it's still fun to think about.

Chris and I are halfway to Chapel Hill before I realize my phone is dying and I forgot to pack my charger. "Do you have a car charger?" I ask her.

She's singing along to the radio. "Nope."

"Shoot!" We've eaten up most of her phone battery using the GPS, too. I feel a little uneasy about traveling out of state without a full charge on my phone. Plus, I told Kitty not to tell Daddy where I was going. What if something were to happen? "What time are we getting back, do you think?"

"Quit worrying, Granny Lara Jean. We'll be fine." She rolls down her window and mine and starts fumbling around for her purse. I get her purse from the floor of the backseat and pull out her cigarettes before she wrecks the car. When we're at a red light, she lights her cigarette and inhales deeply. "We'll be like pioneers. It just adds to the adventure. Our forefathers didn't have cell phones either, you know."

"Just remember, we're only going to look. I'm still going to William and Mary."

"You just remember—options are everything," Chris says.

That's what Margot's always telling me. Those two have more in common than they think.

We spend the rest of the trip surfing radio stations and singing along and talking about whether or not Chris should dye her hair pink in the front. I'm surprised by how fast the time goes. We get to Chapel Hill in just under three hours and thirty minutes, like Chris said we would. We find a parking spot right on Franklin Street, which I guess is their main street. The first thing that strikes me is how similar UNC's campus is to UVA's. Lots of maple trees, lots of green, lots of brick buildings.

"It's so pretty, isn't it?" I stop to admire a pink flowering dogwood tree. "I'm surprised they have so many dogwood trees, since it's Virginia's state flower. What do you suppose is North Carolina's state flower?"

"No idea. Can we please eat? I'm starving." Chris has the attention span of a fly, and when she is hungry, everybody better watch out.

I put my arm around her waist. I'm suddenly feeling very tender toward her for taking me on this trip to see what might have been. "Let's fill that belly up, then. What do you want? Pizza? A hoagie? Chinese food?"

She puts her arm around my shoulder. Her mood is already picking up at the mention of different cuisines. "You pick. Anything but Chinese food. Or pizza. You know what, let's get sushi."

A couple of guys pass on the street, and Chris calls out, "Hey!"

They turn around. "What's up?" one says. He's black, handsome, tall, with muscular arms in a CAROLINA WRESTLING T-shirt.

"Where's the best sushi around here?" Chris asks.

"I don't eat sushi, so I can't really say." He looks at his red-haired friend, who is less cute but still cute. "Where do you go?"

"Spicy Nine," he says, eyeing Chris. "Just go down Franklin that way and you'll run right into it." He winks at her, and they go back to walking in the other direction.

"Should we go after them?" she says, her eyes following them as they walk away. "Find out what they're up to tonight?"

I steer her in the direction they pointed us to. "I thought you were hungry," I remind her.

"Oh yeah," she says. "So that's one point in the UNC column, am I right? Hotter guys?"

"I'm sure William and Mary has good-looking guys too." Quickly I add, "Not that it matters to me, because I obviously have a boyfriend." Who still hasn't called, mind you. My phone is down to 5 percent, so by the time he does, it'll be too late.

After we eat sushi, we wander around on Franklin Street, stopping in stores. I consider buying a UNC Tar Heels basketball hat for Peter, but he probably wouldn't wear it, since he'll be a Wahoo.

We pass a pole with signs on it, and Chris stops short. She points to a sign for a music hall called Cat's Cradle. A band called Meow Mixx is playing tonight. "Let's go!" Chris says.

"Have you ever heard of Meow Mixx before?" I ask. "What kind of music do they play?"

"Who cares. Let's just go!" She grabs my hand. Laughing, we run down the street together.

There's a line to get inside, and the band has already started to play; snatches of dancey music float through the open door. A couple of girls are waiting in line in front of us, and Chris throws her arms around me and tells them, "My best friend just got into UNC."

I feel warm inside hearing Chris call me her best friend—to know that we still matter to each other, even though she has her work friends and I have Peter. It makes me feel sure that when she's in Costa Rica, or Spain, or wherever she ends up, we'll still be close.

One of the girls hugs me and says, "Congratulations! You're going to love it here." Her hair is in milkmaid braids, and she's wearing a T-shirt that says HILLARY IS MY PRESIDENT.

Adjusting the lollipop enamel pin in her hair, her friend says, "Put down Ehaus or Craige for your dorm. They're the most fun."

I feel sheepish as I say, "Actually, I'm not coming here; we just came to visit. For fun."

"Oh, where are you going?" she asks me, a slight frown on her freckled face.

"William and Mary," I tell her.

"It's not definite though," Chris butts in.

"It's pretty definite," I say.

"I came here over Princeton," the braided girl tells me. "That's how much I loved it when I visited. You'll see. I'm Hollis, by the way."

We all introduce ourselves and the girls tell me about the English department, and going to basketball games at the Dean Dome, and the places on Franklin Street that don't card. Chris, who zoned out during the English department part of the conversation, is suddenly all ears. Before we go inside, Hollis gives me her number. "Just in case you come here," she says.

When we get inside, the venue is pretty full, lots of people standing near the stage, drinking beers and dancing to the music. The band is actually just two guys with guitars and a laptop, and their sound is sort of electronica pop. It fills the whole room. It's a mixed crowd in the audience: some older guys in rock band T-shirts and beards, closer to my dad's age, but also a lot of students. Chris tries to wipe off the stamp on her hand to get us beers, but is unsuccessful. I don't mind, because I don't really like beer, and also, she still has to drive us back tonight. I start asking around to see if anyone has a phone charger, which Chris slaps my arm for. "We're on an adventure!" she yells. "We don't need cell phones for an adventure!"

Then she grabs my hand and pulls me along with her to the edge of the stage. We dance our way to the middle, and we jump along to the music, even though we don't know any of the songs. One of the guys went to UNC, and midway through the show, he leads the crowd in the Tar Heels fight song. "I'm a Tar Heel born, I'm a Tar Heel bred, and when I die I'm a Tar Heel dead!" The crowd goes nuts, the whole room is shaking. Chris and I don't know the words, but we shout, "Go to hell, Duke!" along with everyone else. Our hair swings wildly in our faces; I'm sweaty, and suddenly I'm having the best time. "This is so much fun," I scream in Chris's face.

"Same!" she screams back.

After the second set Chris declares that she is hungry, so we are off into the night.

We walk up the street for what feels like ages when we find a place called Cosmic Cantina. It's a tiny Mexican place with a long line, which Chris says must mean they either have good food or really cheap food. Chris and I inhale our burritos; they are stuffed full with rice and beans and melting cheese and homemade pico de gallo. It tastes pretty plain, except for the hot sauce. So hot my lips burn. If my phone weren't dead and Chris's phone weren't nearly dead, I'd have searched online for the best burrito in Chapel Hill. But then we might not have found this place. For some reason it's the best burrito of my life.

After we eat our burritos, I say, "What time is it? We should head back soon if we want to get back before one."

"But you've barely seen any of campus," Chris says. "Isn't there anything you want to see in particular? Like, I don't know, a boring library or something?"

"Nobody knows me like you do, Chris," I say, and she bats her eyelashes. "There is one place I want to see . . . it's in all the brochures. The Old Well."

"Then let's go," she says.

As we walk, I ask her, "Does Chapel Hill seem like Charlottesville to you?"

"No, it seems better."

"You're just like Kitty. You think everything new is better," I say.

JENNY HAN

"And you think everything old is better," she counters.

She has a point there. We walk the rest of the way in companionable silence. I'm thinking about the ways UNC does and doesn't remind me of UVA. The campus is quiet, I guess because most kids have gone home for summer break. There are still people walking around, though: girls in sundresses and sandals and boys in khaki shorts and UNC baseball caps.

We cross the green lawn, and there it is: the Old Well. It sits between two brick residence halls. It's a small rotunda, like a mini version of the one at UVA, and there is a drinking fountain in the center. There's a big white oak tree right behind it, and there are azalea bushes all around, hot pink like a lipstick color Stormy used to wear. It's enchanting.

"Are you supposed to make a wish or something?" Chris asks, stepping up to the fountain.

"I think I heard that on the first day of classes, students take a sip of water from the fountain for good luck," I say. "Either good luck or straight As."

"I won't need straight As where I'm going, but I'll take the luck."

Chris bends down to take a sip, and a couple of girls walking by caution, "Frat guys pee in that fountain all the time—don't do it."

Her head snaps back up and she jumps away from the fountain. "Ew!" Hopping down, she says, "Let's take a selfie."

"We can't; our phones are dead, remember? We'll just have to have the memory in our hearts like the old days."

"Good point," Chris says. "Should we hit the road?"

I hesitate. I don't know why, but I'm not ready to leave just yet. What if I never get to come back? I spot a bench facing one of the brick buildings and go over and sit down, "Let's stay a little bit longer."

I hug my knees to my chest and Chris sits down next to me. Fiddling with the stack of bracelets on her arm, she says, "I wish I could come here with you."

"To college or to UNC?" I'm so caught off guard by the pensive note in her voice that I don't stop to correct her, to remind her that I won't be coming here either.

"Either. Both. Don't get me wrong. I'm psyched about Costa Rica. It's just . . . I don't know. Like, what if I'm missing out by not going to college at the same time as everybody else." She looks at me then, a question in her eyes.

I say, "College will be here waiting for you, Chris. Next year, the year after. Whenever you want it."

Chris twists around and looks out at the lawn. "Maybe. We'll see. I can picture you here, Lara Jean. Can't you?"

I swallow. "I have a plan. William and Mary for a year, then UVA."

"You mean you and Peter have a plan. That's why you're holding back."

"Okay, Peter and I have a plan. But it's not the only reason."

"But it's the main one."

I can't deny it. The thing that's missing no matter where I go, if it's William and Mary or if it's here, is Peter.

"So why not go here for a year, then?" Chris asks me.

"What's the difference if you're here or William and Mary? An hour? Either way, you're not at UVA. Why not be here?" She doesn't wait for me to answer her; she hops up and runs out onto the lawn, and she kicks off her shoes and does a series of cartwheels.

What if I came here and I ended up loving it? What if, after a year, I didn't want to leave? What then? But wouldn't it be great if I loved it? Isn't that the whole point? Why bet on not loving a place? Why not take a chance and bet on happiness?

I lie down and stretch my legs out on the bench and look up at the sky. There is a canopy of tree branches high above my head—one tree sits by the building; the other is planted in the lawn. Their branches reach across the walkway and meet in the middle. What if Peter and I could be like these two trees, far apart but still touching? Because I think maybe I could be happy here. I think maybe I could picture myself here too.

What was it Stormy said? The last day I saw her, the day she gave me her ring? *Never say no when you really want to say yes.*

When Chris pulls up to my house, it's just after three a.m. and every single light is on. Gulp. I turn to Chris. "Come in with me?" I plead.

"No way. You're on your own. I've gotta go home and deal with my own mom."

I hug Chris good-bye, get out of the car, and trudge up to the front steps. The door flies open as soon as I'm fumbling around in my bag for my keys. It's Kitty, in her big sleep T-shirt. "You're in trouble," she whispers.

I step inside, and Daddy's right behind her, still dressed in his work clothes. Trina's on the couch, giving me a look like, *You're in for it, and I feel sympathy for you, but also, you could've at least called.* "Where have you been all night!" he shouts. "And why weren't you answering your phone!"

I shrink backward. "I ran out of battery. I'm sorry. I didn't realize it had gotten so late." I briefly consider making a joke about how this is why millenials should wear watches, to lighten the mood, but I don't think a joke will do the trick this time.

Daddy starts pacing around the living room. "So why didn't you use Chris's phone!"

"Chris's phone died too. . . ."

"We've been worried half to death! Kitty says you left with Chris without saying where you were going. . . ." At this, Kitty gives me a look. "I was five seconds from calling the police, Lara Jean! If you hadn't walked in the door when you did—"

"I'm sorry," I begin. "I'm really sorry."

"This is just so irresponsible." Daddy's muttering to himself, not even listening. "Lara Jean, you might be eighteen, but—"

From the couch, Trina says, "Dan, please don't say, 'but you're still living under my roof.' It's such a cliché."

Daddy spins around and says to her, "It's a cliché for a reason! It's a good line! It's a very good line."

"Lara Jean, just tell them where you were," Kitty says, impatient.

Daddy shoots an accusing look her way. "Kitty, did you know where she went?"

"She made me swear not to tell!"

Before he can reply, I say, "I was in North Carolina with Chris."

He throws his hands up in the air. "In North Carolina! What in the—what in the world? You crossed state lines without even telling me? With a dead phone battery, to boot!"

I feel sick to my stomach for worrying him. I don't know why I didn't call. I could've borrowed somebody's phone. I guess I just got carried away with the night, with being there. I didn't want to think about home or real life. "I'm sorry," I whisper. "I'm really, really sorry. I should've called."

He shakes his head. "Why were you in North Carolina?"

"I was in North Carolina because . . ." I pause. If I say it now, that's it. "Because I got into UNC."

Daddy's eyes widen. "You did? That's—that's wonderful. But what about William and Mary?"

Smiling, I lift my shoulders into a shrug.

Trina lets out a scream and jumps up from the couch, dropping the flannel blanket she had wrapped around her and nearly tripping herself in the process. Daddy grabs me into his arms and sweeps me into a hug, and Trina joins in. "Oh my God, Lara Jean!" she says, slapping me on the back. "You're gonna be a Tar Heel!"

"I'm happy you're happy," Daddy says. He wipes a tear from his eyes. "I'm still furious with you for not calling. But I'm also happy."

"So you're really going, then?" Kitty asks from her perch on the stairs.

I look over at her. I smile shakily and say, "Yeah, I'm going." Peter and I will find a way. We'll make it work.

I tell them every little detail of the night: going to a show at Cat's Cradle, eating burritos at Cosmic Cantina, the Old Well. Trina makes popcorn, and it's nearly dawn before any of us goes to sleep. As Daddy shuffles off to bed, Trina whispers to me, "Your daddy just aged ten years in one night. Look at him walking like he needs a cane. Thanks to you, I'm marrying an old man." We both start laughing, and neither of us can stop. I think we're delirious from lack of sleep. Trina rolls onto her back and kicks her legs in the air, she is laughing so hard. Kitty, who has fallen asleep on the couch, wakes up and says, "What's so funny?" which only makes us laugh harder. On his way up the stairs, Daddy stops and turns around and shakes his head at the two of us.

"You guys are already ganging up on me," he says.

"Face it, Daddy. You've always lived in a matriarchy." I blow him a kiss.

He frowns. "Hey, don't think I've forgotten about you staying out all night without even a phone call home."

Whoops. Maybe too soon for such gaiety. As he trudges up the stairs, I call out, "I truly am sorry!"

Sorry for not calling, but not sorry for going.

25

WHEN I WAKE UP, I LOLL ABOUT IN MY
bed for a while, stretching out my arms and legs like a big X,
reaching north, south, east, west. Last night feels like a dream.
Is it really true? Am I really going to UNC?

Yes, yes I really am. How crazy, how thrilling that your
whole life trajectory can change in just one night. I've always
been scared of change, but right now I don't feel that way. I
feel excited. I'm seeing now what a privilege it is, to be excited
about where I'm going. Peter and Chris and Lucas, they're
going where they want to go, but my future felt like a second
choice because it was, no matter how great a school William
and Mary is. UNC is a choice I didn't even know I had, like a
door that magically appeared, a door that could lead anywhere.

When I'm done with my reverie, I look at my clock
and see that I've slept the whole day away. I sit up, turn
my phone on, and see all the missed calls and voice mails
from my dad and Kitty from the night before. I delete those
without listening to them, so I don't have to hear the anger
in Daddy's voice; then I see that Peter left me a voice mail
too. When I see his name on my phone, my heart does a
little dive into my stomach. There are texts, too, wondering where I am. I call him back, but he doesn't answer, so I
figure he must be training. I leave a message telling him to

just come over when he gets back home. We're supposed to go to Steve Bledell's party tonight. I'm nervous to tell Peter the news. Our plan was set, and now I'm changing things around, but it's not like I knew this door would open for me. He'll understand. I know he will.

I flop back on my bed and FaceTime Margot. She's outside walking, on her way somewhere. "What's up?" she asks.

"Guess what."

"What!"

"I got into UNC!"

She promptly screams and drops her phone. Thankfully, it falls in the grass. She scrambles to pick it up. She's still screaming. "Oh my God! This is amazing! This is the best news! When did you find out?"

I roll onto my stomach. "Yesterday! Chris and I went to visit last night, and Gogo, it was so much fun. We went to see a band play, and we danced and we screamed ourselves silly. My throat is sore!"

"So wait—you're going, right?"

"Yes!"

Margot screams again, and I laugh. "What's UNC's campus like?" she demands.

"Well, it's a lot like UVA."

"I've heard that. I've heard the campuses are very similar. The towns, too. Both liberal, but Chapel Hill maybe even a little more so. Lots of great minds there. I can't wait to look at the course book with you." She starts walking again. "You're going to love it there. Maggie Cohen, she was a year above me, she *loves* it. You should talk to her." Beaming, Margot says to me, "This is when everything begins, Lara Jean. You'll see."

After I get off the phone with Margot, I take a bubble bath and do all my rituals: face mask, loofah, brown sugar–lavender scrub. In the bath, I practice what I'm going to say to Peter. *There are two trees, on opposite sides, and their branches meet in the middle. . . .* I stay in for so long, Kitty screams at me to hurry up. When I get out of the tub, I dry my hair and then curl it; I redo my nails and I even apply the lemon cuticle cream I bought but never remember to use.

Daddy, Trina, and Kitty have gone out to see a movie, so I'm all alone in the house when Peter arrives around eight. He's wearing new UVA sweats; his hair is freshly washed and still damp. He smells like Dove soap, which I love on him. He pulls me in for a hug, leaning his body weight into me. "I'm so sore," he says, falling onto the living room couch. "Can we not go to Steve's tonight? I just want to stay here and hang out with you and not have to talk to people. I'm fucking exhausted."

"Sure," I say, and take a deep breath to tell him my news, but then he looks up at me with weary eyes.

"Those guys on the team are in incredible shape. It was hard to keep up."

I frown. "Hey, you're in good shape too."

"Not as good as them. I need to get my act together." He rubs the back of his neck. "So are you finally gonna tell me where you were last night?"

I sit down on the couch and face him, my legs tucked

under my butt. I put the backs of my hands to my cheeks, which feel flushed. Then I put them in my lap. "Well, okay." I pause. "Are you ready for this?"

He laughs. "Yeah, I'm ready."

"Okay. This is so crazy, but I was in North Carolina with Chris."

Peter raises his eyebrows. "Weird. Okay. Go on."

"I was there because . . . I got into UNC!"

He blinks. "Wow. That's . . . wow. That's awesome."

I take another deep breath. "I didn't think I'd want to go there, but then when Chris and I visited, the town was really charming, and the people were really nice, and there's this bench, by the Old Well, where if you lie down and look up, two trees on opposite sides, they meet in the middle. Their branches touch, like this." I start to demonstrate, and then I stop, because I realize Peter isn't really listening. He's staring into space. "What are you thinking?"

"Does this mean you're going there now and not William and Mary?"

I hesitate. "Yes."

He nods to himself. "I'm happy for you, I am. It just sucks that you're going to be so far away. Like, if I had to get in my car and drive to Chapel Hill right now, I'd fall asleep at the wheel. How far away is Charlottesville from Chapel Hill? Four hours?"

I feel a sinking sensation in my stomach. "Three hours and twenty-five minutes. I know it sounds long, but I swear it goes by fast!"

"That's double how long it takes to get from Charlottesville to William and Mary. And that's without traffic." He drops his head back against the couch.

"It's not double," I say quietly. "It's an extra hour and a half."

He looks over at me, and I see the regret in his eyes. "I'm sorry. I'm just really wiped right now. This is going to be a lot harder than I thought it would be. Not you and me, but college. I'm going to be at practice 24/7, and when I'm not at practice, I'm training or I'm in class or I'm sleeping. It's gonna be intense. Nothing like high school. It's a lot of pressure. And . . . I didn't think you'd be so far away."

I've never seen him like this before. He looks so defeated. When it comes to lacrosse, to school, he's always so easygoing, so confident. Everything's always come easily for him. "Peter, you're going to be great. You're just starting out. Once you get the hang of things, it'll be like always." Shyly I say, "And . . . we'll get the hang of things too."

All of a sudden he sits up straight. "You know what? Let's go to that party."

"Are you sure?"

"Sure. You're all dressed up. Let's not waste your hair." He pulls me toward him. "Let's celebrate your big W."

I put my arms around him and hug him to me. His shoulders feel tight; I can feel the tension in his back. Most boys wouldn't notice a thing like that: that I curled my hair, put on a blouse. I try to concentrate on that and not on how he didn't really congratulate me.

26

AT STEVE BLEDELL'S HOUSE, A BUNCH OF
people are in the family room smoking pot and watching
soccer on the huge flat-screen TV mounted on the wall.
Lucas is here, and when I tell him my big news, he picks me
up and spins me around. "You're getting out of here too!"
he shouts.

"Well, I'm only going next door to North Carolina," I say,
laughing. What an unexpected thrill to say those words out
loud. "It's not that far."

"But it's *away*." Lucas sets me back down on the floor and
puts his hands on my cheeks. "This is going to be very good
for you, Lara Jean."

"You think?"

"I know it."

I'm in the kitchen getting myself a Coke when Genevieve walks in, barefoot, wearing a Virginia Tech hoodie
and carrying a beer in a Virginia Tech koozie. She sways on
her feet before saying, "I heard you got into Chapel Hill.
Congrats."

I wait for the whammy, the underhanded little dig, but it
doesn't come. She just stands there, a little drunk but sober
enough. "Thank you," I say. "Congrats on Tech. I know you
always wanted to go there. Your mom must be happy."

"Yeah. Did you hear Chrissy's going to Costa Rica? Lucky bitch." She takes a sip of her beer. "Chapel Hill and here are pretty far away, huh?"

"Not that far. Just three hours," I lie.

"Well, good luck with that. I hope he stays as devoted to you as he is today. But knowing him, I seriously doubt it." Then she lets out a loud belch, and the look of startled surprise on her face is so funny, I almost laugh out loud. For a second it looks like she might too, but she stops herself, glares, and leaves the kitchen.

I only catch glimpses of Peter throughout the night, talking to other people, swigging on his beer. He seems to be in a better mood. He's smiling; his face is a little flushed from the beer. He's drinking a lot more than I've seen him drink.

Close to one, I go looking all around the house for Peter, and when I find him, he's with a bunch of people playing flip cup on the Ping-Pong table in Steve's garage. They are all cracking up over something he just said. He sees me standing at the top of the steps and beckons to me. "Come play with us, Covey," he says, too loudly.

My feet stay planted on the steps. "I can't. I have to get home."

His smile slips. "All right, I'll take you."

"No, it's fine, I'll get a ride or call an Uber to come get me." I turn to leave, and Peter follows me.

"Don't do that. I'll take you," he says.

"You can't. You're drunk." I try not to make the words sound mean, but it is what it is.

He laughs. "I'm not drunk. I've only had three beers over the course of, what, three hours? I'm fine. You don't drink so you don't know, but that's nothing. I promise."

"Well, I can smell your breath, and I know you wouldn't pass a breathalyzer."

Peter peers at me. "Are you mad?"

"No. I just don't want you driving me home. You shouldn't drive yourself home either. You should just spend the night here."

"Aw, you are mad." He leans closer to me and looks around before he says, "I'm sorry for before. I should've been more excited for you. I was just tired is all."

"It's fine," I say, thought it isn't, not completely.

Stormy used to have a saying. Leave with the one you came with, unless he's a drunk—then find your own way home. I end up getting a ride home from Lucas, and I make it before my curfew, just. After last night, I can't be pushing it.

Peter keeps texting me, and I'm petty enough to be glad he's not enjoying himself anymore. I make him wait long minutes before I text back a terse reply not to drive home tonight, and he texts back a picture of him lying on Steve's couch, with somebody's jacket as a blanket.

I can't sleep, so I go downstairs to make myself a grilled cheese sandwich. Kitty's down there too, watching late-night TV and playing a game on her phone. "Want a grilled cheese?" I ask.

"Sure," she says, looking up from her phone.

I make Kitty's first. I keep pressing the sandwich into

the pan, so the bottom gets crispy and the sandwich flattens. I cut off another dab of butter and watch it melt into a puddle, still feeling a bit out of sorts from the night, when out of nowhere it comes to me. Direct contact. The bread needs direct contact with the hot pan to get the right amount of crisp.

That's it. That's the answer to my chocolate chip cookie problem. All this time, I've been using my Silpat baking sheet so the cookies don't stick to the pan. Parchment paper is the answer. It's whisper thin, unlike Silpat. With parchment paper, the dough has more direct contact with heat, and therefore the dough spreads more! Voilà, thinner cookies.

I'm so determined, I start grabbing ingredients from the pantry. If I make the dough right this minute, it can rest all night, and I'll be able to test my theory tomorrow.

I sleep in again, because there's no school thanks to teacher meetings and because I was up till three making my dough and watching TV with Kitty. When I wake up, just like the day before there are texts from Peter.

> I'm sorry.
> I'm a dick.
> Don't be mad.

I read his texts over and over. They're spaced minutes apart, so I know he must be fretting over whether I'm still mad or not. I don't want to be mad. I just want things to go back to how they were before.

I text back:

Do you want to come over for a surprise?

He immediately replies:

ON MY WAY

"The perfect chocolate chip cookie," I intone, "should have three rings. The center should be soft and a little gooey. The middle ring should be chewy. And the outer ring should be crispy."

"I can't hear her give this speech again," Kitty says to Peter. "I just can't."

"Be patient," he says, squeezing her shoulder. "It's almost over, and then we get cookies."

"The perfect cookie is best eaten while still warm, but still delicious at room temperature."

"If you don't quit talking, they won't be warm anymore," Kitty grumbles. I shoot her a glare, but truthfully, I'm glad she's here to be a buffer between Peter and me. Her presence makes things feel normal.

"In the baking world, it is a truth universally acknowledged that Jacques Torres has perfected the chocolate chip cookie. Peter, you and I tasted it for ourselves just a few months ago." I'm really stretching it now to make them suffer. "How will my cookie measure up? Spoiler alert. It's amazing."

Kitty slides off her stool. "That's it. I'm out of here. A chocolate chip cookie isn't worth all this."

I pat her on the head. "Oh, naive little Kitten. Dear, foolish girl. This cookie is worth all this and more. Sit or you will not partake."

Rolling her eyes, she sits back down.

"My friends, I have finally found it. My white whale. My golden ring. The cookie to rule them all." With a flourish, I whisk off the tea towel and present them with my flat, chewy, non-puffy cookies, artfully arranged on the plate.

To my dismay, Peter shoves one in his mouth whole. With his mouth full he says, "Delicious!"

He's still worried that I'm upset, so he'll say anything right now. "Eat slower. Savor it, Peter."

"I am, trust me."

Kitty is the true critic to please. Eagerly I say, "I used muscovado sugar. Can you taste that hint of molasses?"

She is munching thoughtfully. "I can't taste the difference between this one and the one you made two batches ago."

"This time I used chocolate fèves and not chunks. See the way the chocolate melts in streaks?"

"What's a fève?"

"It's a disc."

"Then just say disc. Also didn't Daddy get mad because you spent thirty dollars on chocolate?"

"I wouldn't say he was *mad*. Maybe annoyed. But I think

he'll agree that it's worth it." Kitty gives me a look, like, *Yeah, right*, and I mumble, "It's Valrhona, okay? It doesn't come cheap. And also, it was a two-pound bag! Look, that isn't the point. Can't you tell how much crispier the edges are, and how much chewier it is in the center? Do I need to explain to you guys again about Silpat versus parchment paper?"

"We got it," Kitty says.

Peter hooks his finger into the loop of my jeans and pulls me closer. "Best cookie of my life," he declares. He's really laying it on thick, but I'm not quite done being mad.

"You guys are so corny," Kitty says. "I'm taking my share of the cookies and getting out of here." She starts stacking cookies on a napkin, rapid-fire.

"Only take three!"

She puts two back, then heads upstairs.

Peter waits until she is gone before he asks, "Are you still pissed at me? I'll never drink on a night I'm supposed to drive you ever again, I promise." He gives me his winning smile.

"Are you really okay with me going to UNC?" I ask him.

His smile fades, and there is a slight hesitation before he nods. "It's like you said. We'll get the hang of it, whatever it is." For the briefest of moments his eyes search mine, and I know he's looking for reassurance. That's when I put my arms around him and hug him tight to me, tight enough that he knows I'm here; I won't let go.

27

NOW THAT I'VE MADE MY DECISION TO GO to UNC, there are suddenly things to do, and right away. I inform William and Mary I'm not coming; I send in my deposit to UNC. I tell my guidance counselor, Mrs. Duvall, who is overjoyed. She tells me I'm the only one from our class going there, and she can't wait to add it to the list of accepted schools. "I knew you'd make me proud," she says, nodding her head. "I knew it."

Our caps and gowns have arrived, and Peter and I go to the gym to pick ours up, along with graduation announcements.

We sit down on the bleachers to try our caps on, and Peter tilts mine to the side and says, "You look cute."

I blow him a kiss. "Let me see your announcements." I want to see his name all fancy in calligraphy.

He passes me the box and I open it. I run my fingers along the embossed letters. *Peter Grant Kavinsky.* Then I say, "Have you given any more thought to inviting your dad?"

Peter looks around to see if anyone's listening before saying in a low voice, "Why do you keep bringing that up?"

I reach out and touch Peter's cap. "Because I think that, deep down, you want him to be there. If only so he can see all that you've accomplished and all that he's missed out on."

"We'll see," he says, and I leave it at that. It's Peter's decision.

On the way home from school Peter asks me, "Wanna see a movie tonight?"

"I can't," I say. "Trina's friend Kristen is coming over to go over final details of Trina's bachelorette party."

He gives me a sly look. "Are you guys going to a strip club?"

"No! Ew. Like I would ever want to see any of that."

"See any of what?" he demands.

"Oiled-up muscles." I shudder. "I'm just glad you don't have big muscles."

Peter frowns. "Hey, I'm built."

I squeeze his bicep, and he automatically flexes against my fingers. "You're nice and lean with little muscles."

"You really know how to emasculate a guy, Covey," he says as he turns down my street.

I feel bad, because now I'm remembering how he said he wasn't in the same shape the other guys on the lacrosse team were in. "I like you just the way you are," I quickly say, and he laughs, so he can't be that hurt.

"What's your dad doing for his bachelor party?"

I laugh. "Have you met my dad? He's the last person who would ever have a bachelor party. He doesn't even have any guy friends to have a party with!" I stop and consider this. "Well, I guess Josh is the closest thing he has. We haven't seen much of him since he went to school, but he and my dad still e-mail every so often."

"I don't get what your family sees in that guy," Peter says sourly. "What's so great about him?"

It's a touchy subject. Peter's paranoid my dad likes Josh better than him, and I try to tell him it's not a contest— which it definitely isn't. Daddy's known Josh since he was a kid. They trade comic books, for Pete's sake. So, no contest. Obviously my dad likes Josh better. But only because he knows him better. And only because they're more alike: Neither of them is cool. And Peter's definitely cool. My dad is bewildered by cool.

"Josh loves my dad's cooking."

"So do I!"

"They have the same taste in movies."

Peter throws in, "And Josh was never in a hot tub video with one of his daughters."

"Oh my God, let it go already! My dad's forgotten about that." "Forgotten" might be too strong of a word. Maybe more like he's never brought it up again and he hopefully never will.

"I find that hard to believe."

"Well, believe it. My dad is a very forgiving, very forgetful man."

As we're pulling into my driveway, Peter suddenly says, "What if I threw your dad a bachelor party? We could do steaks, maybe cigars—"

"My dad doesn't smoke cigars."

"Well, just steaks, then. Geez."

"Steaks and no strip club."

"Oh my God, give me a little credit, Covey! Besides, I'm not twenty-one yet. I doubt I could even get in."

I give him a dirty look.

Quickly he says, "Not that I would even want to. And I definitely wouldn't want to go to one with my girlfriend's dad." He shudders. "That's sick."

"So then what's the plan? Grill some steaks?"

"No. We'll go to a nice steakhouse. We'll get dressed up; it'll be a real guys' night. Maybe we'll even wear suits."

I suppress a smile. Peter will never admit it, but he loves to get dressed up. So vain. "Sounds good."

"Will you ask him about it?" he asks.

"I think *you* should ask him."

"If he says yes, who should I invite?"

"Josh?" I suggest it half-heartedly, knowing he won't agree.

"No way. Doesn't he have any work friends?"

"He doesn't have that many close friends at work," I say. "Just Dr. Kang. . . . You could invite my uncle Victor. And sometimes he goes on bike rides with Mr. Shah from down the street."

"Can you get me their e-mails ASAP?" Peter asks me. "I want to get the invites out as soon as I get the okay from your dad. When's the bachelorette? The weekend after next?"

My heart surges. I'm so touched by how eager Peter is to impress my dad. "It's the third Friday of the month. We're waiting for Margot to come home."

★ ★ ★

Kitty was suspiciously serene about not being invited to Trina's bachelorette night, and I thought to myself, Wow, Kitty's really growing up. She gets that it's not about her; she understands that the night is about Trina.

But of course Kitty always has a long game.

For the first time in a while, she's riding to school with us. She wanted Peter to take her in his Audi, but I put my foot down and said I needed to get to school too. So we're all in his mom's minivan like old times.

However, Kitty is up front and I am in the backseat.

From the passenger seat Kitty sighs heavily and rests her head against the window.

"What's up with you?" Peter asks.

"The bridesmaids won't let me go on the bachelorette night," she says. "I'm the only one left out."

I narrow my eyes at the back of her head.

"That's bullshit!" Peter looks at me in the rearview mirror. "Why won't you guys let her go?"

"We're going to a karaoke bar! We can't bring Kitty in because she's too young. Honestly, I think I was barely allowed to go."

"Why can't you guys just go to a restaurant like we're doing?"

"Because that's not a real bachelorette."

Peter rolls his eyes. "It's not like you guys are going to a strip club or something—wait, did you change your mind? Are you going to a strip club?"

"No!"

"Then what's the big deal? Just go somewhere else."

"Peter, it's not my decision. You'll have to take it up with Kristen." I smack the back of Kitty's arm. "Same goes for you, you little fiend! Quit trying to weasel your way in by manipulating Peter. He has no power here."

"Sorry, kid," Peter says.

Kitty slumps in her seat and then straightens. "What if I came to the bachelor night instead?" she suggests. "Since you're just going to a restaurant?"

Peter stutters, "Uh—uh, I don't know, I'd have to talk to the guys. . . ."

"So you'll ask? Because I like steak too. I like it so much. I'll order steak with a baked potato on the side, and for dessert I'll have a strawberry sundae with whipped cream." Kitty beams a smile at Peter, who smiles back weakly.

When we get to the elementary school and she hops out, perky and puffed up like a chickadee, I lean forward in my seat and say into Peter's ear, "You just got played."

28

WITH ONLY THREE DAYS LEFT OF SCHOOL, yearbooks arrive. There are several blank pages in the back for signatures, but everybody knows the place of honor is the back cover. Of course I've saved mine for Peter. I never want to forget how special this year was.

My yearbook quote is "I have spread my dreams under your feet; / Tread softly because you tread on my dreams." I had a very hard time choosing between that and "Without you, today's emotions would be the scurf of yesterday's." Peter was like, "I know that's from *Amélie*, but what the hell is a scurf?" and honestly, he had a point. Peter let me write his. "Surprise me," he said.

As we walk through the cafeteria doors, someone holds the door for us, and Peter says, "Cheers." Peter's taken to saying cheers instead of thanks, which I know he learned from Ravi. It makes me smile every time.

For the past month or so, the cafeteria's been half-empty at lunch. Most of the seniors have been eating off-campus, but Peter likes the lunches his mom packs and I like our cafeteria's french fries. But because the student council's passing out our yearbooks today, it's a full house. I pick up my copy and run back to the lunch table with it. I flip to his page first. There is Peter, smiling in a tuxedo. And there is his quote: *"You're welcome."* —*Peter Kavinsky.*

Peter's brow furrows when he sees it. "What does that even mean?"

"It means, here I am, so handsome and lovely to look at." I spread my arms out benevolently, like I am the pope. "You're welcome."

Darrell busts out laughing, and so does Gabe, who spreads his arms out too. "You're welcome," they keep saying to each other.

Peter shakes his head at all of us. "You guys are nuts."

Leaning forward, I kiss him on the lips. "And you love it!" I drop my yearbook in front of him. "Write something memorable," I say, leaning over his shoulder. "Something romantic."

"Your hair is tickling my neck," he complains. "I can't concentrate."

I straighten up and rock back on my heels, arms crossed. "I'm waiting."

"How am I supposed to think of something good with you looking over my shoulder?" he says. "Let me do it later."

I shake my head firmly. "No, because then you never will."

I keep bugging him about it, until finally he says, "I just don't know what to write," which makes me frown.

"Write down a memory, or a hope, or—or anything." I'm disappointed and trying not to show it, but would it be so hard for him to think of something on his own?

"Let me take it home tonight so I can take my time with it," he says hastily.

I spend the rest of the day filling up my yearbook, and people write generic things like *Good luck at UNC,* and *You made freshman year gym fun,* and *Add me on Instagram,* but also more meaningful things, like *I wish you had started coming out more sooner, so I'd know you better.* Ben Simonoff writes, *It's always the quiet ones that are the most interesting. Stay interesting.* I hand the yearbook over to Peter at the end of the day. "Keep it safe," I tell him.

The next morning, he forgets to bring it to school with him, which is annoying, because I want to get the whole senior class's signatures, and I still have a few more to go. Tomorrow is the last day of school.

"Did you at least finish it?" I ask him.

"Yeah! I just forgot it," he says, wincing. "I'll bring it tomorrow, I swear."

Beach Week is a tradition where we're from. It's exactly what it sounds like. The day after graduation, the senior class packs up and goes to Nags Head for a week. Never in a million years did I think I would be going. For one thing, you have to gather up enough friends to rent a house together—like ten friends! Before Peter I didn't have ten friends I could rent a beach house with. Somebody's parent has to rent the house in their name, because no one wants to rent out a house to a bunch of high school kids. Margot didn't go her year. She and Josh went camping with some friends. She said Beach Week wasn't really her thing. A year ago, it wouldn't have been my thing either. But now I have Peter, and Pammy, and Chris and Lucas.

When the topic of Beach Week first came up months ago, Peter asked me if I thought my dad would let me stay at his house. I said no way. Instead I'm staying with a bunch of girls. Pammy's older sister Julia rented the house, and Pammy assured me it had air-conditioning and everything. She said the boys' house was on the beach and we were two rows back, but it was better this way because then we could junk up their house with sand and ours would stay pristine.

My dad said yes at the time, but I'm fairly certain he's forgotten about it, because when I bring up Beach Week tonight at dinner, he looks confused. "Wait, what's Beach Week again?"

"It's when everybody goes to the beach after graduation and parties all week," Kitty explains, stuffing her slice of pizza in her mouth.

I shoot her a look.

"My Beach Week was *insane*," Trina says, and a fond smile crosses her face.

I shoot Trina one too.

Daddy's forehead creases. "Insane?"

"Well it wasn't *that* insane," Trina amends. "It was just a fun girls trip. One last fling with all the girls before college."

"Where's Peter staying?" Daddy asks me, and now his forehead looks as wrinkled as a walnut.

"In a boy house. I told you all about it ages ago and you

said yes, so you can't go back on it now. It's the day after graduation!"

"And there won't be any adult supervision? Just kids?"

Trina puts her hand on Daddy's arm. "Dan, Lara Jean isn't a kid anymore. In a few months she'll be living on her own. This is just practice."

"You're right. I know you're right. That doesn't mean I have to like it." He sighs heavily and stands up. "Kitty, help me clear the table, will you?"

As soon as they're gone, Trina turns to me, and in a low voice she says, "Lara Jean, I know you're not a drinker, but here's a pro tip that you can take with you to Beach Week and college and beyond. Always, always have a buddy system in place. It'll go like this: One night, you get to drink. The next night, your girlfriend gets to drink. That way one person is always sober enough to hold the other person's hair back and make sure nothing bad happens."

Smiling, I say, "Peter will be there. He'll hold my hair back if need be. Or I can just wear it in a ponytail."

"True. I'm just saying, for the future." For when he isn't there. My smile dims, and she quickly goes on to say, "At my Beach Week, we took turns cooking dinner for the house. When it was my turn, I made chicken parmesan and all the smoke detectors went off and we couldn't figure out how to make the beeping stop all night!" She laughs. Trina has such an easy laugh.

"I doubt my Beach Week will get that crazy," I say.

"Well, let's hope it gets a *little* crazy," she says.

29

THIS IS THE LAST TIME WE'LL WALK UP THIS staircase together, Peter taking the stairs two at a time, me nipping at his heels, huffing and puffing to keep up. It's the last day of school for seniors, the last day of my high school career.

When we reach the top of the staircase, I say, "I feel like taking the stairs two at a time is just bragging. Have you ever noticed that only boys ever take stairs two at a time?"

"Girls probably would if they were as tall."

"Margot's friend Chelsea is five eleven, and I don't think she does it."

"So what are you saying—boys brag more?"

"Probably. Don't you think?"

"Probably," he admits.

The bell rings, and people start heading for class.

"Should we just skip first period? Go get pancakes?" He raises his eyebrows at me enticingly, pulling me toward him by the dangling straps of my book bag. "Come on, you know you want to."

"No way. It's the last day of school. I want to say good-bye to Mr. Lopez."

Peter groans. "Goody-goody."

"You knew who I was when you started dating me," I tell him.

"True," he says.

Before we go our separate ways, I hold out my hands and wait expectantly. Peter gives me a curious look. "My yearbook!"

"Oh shit! I forgot it again."

"Peter! It's the last day of school! I only got half the signatures I wanted!"

"I'm sorry," he says, rubbing his hand through his hair and making it go all messy. "Do you want me to go back home and get it? I can go right now." He looks genuinely sorry, but I'm still annoyed.

When I don't say anything right away, Peter starts to head back toward the stairs, but I stop him. "No, don't. It's fine. I'll just pass it around at graduation."

"Are you sure?" he asks.

"Sure," I say. We're not even here the full school day; I don't want him to have to run back home just for my yearbook.

Classes are pretty lax; we mostly just walk around saying good-bye to teachers, the office staff, the cafeteria ladies, the school nurse. A lot of them we'll see at graduation, but not everyone. I pass around cookies that I baked last night. We get our final grades—all good, so no worries there.

It takes me forever to clean out my locker. I find random notes I saved from Peter, which I promptly put in my bag so I can add them to his scrapbook. An old granola bar. Dusty black hair ties, which is ironic because you can never seem to find a hair tie when you need one.

"I'm sad to throw any of this stuff away, even this old granola bar," I say to Lucas, who is sitting on the floor keeping me company. "I've seen it there at the bottom of my locker every day. It's like an old pal. Should we split it, to commemorate this day?"

"Sick," Lucas says. "It's probably got mold." Matter-of-factly he says, "After graduation I probably won't see any of these people again."

I throw him a hurt look. "Hey! What about me?"

"Not you. You're coming to visit me in New York."

"Ooh! Yes, please."

"Sarah Lawrence is so close to the city. I'll be able to go to Broadway shows whenever I want. There's an app for same-day student tickets." He gets a faraway look in his eyes.

"You're so lucky," I say.

"I'll take you. We'll go to a gay bar, too. It'll be amazing."

"Thank you!"

"But everybody else I can take or leave."

"We still have Beach Week," I remind him, and he nods.

"For the rest of our lives, we'll always have Beach Week," he says mockingly, and I throw a hair tie at him.

Lucas can mock me for being nostalgic all he wants. I know these days are special. High school *will* be a time we remember the whole rest of our lives.

After school, Peter and I go to his house because mine is a disaster zone with wedding stuff, and Peter's mom has her book club after work, and Owen has soccer, so we have the house all to ourselves. It seems the only place we're ever truly alone is in his car, so moments like these are rare and of note. My last drive home from high school, and Peter K. is the one who's driving me. It's fitting, to end high school the way I spent it—riding in the passenger seat of Peter's car.

When we go up to his room, I sit down on his bed, which is neatly made, with the comforter pulled in tight; the pillows look fluffed, even. It's a new comforter, probably for college—a cheery red and cream and navy tartan that I'm sure his mom picked out. "Your mom makes your bed, doesn't she?" I ask him, leaning back against the pillows.

"Yes," he says, without an ounce of shame. He flops onto the bed, and I scoot over to make room for him.

Late afternoon light filters in through his pale curtains, and it casts the room in a dreamy kind of filter. If I were going to name it, I would call it "summer in the suburbs." Peter looks beautiful in this light. He looks beautiful in any light, but especially this one. I take a picture of him in my mind, just like this. Any annoyance I felt over him forgetting my yearbook melts away when he snuggles closer to me, rests his head on my chest, and says, "I can feel your heart beating."

I start playing with his hair, which I know he likes. It's so soft for a boy. I love the smell of his detergent, his soap, everything.

He looks up at me and traces the bow of my lip. "I like this part the best," he says. Then he moves up and brushes his lips against mine, teasing me. He bites on my bottom lip playfully. I like all his different kinds of kisses, but maybe this kind best. Then he's kissing me with urgency, like he is utterly consumed, his hands in my hair, and I think, no, these are the best.

Between kisses he asks me, "How come you only ever want to hook up when we're at my house?"

"I—I don't know. I guess I never thought about it before." It's true we only ever make out at Peter's house. It feels weird to be romantic in the same bed I've slept in since I was a little girl. But when I'm in Peter's bed, or in his car, I forget all about that and I'm just lost in the moment.

We're at it kissing again—Peter's shirt is off; mine is still on—when the phone rings downstairs, and Peter says it's probably the repairman calling about when he's coming to fix the pipes. He puts on his shirt and runs downstairs to answer it, and that's when I spot my yearbook on his desk.

I get out of bed and pick it up and flip to the back. It's still empty. When Peter comes back upstairs, I'm sitting on his bed again and I don't mention my yearbook, I don't ask why he still hasn't written in it. I'm not sure why. I tell him I'd better get going, because Margot's coming home from Scotland tonight, and I want to stock the fridge with all her favorite foods.

Peter's face falls. "You don't want to hang out a little longer? I can take you to the store."

"I still have to clean up the upstairs, too," I say, standing up.

He tugs on my shirt and tries to pull me back onto the bed. "Come on, five more minutes."

I lie back down next to him and he cuddles in close, but I'm still thinking about the yearbook. I've been working on his scrapbook for months; the least he can do is write me a nice yearbook message.

"This is good practice for college," he murmurs, pulling me toward him, wrapping his arms around me. "The beds are small at UVA. How big are the beds at UNC?"

My back to him, I say, "I don't know. I didn't get to see the dorms."

He tucks his head in the space between my neck and shoulder. "That was a trick question," he says, and I can feel him smile against my neck. "To check and see if you visited a random UNC guy's dorm room with Chris. Congrats, you passed the test."

I can't help but laugh. Then my smile fades and I give him a test of my own. "Don't let me forget to take my yearbook with me when we leave."

He stiffens for a second and then says in an easy tone, "I have to hunt it down. It's here somewhere. If I can't find it, I'll just bring it over later."

I pull away from him and sit up. Confused, he looks up at me. "I saw my yearbook on your desk, Peter. I know you haven't written anything yet!"

Peter sits up and sighs and scrubs his hand through his hair roughly. His eyes flit over to me and then back down again. "I just don't know what to write. I know you want me to write some great, romantic thing, but I don't know what to say. I've tried a bunch of times, and I just—I freeze up. You know I'm not good at that kind of thing."

Feelingly, I tell him, "I don't care what you say as long as it's from the heart. Just be sweet. Be you." I crawl closer to him and put my arms around his neck. "Okay?" Peter nods, and I give him a little kiss, and he surges up and kisses me harder, and then I don't even care about my dumb yearbook anymore. I am aware of every breath, every movement. I memorize it all, I hold it in my heart.

When we break away, he looks up at me and says, "I went to my dad's house yesterday."

My eyes widen. "You did?"

"Yeah. He invited me and Owen to come over for dinner, and I wasn't going to go, but then Owen asked me to come with him and I couldn't say no."

I lie back down, rest my head on his chest. "How was it?"

"It was fine, I guess. His house is nice." I don't say anything; I just wait for him to go on. It feels like a long time before he says, "You know that old movie you made me watch, where the poor kid was standing outside with his nose pressed to the glass? That's how I felt."

"That old movie" he's referring to is *Willy Wonka and the Chocolate Factory*, when Charlie is watching all the kids go hog wild at the candy store but he can't go inside because he doesn't have any money. The thought of Peter—handsome, confident, easy Peter—feeling that way makes me want to cry. Maybe I shouldn't have pushed him so hard to reconnect with his dad.

"He put up a basketball hoop for those kids. I asked him

for one so many times, but he never did it. His kids aren't even athletic. I don't think Everett's picked up a basketball once in his whole life."

"Did Owen have a good time?"

This he grudgingly concedes. "Yeah, he and Clayton and Everett played video games. My dad grilled hamburgers and steaks. He even wore a damn chef's apron. I don't think he ever helped my mom in the kitchen once the whole time they were married." Peter pauses. "He didn't do the dishes, though, so I guess he hasn't changed that much. Still, I could tell he and Gayle were trying. She baked a cake. Not as good as yours, though."

"What kind of cake?" I ask.

"Devil's food cake. Kind of dry." Peter hesitates before he says, "I invited him to graduation."

"You did?" My heart swells.

"He kept asking about school, and . . . I don't know. I thought about what you said, and I just did it." He shrugs, like he doesn't care much either way if his dad's there or not. It's an act. Peter cares. Of course he cares. "So you'll meet him then."

I snuggle closer to him. "I'm so proud of you, Peter."

He gives a little laugh. "For what?"

"For giving your dad a chance even though he doesn't deserve it." I look up at him and say, "You're a nice boy, Peter K.," and the smile that breaks across his face makes me love him even more.

30

AFTER PETER DROPS ME OFF AT HOME, I end up having just enough time to run to the grocery store and pick up chips and salsa, ice cream, challah bread, Brie, blood-orange soda—you know, all the essentials—and then come home and clean the upstairs bathroom and make up Margot's bed with fresh sheets.

Daddy picks Margot up at the airport on the way home from work. It's the first time she's been home since Trina moved in. When we step inside the house with her suitcases, I see her looking around the living room; I see her eyes flit to the mantel, where there is now framed art that Trina brought over from her house—it's an abstract painting of the shoreline. Margot's expression doesn't change, but I know she notices. How could she not? I moved Mommy and Daddy's wedding portrait into my room the day before Trina moved in. Margot's looking around the whole room now, silently noting everything that is different. The embroidered throw pillows Trina brought with her, a framed picture of her and Daddy on the day he proposed on the side table by the couch, the armchair we switched out for Trina's. All of Trina's little knickknacks, of which there are many. Now that I'm looking at it all through Margot's eyes, it *is* kind of cluttered.

Margot takes off her shoes and opens the door to the shoe

closet and sees how stuffed it is—Trina has a lot of shoes, too. "Geez, this closet is packed," she says, shoving Trina's cycling shoes to the side to make room for her booties.

After we lug her suitcases upstairs and Margot changes into comfy clothes, we come back down for a snack while Daddy fixes dinner. I'm sitting on the couch, chomping on chips, when Margot suddenly stands up and declares that she's going to go through the shoe closet and get rid of all her old shoes. "Right now?" I say, my mouth full of chips.

"Why not?" she says. When Margot gets it into her head to do something, she does it right away.

She dumps everything out of the shoe closet and sits on the floor cross-legged, going through piles, deciding which ones to keep and which to donate to the Salvation Army. She holds up a pair of black boots. "To keep or to toss?"

"Keep them or give them to me," I say, scooping salsa with a tortilla chip. "They look so cute with tights."

She tosses them in the keep pile. "Trina's dog sheds so much," Margot grouses, plucking dog fur off of her leggings. "How do you ever wear black clothes?"

"There's a lint roller in the shoe case. And I guess I don't wear that many black clothes?" I really should wear black more often. Every fashion blog emphasizes the importance of a little black dress. I wonder if there will be a lot of occasions for a little black dress at college. "How often do you get dressed up at Saint Andrews?"

"Not that often. People mostly wear jeans and boots when they go out. Saint Andrews isn't that dressy of a place."

"You don't get dressed up even to go to a wine-and-cheese night at your professor's house?"

"We get dressed up for high table dinners with professors, but I've never been invited to one's house. Maybe they do that at UNC, though."

"Maybe!"

Margot holds up a pair of yellow rain boots. "Keep or toss?"

"Keep."

"You're no help. You've voted to keep everything." She tosses the rain boots into the cardboard giveaway box.

It seems both of my sisters are pretty ruthless about throwing away old things. When Margot's done sorting through everything, I go through the box one more time to see if there isn't anything I can save. I end up taking her rain boots and a pair of patent-leather Mary Janes.

That night I'm heading to the bathroom to brush my teeth when I hear Trina's hushed voice coming from Margot's room. I stop in the hallway to listen like a little spy, like Kitty. "This is a little awkward, but you left this in the bathroom, so I stuck it in a drawer just in case you wanted to keep it private."

Margot's cool voice returns, "Keep it private from whom? Kitty?"

"Well, from your dad. Or whoever. I just wasn't sure."

"My dad's an obstetrician. It's not like he's never seen birth-control pills before."

"Oh, I know. I just . . ." Lamely she says again, "I just

JENNY HAN

wasn't sure. If it was a secret or not, I mean."

"Well, thanks. I appreciate the thought, but I don't keep secrets from my dad."

I scurry back to my bedroom before I hear Trina's reply. Eek.

The day before graduation, Peter comes over to hang out at the house. I'm sewing little flowers onto my graduation cap, Kitty's watching TV on the floor on her beanbag, and Margot's shelling beans into a mixing bowl. She has a recipe she wants to try out for dinner tonight. A wedding show is on the TV, one of those who-had-the-best-wedding type programs.

"Hey, for your dad's wedding, what about one of those sky-lantern ceremonies, where you light up the lantern and make a wish and release it into the sky?" Peter pipes up. "I saw it in a movie."

I'm impressed. "Peter, that's a really nice idea!"

"I saw that in a movie too," Kitty says. "*Hangover Part Two*?"

"Yeah!" I give them both a look. Peter is quick to ask, "Isn't that an Asian tradition? Could be nice."

"It's not a Korean tradition, it's Thai," Kitty says. "Remember, the movie takes place in Thailand?"

"Not that it matters, because it's not like Trina is even Asian," says Margot. "Why would she need to appropriate Asian culture into her wedding just because we're Asian? It doesn't have anything to do with her."

"I wouldn't go that far," I say. "She wants us to feel

included. The other day she was saying it might be nice to acknowledge Mommy in some way."

Margot rolls her eyes. "She didn't even know her."

"Well, she knew her a little. They were all neighbors, after all. I don't know, I thought during the ceremony, like, maybe the three of us could light a candle. . . ." I trail off because Margot doesn't look at all convinced. "It was just an idea," I say, and Peter makes a *yikes* face at me.

"I don't know, I think that sounds kind of awkward? I mean, this wedding is about Trina and Daddy starting a new life together, not the past."

"That's a good point," Peter agrees.

Peter works hard to impress Margot. He's always taking her side. I pretend to be annoyed by it, but really I am touched. Of course he should take her side. It's his job to take her side. It shows that he gets how important her good opinion is to me, and he gets the place she has in my life. I could never be with someone who didn't understand how important my family is to me.

When Margot leaves to take Kitty to piano lessons, Peter says, "Your sister is really not loving Ms. Rothschild, huh." Peter still hasn't gotten the hang of calling Ms. Rothschild Trina, and he likely never will. In our neighborhood, none of the kids growing up called the adults by their first names. Everyone was Miss or Mrs. or Mr., except for Daddy, who was Dr.

"I wouldn't say Gogo *dislikes* Trina," I say. "She likes her; she just isn't used to her yet. You know how Trina is."

"True," he says. "I also know how your sister is. It took her forever to warm up to me."

"It wasn't forever. You're just used to people liking you from the very first minute they meet you." I give him a sidelong look. "Because you're so very charming." He scowls, because I don't say it like a compliment. "Gogo doesn't care about charm. She cares about real."

"Well, now she loves me," he says, all confidence. When I don't answer right away, he says, "Right? Doesn't she?"

I laugh. "She does."

Later that day, after Peter leaves to help his mom out at her store, Margot and Trina get into a spat over, of all things, hair. I'm in the laundry room, ironing my dress when I hear Trina say, "Margot, when you shower, would you mind picking up your hair out of the drain catch? I was cleaning the tub this morning and I noticed it."

Then comes Margot's quick reply. "Sure."

"Thanks. I just don't want the drain to get clogged."

A minute later Margot's in the laundry room with me. "Did you hear that? Can you believe her? How does she even know it was my hair and not yours or Kitty's?"

"Your hair is lighter, and it's shorter," I point out. "Plus, Kitty and I pick ours up because we know it grosses Trina out."

"Well, dog fur all over my clothes grosses *me* out! Every time I take a breath, I feel like I'm inhaling fur. If she's so concerned about housekeeping, she should vacuum more often."

Trina comes up behind Margot, looking stony-faced, and

says, "I actually vacuum once a week, which is the standard amount."

Margot's gone red. "Sorry. But if you have a dog that sheds as much as Simone, I think twice a week is probably more appropriate."

"Then tell that to your dad, since I haven't seen him pick up a vacuum once in the whole time I've known him." Trina stalks off, and Margot's mouth drops open, and I go back to ironing.

"Don't you think that was a bit much?" she whispers to me.

"She's right, though. Daddy never vacuums. He sweeps, and he mops, but he doesn't vacuum."

"Still!"

"Trina isn't one to be trifled with," I tell her. "Especially not when she's about to get her period." Margot stares at me. "We're synced up. It's only a matter of time before you are too."

Margot and I go to the mall, ostensibly so I can get a new strapless bra for my dress, but really because Margot wants to escape Trina. When we get back, the downstairs rugs are freshly vacuumed and neat as a pin, and Kitty is putting the vacuum cleaner away, which I can tell Margot feels bad about.

At dinner Trina and Margot are cordial to each other, as if nothing happened. Which, in some ways, is worse than a fight. At least when you're in a fight, you're in it with someone.

31

THE DAY OF MY GRADUATION, I WAKE UP
early and lie in bed listening to the sounds of the house
waking up. Daddy is puttering around downstairs making
coffee; Margot has the shower running; Kitty is probably still
sound asleep. Trina, too. They're both late sleepers.

I will miss these house sounds when I'm gone. A part of
me is already homesick for them. Another part of me is so,
so excited to take this next step, and I never thought I would
be, not after things didn't turn out the way I'd hoped.

For my graduation present, Margot gives me a college kit. A
pink satin eye mask with my name embroidered on it in pale
silvery blue. A USB drive shaped like a gold tube of lipstick.
Earplugs that look like circus peanuts, pink fuzzy slippers, a
nylon makeup bag covered in sketches of bows. I love every
single thing in the kit equally.

Kitty makes a beautiful card. It's a collage of pictures of us,
but she's used some sort of app to turn the pictures into line
drawings, like a coloring book. She's colored them all with
coloring pencils. On the inside she's written, *Congratulations.*
Have fun at college. P.S. I'll miss you an 11. Tears spring to my
eyes, and I scoop Kitty into my arms and hug her tightly, for
so long that she says, "All right, all right—enough already,"

but I can tell she is pleased. "I'm going to frame it," I declare.

My gift from Trina is a vintage tea set—cream with pink rosebuds and rimmed in gold. "It was my mom's," she tells me, and I feel like I could cry, I love it so much. When I hug her, I whisper in her ear, "This is my favorite gift," and she winks at me. Winking is one of Trina's talents. She's great at it, very natural.

Daddy sips from his coffee and then clears his throat. "Lara Jean, your gift from me is one that Margot and Kitty will also partake in."

"What is it, what is it?" Kitty presses.

"Hush, it's my gift," I say, looking at Daddy expectantly.

Grinning, he says, "I'm sending you three girls to Korea with Grandma this summer. Happy graduation, Lara Jean!"

Kitty screams and Margot is beaming, and I'm in shock. We've been talking about going to Korea for years. Mommy always wanted to take us. "When, when?" Kitty asks.

"Next month," Trina says, smiling at her. "Your dad and I will go on our honeymoon, and you guys will jet off to Korea."

Next month?

"Aw, you guys aren't coming?" Kitty pouts. Margot, on the other hand, is smiling. Ravi's visiting family in India over the summer, and she doesn't have any big plans.

"We really want to come, but I can't take that much time away from the hospital," Daddy says, regretful.

"For how long?" I ask. "How long will we go?"

"For all of July," Daddy says, gulping the rest of his coffee.

"Grandma and I have set the whole thing up. You're going to stay at your great-aunt's in Seoul, you'll take Korean language classes a few times a week, and you're going on a tour of the whole country, too. Jeju, Busan, the works. And Lara Jean, something special for you—a Korean pastry-making class! Don't worry, it'll be in English."

Kitty starts doing a little dance in her seat.

Margot looks at me then, her eyes shining. "You've always wanted to learn how to bake Korean cream cakes! We'll go shopping for face masks and stationery and cute things, like, every day. By the time we come back, we'll be able to watch Korean dramas without subtitles!"

"I can't wait," I say, and Margot and Kitty and Daddy start discussing all the logistics, but Trina looks over at me closely. I keep the smile on my face.

A whole month. By the time I get back, it'll be nearly time to leave for college, and Peter and I will have spent the summer apart.

At graduation all the girls wear white dresses. All white everything. I'm wearing Margot's dress from two years ago—sleeveless with Swiss dots and a crisp knee-length skirt. Trina's taken up the hemline for me because I'm shorter. Margot wore it with Converse, and I'm wearing white patent-leather sandals with a T-strap and little perforations.

In the car on the way over, I smooth down my skirt and say to Kitty, "Maybe you could wear this dress for your high school graduation too, Kitten. And you'll pose by the oak tree just like we did. It'll be a beautiful triptych." I wonder what shoes Kitty will wear. She's about as likely to wear white stilettos as she is white Reeboks or white roller skates.

Kitty makes a sour-lemon face. "I don't want to wear the same dress as you and Margot. I want my own dress. Besides, it'll *really* be out of style by then." She pauses. "What's a triptych?"

"It's, um, three pieces of art that come together and make one." Furtively, I google "triptych" on my phone to make sure I'm telling her the right thing. "It's, like, three panels, sort of hinged side by side. They're meant to be appreciated together."

"You're reading that off your phone."

"I was just double-checking," I say. I smooth my dress down again, making sure my cap is in my bag. I'm graduating from high school today. It snuck up on me—growing up, I mean. In the driver's seat, Trina's looking for a parking spot, and Margot's next to her, texting on her phone; Kitty's next to me, looking out the window. Daddy has driven separately, to pick up Grandma. Nana, Daddy's mom, is in Florida with her boyfriend and won't be able to make it. I only wish my own mom were here for this. All these big moments she's missing, that she'll keep missing. I have to believe that she knows, that somehow she still sees. But I also just wish I could have a hug from my mom on my graduation day.

★ ★ ★

Throughout the valedictorian speech, I keep looking out in the crowd for Peter's family. I wonder if his dad is sitting with Peter's brother and his mom, or separately. I wonder if I'll get to meet Peter's two half brothers too. I've already spotted my own family—they are hard to miss. Every time I look in their direction, they all wave madly. Plus, Trina's wearing a wide brimmed Kentucky Derby hat. Whoever is sitting in the row behind her probably can't see a thing. Margot exercised a lot of self-control by not rolling her eyes when Trina came downstairs wearing it. Even Kitty said it was "a bit much," but Trina asked me what I thought and I said I loved it, which I kind of do.

Our principal calls my name, "Lara Jean Song Covey," but he pronounces it Laura, which trips me up for a second.

When I accept my diploma from him and shake his hand, I whisper, "It's *Lara*, not *Laura*."

My plan was to blow my family a kiss as I walked across the stage, but I get so nervous that I forget. Over the applause I can hear Kitty's whoop, Daddy's whistle. When it's Peter's turn, I clap and scream like crazy, and of course everyone else does too. Even the teachers clap extra loud for him. It's so obvious when teachers have favorites. Not that I could blame them for loving Peter. We all do.

After we are declared graduates, after we throw our caps in the air, Peter makes his way past the throngs of people to find me. As he moves through the crowd, he's smiling, making jokes, saying hi to people, but there's something wrong. There's a blankness in his eyes, even as he grabs me for a hug. "Hey," he says, kissing me swiftly on the lips. "So we're officially college kids now."

Looking around, I straighten my robe and say, "I didn't see your mom and Owen in the stands. Did your dad sit with them? Are your brothers here? Should I come over now or after I take pictures with my family?"

Peter shakes his head. He doesn't quite meet my eyes. "My dad couldn't come last minute."

"What! Why?"

"There was some kind of emergency. Who knows."

I'm stunned. His dad seemed so sincere when I saw him at the lacrosse game. "I hope it was a really big emergency to miss his own son's high school graduation."

"It's fine." Peter shrugs like he doesn't care either way, but I know that can't be true. His jaw is set so tight, he could break his teeth.

Over his shoulder I see my family making their way through the crowds to get to me. You can't miss Trina's hat, even in this swarm of people. My dad's carrying a big bouquet of all different-colored roses. Grandma's wearing a cranberry-colored suit; her hair is freshly permed.

I feel so rushed and panicky for more time with Peter, to comfort him, to just be at his side. I grab his hand. "I'm sorry," I say, and I want to say more, of course I do, but my family arrives, and everyone's hugging me. Peter says hi to my grandma and takes some pictures with us before he escapes to find his mom and brother. I call out to him, but he's too far away, and he doesn't turn around.

After we take pictures, Daddy, Trina, Grandma, Kitty, Margot, and I go to a Japanese restaurant for lunch. We order plates and plates of sashimi and sushi, and I wear a napkin bib so soy sauce doesn't fling onto my white dress. Trina sits next to Grandma and chatters in her ear about all manner of things, and I can just hear Grandma thinking, *Damn, this girl talks a lot*—but she's trying, and that's what Grandma appreciates. I'm trying to be festive and appreciative and in the moment, since this lunch is in my honor, but all I can think of is Peter and how hurt I am on his behalf.

Over mochi ice cream, Grandma tells us about all the places she wants to take us in Korea: the Buddhist temples, the outdoor food markets, the skin clinic where she goes to get her moles lasered off. She points at a tiny mole on Kitty's cheek and says, "We'll get that taken care of."

Daddy looks alarmed, and Trina's quick to ask, "Isn't she too young?"

Grandma waves her hand. "She'll be fine."

Then Kitty asks, "How old do you have to be to get a nose job in Korea?" and Daddy nearly chokes on his beer.

Grandma gives her a threatening look. "You can never, ever change your nose. You have a lucky nose."

Kitty touches it gingerly. "I do?"

"Very lucky," Grandma says. "If you change your nose, you'll change your luck. So never do it."

I touch my own nose. Grandma's never said anything about my nose being lucky.

"Margot, you can get new eyeglasses in Korea," Grandma

says. "It's very cheap to buy eyeglasses in Korea. All the newest fashions."

"Ooh," Margot says, dunking a piece of tuna in her soy sauce. "I've always wanted red frames."

Grandma turns to me and asks, "What about you, Lara Jean? Are you excited about the cooking class?"

"*So* excited," I say brightly. Underneath the table I text Peter.

> Are you okay?
> We're almost done at lunch.
> Come over anytime.

The ride home from the restaurant is just Daddy and me, because Trina, Margot, and Kitty are driving Grandma back home. When Margot said she'd ride with us, Grandma insisted that Margot come along with them. She knows Margot isn't crazy about Trina; I know she's just trying to matchmake them a bit. Grandma doesn't miss a beat.

On the drive home, Daddy looks over at me from the driver's seat with misty eyes and says, "Your mom would've been so proud of you today, Lara Jean. You know how much she cared about your education. She wanted you to have every opportunity."

Fingering the tassel on my graduation cap in my lap, I ask him, "Do you think Mommy was sad she never got to get her master's? I mean, not that she ever regretted having Kitty or anything. Just, do you think she wished things happened differently?"

He's taken aback. Glancing at me, he says, "Well, no. Kitty really was a happy surprise. I'm not just saying that. We always wanted a big family. And she planned on going back after Kitty was in preschool full-time. She never gave up that plan."

"She didn't?"

"No way. She was going to get her master's. In fact she was going to take a class that fall. She just . . . ran out of time." Daddy's voice chokes a little. "We only had eighteen years together. We had as many years as you've been alive, Lara Jean."

A lump gathers in my throat. When you think about it, eighteen years with the person you love isn't much time at all. "Daddy, can we stop by the drugstore? I want to get some photo paper." Peter and I took a picture together in our caps and gowns this morning, before the ceremony. It'll be the last page of his scrapbook, our last high school chapter.

32

PETER COMES OVER AFTER HAVING DINNER
with his mom and Owen. When he rings the bell, I run to
the front door and the first thing I do is ask if he's spoken to
his dad, but he brushes me off, the very picture of noncha-
lance. "It's fine," he says, taking off his shoes. "I didn't even
want him to come in the first place."

This stings, because it feels like maybe he's blaming me,
and maybe he should—after all, I was the one who kept
pushing him to invite his dad. I should've listened to him
when he said no.

Peter and I go upstairs to my room, and I hear my dad
jokingly call out, "Keep the door open!" the way he always
does, which makes Peter wince.

I sit down on the bed, and he sits far away from me at my
desk. I go over to him and put my hand on his shoulder. "I'm
sorry. This is my fault. I never should have pushed you to
invite him. If you're mad at me, I don't blame you one bit."

"Why would I be mad at you? It's not your fault he sucks."
When I don't say anything, he softens. "Look, I'm really not
sad. I'm not anything. You'll meet him another time, okay?"

I hesitate before saying, "I've actually already met him
before."

He stares at me in disbelief. *"When?"*

I swallow. "I accidentally met him at one of your lacrosse games. He asked me not to mention it—he didn't want you to know he was there. He just wanted to watch you play. He said he missed it." The muscle in Peter's jaw jumps. "I should have told you. I'm sorry."

"Don't be. It's like I said, I don't give a shit what he does." I start to say something in return, but he interrupts before I can. "Can we just not talk about him anymore? Please?"

I nod. It's killing me to see the hurt in his eyes that he's trying so hard to hide, but I feel like if I keep pressing him, it'll make things worse. I just want to make him feel better. Which is when I remember his gift. "I have something for you!"

Relief washes over his face, the tension in his shoulders loosens. "Aw, you got me a graduation gift? I didn't get you anything, though."

"That's okay, I didn't expect anything." I jump up and get his scrapbook out of my hatbox. As I present the scrapbook to him, I find my heart is jumping all over the place. With excitement, and with nervousness. This will cheer him up, I know it will. "Hurry up and open it!"

Slowly he does. The first page is a picture I found in a shoe box when Kitty and I were cleaning out the attic to make room for Trina's boxes. It's one of the few from our middle school days in the neighborhood. It's the first day of school; we're waiting for the bus. Peter's arms are slung around John McClaren and Trevor Pike. Genevieve and I have our arms linked; she is whispering a secret to me, probably about Peter.

I am turned toward her and not looking at the camera. I'm wearing a heather-gray camisole of Margot's and a jean skirt, and I remember feeling very grown-up in it, like a teenager. My hair is long and straight down my back, and it looks pretty much the same as it does now. Genevieve tried to convince me to cut it short for middle school, but I said no. We all look so young. John with his rosy cheeks, Trevor with his chubby ones, Peter with his skinny legs.

Underneath the picture I wrote, *THE BEGINNING*. "Aww," he says tenderly. "Baby Lara Jean and Baby Peter. Where'd you find this?"

"In a shoe box."

He flicks John's smiling face. "Punk."

"Peter!"

"Just kidding," he says.

There's our homecoming picture. Last Halloween, when I dressed up as Mulan and Peter wore a dragon costume. There's a receipt from Tart and Tangy. One of his notes to me, from before. *If you make Josh's dumb white-chocolate cranberry cookies and not my fruitcake ones, it's over.* Pictures of us from Senior Week. Prom. Dried rose petals from my corsage. The *Sixteen Candles* picture.

There are some things I didn't include, like the ticket stub from our first real date, the note he wrote me that said, *I like you in blue.* Those things are tucked away in my hatbox. I'll never let those go.

But the really special thing I've included is my letter, the one I wrote to him so long ago, the one that brought us together. I wanted to keep it, but something felt right about Peter having it. One day all of this will be proof, proof that we were here, proof that we loved each other. It's the guarantee that no matter what happens to us in the future, this time was ours.

When he gets to that page, Peter stops. "I thought you wanted to keep this," he said.

"I wanted to, but then I felt like you should have it. Just promise you'll keep it forever."

He turns the page. It's a picture from when we took my grandma to karaoke. I sang "You're So Vain" and dedicated it to Peter. Peter got up and sang "Style" by Taylor Swift. Then he dueted "Unchained Melody" with my grandma, and after, she made us both promise to take a Korean language class at UVA. She and Peter took a ton of selfies together that night. She made one her home screen on her phone. Her friends at her apartment complex said he looked like a movie star. I made the mistake of telling Peter, and he crowed about it for days after.

He stays on that page for a while. When he doesn't say anything, I say, helpfully, "It's something to remember us by."

He snaps the book shut. "Thanks," he says, flashing me a quick smile. "This is awesome."

"You're not going to look at the rest of it?"

"I will, later."

Peter says he should get back home so he can pack for Beach Week, and before we go back downstairs, I ask him again if he's okay, and he assures me that he is.

After Peter leaves, Margot comes up to my room and helps me pack. I'm sitting cross-legged on the floor, arranging my suitcase, and she's passing me piles. I'm still feeling worried about Peter, so I'm glad to have her company to take my mind off things.

"I can't believe you're already graduated," Margot says, folding a stack of T-shirts for me. "In my head you're still the same age you were when I left." Teasingly she says, "Forever sweet sixteen, Lara Jean."

"Almost as grown-up as you now, Gogo," I say.

"Well, you'll always be shorter than me, at least," she says, and I throw a bikini top at her head. "Pretty soon we'll be packing you up for college."

I stuff a curling iron into the pocket of my suitcase. "Margot, when you first went to college, what did you miss most about home?"

"Well, you guys, obviously."

"But what else? Like, what were the unexpected things you missed?"

"I missed giving Kitty a kiss good night after she'd had a bath and her hair was clean."

I make a snorty sound. "A rare occasion!"

Margot takes her time, thinking about what else. "I missed a good hamburger. Hamburgers taste different in Scotland. More like . . . meat loaf. Meat loaf on a bun. Hmm, what else? I missed driving you guys around. I felt like the captain of a ship. I missed your baked goods!"

"Which ones?" I ask.

"Hmm?"

"Which ones did you miss the most?"

"Your lemon cake."

"If you'd told me, I would've sent you one."

Smiling, she says, "I'm pretty sure sending a cake overseas is exorbitantly expensive."

"Let's make one now," I say, and Margot kicks her legs up happily.

So we go downstairs and that's what we do. Kitty is asleep; Daddy and Trina are in their bedroom with the door closed. As much as I love Trina, that's a strange thing to get used to as well. Daddy's door was never closed. But I suppose he needs his time too, time where he's not a dad. Not even for sex, but just to talk, to take a breath. But also for sex, I guess.

Margot's measuring flour when I ask, "Did you have on music when you and Josh first did it?"

"You made me lose count!" Margot dumps all the flour back in the canister and starts over again.

"Well, did you?"

"No. Nosy! I swear, you're worse than Kitty."

I roll a lemon around on the counter to warm it up before I start squeezing. "So it was just . . . silent?"

"It wasn't *silent*. There was the sound of someone mowing their lawn. And his mom had the dryer going. Their dryer is really loud. . . ."

"But his mom wasn't home, right?"

"No way! I couldn't do that. My roommate brought someone home once and I pretended to be asleep, but honestly, I was trying not to laugh. The guy was a heavy breather. He was a moaner, too."

We both giggle.

"I hope my roommate doesn't do that."

"Just set up ground rules in the beginning. Like who can use the room when, that kind of thing. And just remember that you should try to be understanding, because Peter will be visiting a lot, and you don't want to use up her goodwill." She pauses. "You guys haven't had sex yet, right?" Quickly she adds, "You don't have to say if you don't want to."

"No," I say. "I mean, not yet."

"Are you thinking about it?" Margot asks, trying to sound casual. "Because of Beach Week?"

I don't answer her right away.

I hadn't been thinking about it, not Beach Week specifically, anyway. The thought of Peter and me having sex in the future, for it to be as commonplace as us going to the movies or holding hands—it's a little strange to imagine. I just wouldn't want it to be less special, after we do it. I want it to always be a sacred thing, not something to take for granted because everybody else does it, or because we've done it before. I suppose anything can become ordinary or commonplace if you do it enough times, but my hope is that this never is. Not for us. "I think I definitely want music," I say, straining lemon juice into a glass measuring cup. "That way if I'm a heavy breather or he's a heavy breather, we won't really know. And it'll be more romantic. Music makes everything more romantic, doesn't it? One second you're walking your dog in the suburbs, and then you put on Adele, and it's like you're in a movie and you've just had your heart brutally broken."

Margot says, "In movies they never put on a condom, so make sure you're in real life for that part."

That's enough to shake me out of my reverie. "Daddy gave me a whole kit. He left it in the upstairs bathroom for me. Condoms, cream, dental dams." I burst out laughing. "Isn't 'dental dam' the unsexiest word you ever heard?"

"No, I think 'gonorrhea' is!"

Abruptly I stop laughing. "Peter doesn't have gonorrhea!" Now Margot's the one cracking up. "He doesn't!"

"I know, I'm just teasing. But I think you should pack your kit just in case things go in that direction."

"Gogo, I'm not planning on having sex at Beach Week."

"I said just in case! You never know." She pushes her hair out of her face and in a serious tone, she says, "I'm really glad my first time was with Josh, though. It should be with someone who really knows you. Someone who loves you."

Before I go to bed, I open up that kit and take out the condoms and pack them deep in the bottom of my suitcase. Then I pick out my prettiest bra and underwear set, pale pink edged in electric blue lace, never been worn, and I pack that too. Just in case.

33

PETER'S AT MY HOUSE BRIGHT AND EARLY
to pick me up. Everyone else is caravanning down together,
but Peter wanted it to be just him and me in his two-seater.
He's in a good mood; he's brought donuts for us like old
times. He says they're all for me, though. Ever since he
came back from that training weekend with his lacrosse
team, he's been in fitness mode.

We're moving stuff around in his car to make room for
my suitcase when Kitty comes running out to say hi. She
spots the bag of donuts resting on top of my bag and she
snags one. Her mouth full, she says, "Peter, did Lara Jean tell
you the news about Korea?"

"What news?" he says.

My head snaps up and I throw Kitty a look. "I was just
about to. Peter, I didn't get a chance to tell you yesterday. . . .
My dad's sending us to Korea for my graduation present."

"Wow, that's cool," Peter says.

"Yeah, we're going to see our relatives and do a tour
around the country, too."

"When?"

I glance over at him. "Next month."

"For how long?" he asks.

"A month."

He looks at me in dismay. "A *month*? That long?"

"I know." We're already in mid-June. Only two months of summer left from here and then he'll still be here and I'll be in Chapel Hill.

"A month," he repeats. Before Peter, I wouldn't have thought twice about going to Korea for a month. I would have rejoiced. And now . . . I'd never say so to Daddy or Margot or Kitty, but I don't want to go. I just don't. I do. But I don't.

When we're in the car, on our way, I say, "We'll Face-Time every day. It's a thirteen-hour time difference, so if I call you at night, it'll be your morning."

Peter looks gloomy. "We were gonna go to Bledell's for his Fourth of July weekend, remember? His dad got a new boat. I was going to teach you how to wakeboard."

"I know."

"What am I going to do when you're all the way over there? The summer's going to suck. I wanted to take you to Pony Pasture." Pony Pasture is a little park on the James River in Richmond; there are big stones you can lie out on, and you can float down the river on inner tubes. Peter's gone before, with friends from school, but I never have.

"We can go when I come back," I say, and he nods half-heartedly. "And I'll bring back lots of presents. Face masks. Korean candy. A present a day!"

"Bring me back some tiger socks."

"If they make them big enough," I say, just to make a joke, just to make him smile. This week will have to be the most perfect, the best ever, to make up for the fact that I'll be gone all summer.

Peter's phone buzzes, and he ignores the call without looking to see who it is. A minute later it buzzes again, and Peter's face goes tight.

"Who is it?" I ask.

"My dad," he says shortly.

"I hope he's calling to apologize and explain how he could miss his own son's graduation."

"I already know why. He told my mom Everett had an allergic reaction so they took him to urgent care."

"Oh," I say. "I guess that's a pretty good excuse. Is Everett okay?"

"He's fine. I don't think he's really even that allergic. When I eat strawberries, my tongue itches. Big deal." With that, Peter turns on the music, and we don't talk for a while.

The girls' house is second row, with a view of the beach. It's on stilts, like all the other houses in the second row. There are three levels, with the kitchen and living room on the bottom level, and the bedrooms on the top levels. Chris and I share a room with two beds on the top level. It's like we are at the top of a lighthouse. The bedspreads are turquoise with seashells on them. Everything smells a little mildewy, but it's not a bad house.

All of the girls in the house have taken up different roles, except for Chris, whose main role has been to sleep on the beach all day with a water bottle of beer. The first day she came back with her chest and face lobster red; the only unburned part of her was where her sunglasses were. She was embarrassed but she played it off, saying it's her base tan for Costa Rica. Pammy is the den mom. She promised her parents she wouldn't drink, so she's taken it upon herself to check on the other girls and bring water and Advil to their beds in the morning. Kaila's really good with a flatiron. She can even curl with it, something I've never managed to quite get the hang of. Harley's good at coordinating and making plans with the other houses.

I'm the cook. When we first got to the house, we went out and did a big shopping trip and bought cold cuts, granola, dried pasta and jars of sauce, salsa, cereal. The one thing we didn't buy was toilet paper, which we ran out of on the second day. Every time we leave the house to eat lunch or dinner out, one of us steals a wad of toilet paper from the restaurant bathroom. Why we don't just go buy more, I don't know, but it's turned into kind of a game. Chris is the clear winner, because she managed to get an economy-size roll out of the dispenser, and she smuggled it out under her shirt.

The boys come over every day to freeload and also because their house is already filled with sand. We've nicknamed it the Sandcastle. Just sitting on their couch, it's like getting a body scrub, and you stand up feeling exfoliated and not in a good way.

I wonder if this is what it would feel like to live in a sorority house. At first it's kind of charming, like those boarding houses in the 1940s, borrowing nail polish and playing music while we get ready, eating ice cream in bed. But then on Wednesday, Kaila and Harley get into a screaming fight at one in the morning over who left the flatiron on and our neighbors call the police. That same night Pammy gets drunk, and I sit next to her on the beach for hours while she cries, because she feels guilty about breaking her word to her parents. The next night, some of the girls go out to a club and bring back three guys from Montana. One has shifty eyes and I make sure to lock my bedroom door that night. In my and Chris's room, I text Peter, who's already gone back to his house. He comes right back and camps out downstairs "to keep my eye on them."

Peter and I spend our days at the beach, where I sit and read and he goes for long runs. Since we've been here, he goes running all the time, because he can't work out like he does at home, in the gym. He goes for a long run in the morning before it gets hot, a short one midday, and another long one at dusk. Except for the day I make him go with me to the Wright Brothers museum in Kill Devil Hills. I went there as a kid with my family, before Kitty was born, but I was too little to climb up to the monument. We go all the way to the top and take in the view.

All week, Peter has been as winsome and winning as ever, especially in front of other people—always with an easygoing smile on his face, always the first to suggest an activity, a game. But with me he's been distant. Like even though he's right here next to me, he feels far away.

Unreachable. I've tried to broach the topic of his dad again, but he just laughs it off. He hasn't brought up my trip to Korea again either.

Every night there's a party at one of the houses—except ours. We never host, because Pammy is worried about losing our security deposit. The nice thing about it is, all the different groups are hanging out in a way that people didn't in high school. There is something freeing about knowing it's all over. We won't all be together like this again, so why not? In that spirit, Chris hooks up with Patrick Shaw, a guy from Josh's anime club.

Tonight the party is at Peter's house. I have no idea how they're getting their security deposit back, because the place is in sandy shambles: One of the wicker chairs on the deck is broken, there are beer cans everywhere, and someone sat down on the beige living room couch in a wet orange towel and now there's a big orange spot in the middle. I'm making my way through the kitchen when I see John Ambrose McClaren, going through the refrigerator.

I freeze. Peter's been in such an unpredictable mood; I don't know what he'll do when he sees John at his house.

I'm trying to decide if I should go find Peter and tell him John's here, when John's head pops up behind the refrigerator door. He's holding a carrot and munching on it. "Hey! I thought I might see you here."

"Hi!" I say, cheerfully, as if I weren't just contemplating backing away before he saw me. I come over and he gives me a one-armed hug, because he's still holding the carrot. "Have you seen Peter?" I ask him. "This is the house he's staying in."

"Nah, we just got here." John looks tan, his hair is bleached from the sun, and he's wearing a worn blue-and-white-checked shirt and khaki shorts. "Where are you staying?"

"Really close to here. What about you?"

"We got a house in Duck." He smiles and then offers me his carrot. "Want a bite?"

I laugh. "No thanks. So where did you decide on for school?"

"William and Mary." John holds his hand up for a high five. "So I'll see you there, right?"

"Actually . . . I'm going to Chapel Hill. I got in off the wait list."

John's jaw drops. "Are you serious? That's awesome!" He pulls me in for a hug. "That's amazing. It's actually the perfect place for you. You're going to love it there."

I'm looking toward the kitchen door, thinking of how I can gracefully exit this conversation, when Peter strolls into the kitchen with a beer in his hand. He stops short when he sees us. I'm cringing inside, but he just grins and shouts, "McClaren! What up!" They do a guy hug, where they pull each other in and then just kind of bump into each other. When they back away, Peter's eyes linger on the carrot in John's hand. Every day, Peter's made himself a carrot-and-berry protein shake, and I just know he's smarting over John taking one. He's counted out exactly how many carrots he needs for the rest of the week.

"Lara Jean was just telling me she got into Carolina," John says, resting his back against the countertop. "I'm so jealous."

"Yeah, you always wanted to go there, right?" Peter's eyes are still on the carrot.

"Ever since I was a kid. It was my top choice." John gives me a playful nudge. "This girl snuck in there like a thief in the night. Took my spot right out from under me."

Smiling, I say, "Sorry about that."

"Nah, I'm just kidding with you." John takes a bite of his carrot. "I really might transfer, though. We'll see."

Peter puts his arm around my waist and takes a swig of beer. "You should. We could all go to a Tar Heels game together." He says it genially enough, but I can hear the tension underneath.

John doesn't miss it either. "For sure," he says. Then he polishes off the rest of his carrot and tosses the stem into the sink. "I want you guys to meet my girlfriend, Dipti. She's around here somewhere." He pulls his phone out of his pocket and sends her a text.

We're still standing around when she finds us. She is taller than me, sporty-looking, shoulder-length black hair, dark skin, maybe Indian. She has a nice white smile and one dimple. She's wearing a silky white romper and sandals. I'm regretting my decision to wear a UVA T-shirt of Peter's and cutoffs. We introduce ourselves, and then she hops up on the countertop and asks, "So how do you guys know each other?"

"McClaren was my BFF back in middle school," Peter says. "They used to call us Butch Cassidy and the Sundance Kid. Who do you think was Butch and who do you think was the Sundance Kid, Dipti?"

She laughs. "I don't know. I never saw that movie."

"Butch was the main guy." Peter points to himself. "And the Sundance Kid over there"—he points to John—"he was the sidekick." Peter cracks up, and I'm cringing inside, but John just shakes his head in his good-natured way. Peter grabs John's bicep. "Yo, have you been working out?" To Dipti he says, "This kid used to have spaghetti arms and read all day, but now look at him. He's a stud."

"Hey, I still read," John says.

"When Peter and I first got together, I thought maybe he didn't know how to read," I say, and John doubles over laughing.

Peter laughs too, but not as heartily as he was a second ago.

When it gets late, Peter says I should just stay over instead of going back to my house. I say no, because I don't have my toothbrush or any of my things, but really, I'm just annoyed with him for the way he acted in front of John.

On the walk back to my house, Peter says, "Dipti seems cool. Good for McClaren. Doubt they'll stay together, though. They'll probably visit each other once and be broken up by Christmas, if that."

I stop walking. "That's a lousy thing to say."

"What? I'm just being honest."

I face him, and salty beach wind whips my hair around my face. "Okay, if you're 'just being honest,' then maybe I will be too." Peter raises an eyebrow and waits for me to continue. "You acted like a jerk tonight. Insecurity is not a good look on you, Peter."

"Me?" Peter makes a derisive sound. "Insecure? About what? McClaren? Please. Did you see how he just went into my fridge and ate my carrots?"

I start walking again, faster. "Who cares about your carrots!"

He jogs to catch up with me. "You know I'm trying to get in shape for lacrosse!"

"You're ridiculous, do you know that?" We are now standing in front of my house. Angry walking sure gets you places in a hurry. "Good night, Peter." I turn on my heel and start walking up the steps, and Peter doesn't try to stop me.

34

THE NEXT MORNING, I WAKE UP UNSURE if Peter and I are in a fight. Last night felt like a fight, only I'm not sure if he's mad at me or if I'm supposed to be mad at him. It's an unsettling feeling.

I don't want to be mad at him. I leave for Korea on July 1. We don't have time to get into dumb fights over carrots and John Ambrose McClaren. Every second we have left together is precious.

I decide to make him French toast as a peace offering. His favorite breakfast food, besides donuts, is French toast. In the kitchen I find a box of sugar in the cabinet, milk, half a loaf of bread, a couple of eggs, but no cinnamon. The cinnamon is essential.

I take Pammy's car keys and drive to the little market near our house, where I buy a shaker of cinnamon, butter, a dozen eggs, and a new loaf of white bread, because I figure I might as well make toast for Peter's whole house while I'm at it. At the last second, I throw in a bag of carrots.

Everyone at his house is still asleep, and the place looks even worse than it did the night before. Beer bottles all over the place, empty bags of chips strewn about, bathing suit trunks drying on furniture. Dirty dishes are piled high in the sink, and I have to wash a bowl and a spatula caked in old egg in order to start cooking.

Because the bread is fresh, my first few pieces end up disintegrating in the egg mix, but I get the hang of it on the third try, dipping the bread for only a few seconds before I drop it in the frying pan.

The boys drift downstairs, and I keep frying more French toast. Every time the stack dwindles, I add more. Peter's the last one down, and when I offer him a piece, one of the good crispy ones, he shakes his head and says he'd better not, because of his diet. He doesn't meet my eyes as he says it. He just doesn't want to eat something I made.

After breakfast I don't stick around, and again Peter doesn't try to stop me. I drive back home and wake up Chris, who is still in last night's clothes. "I have a piece of French toast for you downstairs," I say. I brought her the piece I saved for Peter.

There's a cookout that night, at a house a few streets down from ours. Our house brings tubs of neon-yellow potato salad and all the wine coolers we have left. Since it's the last night, we are emptying out the fridge.

Out on the deck, I end up in a conversation with Kaila and Emily Nussbaum, one of Genevieve's friends. I've barely seen Genevieve at all this week, because she's here with her church friends, and her house is a mix of people from other schools.

Emily asks me, "So are you and Kavinsky really going to stay together?"

Right this second? I have no idea, seeing as how we've barely said two words to each other all night. Of course I don't say that. Whatever I say to Emily will get right back to Genevieve. Gen might have moved on, but she would surely still take pleasure in Peter and me being in a fight. I say, "Yes, we're staying together. UNC and UVA aren't that far."

Kaila sucks up rum and Diet Coke out of her straw, giving me a sidelong look. "You know, you're an interesting girl, Lara Jean. You seem shy and kind of babyish at first, but you're actually very confident. That was a compliment, by the way."

"Thanks," I say. If someone is giving you a compliment, I don't think they should have to tell you they're giving you one; it should probably be obvious to the person receiving it. I take a sip of the drink Chris made me, and I nearly spit it out because she made it so strong. She called it a grown-up Shirley Temple, whatever that means.

"I can see why Kavinsky likes you," Kaila says. "I hope it works out."

"Thank you," I say.

Emily puts her feet up on my chair and says, "If Blake broke up with me, I would freak out. I would be absolutely devastated."

"Well, you guys are super intense. You'll probably get married right after college."

"No way," Emily says, but she's obviously pleased.

"Y'all are going to the same school. It's different." Kaila regards me. "I don't think I could ever do long distance."

"Why not?" I ask.

"I like seeing my man every day. I don't want to wonder what he's up to. Like, am I a possessive person? Yes. But also, I don't want to have to play catch-up at the end of the day. I need to be a part of his daily life and he needs to be a part of mine." She crunches ice with her teeth.

That's what happened with Margot and me when she went to college. The distance came slowly, like seawater filling up a boat, without us even realizing it. Before you know it you're underwater. We made it through, but we're sisters. Sisters always find their way back to each other. I don't think it's the same for boyfriends. The thought of it happening to Peter and me fills me with such sadness. How will we ward it off? By talking every day? Visiting at least once a month? He said it himself—his life is going to be so busy and so full because of lacrosse. He's already changing, with his healthy diet and his workouts. And we're fighting, and we never fight, not really. Not the kind of fights you can't take back. So what now? How do we negotiate this next step?

I stay a few more minutes, and when Emily and Kaila start talking about whether or not to rush a sorority, I make my escape to find Peter. Between this conversation and last night's fight, I just want him close, while we're still in the same vicinity. I find him standing around with a bunch of guys who are building a bonfire. He already seems so far away, and I want so badly for things to feel normal between us again. I take big sip of my grown-up Shirley Temple, for courage. Our eyes meet, and I mouth, *Do you want to go?* He nods. I start to head back inside, and he follows me.

As I take another sip of my grown-up Shirley Temple, he asks, "What are you drinking?"

"Something Chris made me."

He takes the red Solo cup from me and tosses it in the trash on our way out.

Our walk back to my house is pretty quiet, except for the sound of the ocean waves. I don't think either of us knows what to say, because whatever is wrong between us, we both know it wasn't John Ambrose McClaren, or the carrots.

As we make our way down the street, I hear Peter's subdued voice. "Are you still mad about last night?"

"No."

"Okay, good," he says. "I saw the carrots you bought in the fridge. Sorry I didn't eat your French toast."

"Why didn't you? I know it wasn't because of your diet."

Peter rubs the back of his neck. "I don't know what my problem was. I've just been in a weird mood."

I look over at him; his face is obscured by the dark. "We only have a little bit of time before I leave for Korea. Let's not waste it." Then I slide my hand in his, and he squeezes it.

The house is completely empty, for the first time all week. All the other girls are still at the party, except for Chris, who ran into somebody she knows through Applebee's. We go up to my room, and Peter takes off his shoes and gets in my bed. "Want to watch a movie?" he asks, stretching his arms behind his head.

No, I don't want to watch a movie. Suddenly my heart is racing, because I know what I want to do. I'm ready.

I sit down on the bed next to him as he says, "Or we could start a new show—"

I press my lips to his neck, and I can feel his pulse jump. "What if we don't watch a movie or a show? What if we . . . do something else instead." I give him a meaningful look.

His body jerks in surprise. "What, you mean like now?"

"Yes." Now. Now feels right. I start planting little kisses down his throat. "Do you like that?"

I can feel him swallow. "Yes." He pushes me away from him so he can look at my face. "Let's stop for a second. I can't think. Are you drunk? What did Chris put in that drink she gave you?"

"No, I'm not drunk!" I had a little bit of a warm feeling in my body, but the walk home woke me right up. Peter's still staring at me. "I'm not drunk. I swear."

Peter swallows hard, his eyes searching mine. "Are you sure you want to do this now?"

"Yes," I say, because I really, truly am. "But first can you put on Frank Ocean?"

He grabs his phone, and a second later the beat kicks in and Frank's melodious voice fills the room. Peter starts fumbling with his shirt buttons and then gives up and starts to pull my shirt up, and I yelp, "Wait!"

Peter's so startled, he jumps away from me. "What? What's wrong?"

I leap off the bed and start rummaging through my suitcase.

I'm not wearing my special bra and underwear set; I'm wearing my normal every day cappuccino-colored bra with the frayed edges. I can't lose my virginity in my ugliest bra.

"What are you doing?" he asks me.

"Just wait one second."

I run to the bathroom and change out of my old bra and underwear and put on the lacy ones. Then I brush my teeth, look at my face in the mirror. This is it. I, Lara Jean Song Covey, am about to lose my virginity to Peter K.

Peter calls out, "Is everything okay?"

"Just a sec!" Should I put my clothes back on or just come out in my bra and underwear? He's never seen me in just my underwear before. Well, I guess he's about to see me without any clothes at all, so I might as well.

I step out of the bathroom, carrying my clothes in front of me like a shield, and Peter does a double take when he sees me and quickly takes his shirt off. I can feel myself blush. I stuff my bra and underwear in my suitcase, and then dig around inside until I find the packet of condoms. I take one out and then climb back into bed and get under the sheets. "Okay, now I'm ready."

"I like your bra," Peter says, peeling the sheet away from me.

"Thank you."

He moves closer to me and kisses my eyelid. First the left, then the right. "Are you nervous?"

"A little."

"We don't have to do anything tonight, Covey."

"No, I want to." I hold up the condom, and Peter's eyebrows shoot up. "From my dad's kit. Remember, I told you he made me a contraception kit?"

Taking the condom from me, he kisses my neck and says, "Can we not talk about your dad right now?"

"Sure," I say.

Peter rolls on top of me. My heart is thrumming in my chest, the way it does whenever I am close to him, but now even more so, because everything's about to change. I'm going somewhere with him I've never gone before. He's careful to keep his weight on his forearms, to not crush me, but I don't mind the weight of his body on mine. His hand is in my hair the way I like; his lips are warm. We're both breathing fast.

And then he's suddenly not kissing me anymore. I open my eyes and he's hovering above me, his brow furrowed. "Is this because we had a fight last night? Because, Covey—"

"It's not because of the fight. I just—I just want to feel close to you." Peter's looking at me so intently, and I can tell he's waiting for more, for me to give him some grand reason. It's pretty simple, really. "It's not all of a sudden. I want to have sex with you because I love you and I want it to be you."

"But why me?"

"Because—because you're my first love, so who else would it be?"

Peter rolls off me and sits up; his head is in his hands.

I sit up too, pulling the sheet up around me. "What's wrong?" He doesn't say anything for what feels like forever.

"Please just say it." I'm starting to feel sick to my stomach.

"I don't want to do this right now."

"Why not?" I whisper.

He can't look at me. "I don't know. . . . I just have a lot on my mind. Between lacrosse, and my dad not showing up at graduation, and now you're leaving for the summer."

"Not the whole summer. Just July. I'll be back at the end of July! Why are you fast-forwarding the whole summer away?"

Peter shakes his head. "It just seems like you're leaving and you don't really care."

"You know it wasn't my choice! My dad surprised me! You're not being fair, Peter."

He looks at me for a long beat. "What about UNC? Are you even planning on transferring to UVA anymore? When it was William and Mary, it was a given, and now it doesn't seem like it."

I wet my lips. My heart is pounding out of control. "I'm not sure. Maybe? But maybe not. UNC feels different to me."

"Yeah, I know. It's obvious."

"Don't make it sound like a bad thing! Would you rather I go somewhere and be unhappy?"

"Temporarily unhappy," he corrects.

"Peter!"

"Come on, Lara Jean. Do you really think that shitty of me?"

"No. I . . . I just don't understand why you're acting this

way. I want to at least give UNC a real chance. I want to give myself a chance." My eyes well up with tears, and it's hard to speak. "And I think you should want that for me too."

Peter flinches like I've hit him. This bed is small, but it feels like he's so far away from me right now. I ache inside, wanting to go to him. But I can't.

Silently he puts his shirt back on. "I think I'm gonna go," he says. Then he gets up, walks out the door, and leaves. I wait for the front door to shut before I start to cry.

35

AS WE PACK UP THE CAR THAT MORNING, I keep thinking Peter might show up to take me home, but he doesn't, and I don't reach out to him, either. I ride back up to Virginia with the girls.

I don't hear anything from Peter until the next day. I get a text that says:

> ```
> I'm sorry for last night. I was a dick.
> We're gonna make this work, I promise.
> I have to do some stuff for my mom but
> can I see you later?
> ```

I text back:

> ```
> Yes.
> ```

He texts back:

> ```
> I really am sorry.
> I love you.
> ```

I'm starting to text back, I love you, too, when my phone rings. It's Peter's house number, and I answer it eagerly.

"I love you, too," I say.

There is surprised silence on the other end, then a little laugh to cover it up. "Hi, Lara Jean. This is Peter's mom."

I am mortified. "Oh! Hi, Mrs. Kavinsky."

She wants me to come over and chat with her. She says Peter isn't home, that it'll be just the two of us. She must have sent him out to run errands for her so she could ask me over. What can I do but go?

I put on a yellow sundress and lipstick, brush my hair, and drive to Peter's house. She answers the door with a ready smile on her face; she's wearing a gingham blouse and Bermuda shorts. "Come on in," she says.

I follow her into the kitchen, and she says, "Lara Jean, would you like something to drink? Sun tea?"

"Sure," I say, climbing onto a stool.

Peter's mom pours me a glass of sun tea out of a plastic frosted pitcher. She hands me the glass and says, "Thank you for coming over here to visit with me, just us girls. There's something I've been wanting to talk to you about."

"Sure," I say again. My skin is prickling.

She takes my hands in hers. Her hands are cool and dry; mine suddenly feel clammy. "Peter's been through a lot, and he's worked so hard. I'm sure you know how disappointing it was for him when his dad didn't come to graduation." Her eyes search mine, and I nod. "He pretends he doesn't care, but he's hurting inside. He came back from Beach Week talking about transferring to UNC for his sophomore year. Did you know that?"

I can feel all the blood rush to my face. "No, I didn't know that. He . . . he hasn't said a word to me about it."

She nods, as if she suspected as much. "If he were to transfer, he wouldn't be able to play for a year. That means he wouldn't keep his athletic scholarship. Out-of-state tuition is very expensive, as I'm sure you know."

It is. Daddy said it would be all right, that Margot only has two more years of college, and Kitty has ages before it's her turn. But I know it's expensive. And I know, even though we don't talk about it, that my dad makes more money than Peter's mom does.

"Peter's dad says he wants to contribute, but his dad isn't someone to be depended on. So I can't count on him." She pauses delicately. "But I'm hoping I can count on you."

I rush to say, "You don't need to worry about me. I'll tell Peter not to transfer to North Carolina."

"Honey, I appreciate that so much, I really do, but it's not just transferring that I'm worrying about. I'm worried about his mind-set. When he gets to UVA, he needs to be focused. He's going there to be a student athlete. He can't be driving down to North Carolina every weekend. It just isn't practical. You're both so young. Peter's already making big life decisions based on you, and who even knows what's going to happen with you two in the future. You're teenagers. Life doesn't always work out the way you think it's going to work out. . . . I don't know if Peter ever told you this, but Peter's dad and I got married very young. And I'd—I'd just hate to see you two make the same mistakes we did." She hesitates. "Lara Jean, I know my son, and he's not going to let you go unless you let him go first."

I blink.

"He'd do anything for you. That's his nature. He's loyal to his very core. Unlike his father." Mrs. Kavinsky looks at me with sympathetic eyes. "I know you care about Peter and you want what's best for him. I hope you'll give what I said some thought." She hesitates, then says, "Please don't mention anything to him. Peter would be very upset with me."

I struggle to find my voice. "I won't."

Her smile is bright, relieved. "You're a sweet girl, Lara Jean. I know you'll do the right thing." She pats my hands and releases them. Then she changes the subject, asking me about my dad's wedding.

When I get back to my car, I flip down the mirror and see that my cheeks are still stained pink. It feels like the time in seventh grade when Chris's mom found her cigarettes and she thought we'd both been smoking them. I wanted to say it wasn't me, but I couldn't. I just shriveled up with shame. That's how I feel right now. Like I've gotten in trouble.

Was it foolish of Peter and me to think that we could be the exception to the rule? Is Peter's mom right? Are we making a huge mistake? Suddenly it feels like every decision we make is so momentous, and I'm so scared to make the wrong one.

Back at home, Daddy, Margot, and Kitty are in the living room debating over where to go for dinner. It's such a normal thing to be discussing on a Thursday evening, but I feel so strange, because it's as if the earth is shifting beneath my feet, and the ground isn't steady anymore, but everyone around me is talking about food.

"What do you feel like, Lara Jean?" Daddy asks me.

"I'm not very hungry," I say, looking down at my phone. What will I say to Peter when he calls? Do I tell him? "I might just stay home."

Daddy peers at me. "Are you all right? Coming down with something? You look pale."

I shake my head. "No, I'm fine."

"How about Seoul House?" Margot suggests. "I've really been craving Korean food."

Daddy hesitates, and I know why. Trina doesn't exactly have the most sophisticated palate. She lives off of Diet Coke and chicken fingers; kale salads are about as adventurous as she gets. When we order sushi, she'll only eat California rolls and cooked shrimp. She doesn't eat any fish at all. But nobody's perfect.

"Trina's not big on Korean food," I say, to spare Daddy having to say it. My phone buzzes, but it's just an email from UNC's housing department.

Incredulous, Margot says, "Are you serious?"

"It's a little spicy for her." Hastily he adds, "But it's fine. She can get the bulgogi sliders or the fried rice."

"I don't want Korean food either," Kitty says.

"We'll go to Seoul House," Daddy says. "Trina will be fine."

As soon as Daddy goes to make a reservation, I say to Margot, "Don't judge Trina for not liking Korean food.

She can't help it if she can't eat spicy stuff."

Kitty is quick to jump in with, "Yeah, don't judge her."

A hurt look flashes across Margot's face, and she protests, "I didn't say anything!"

"We know what you were thinking," I say. I know what she's thinking because I've had the same thought. And I'm now in the curious position of having to defend Trina for something I also think is annoying. It wouldn't kill Trina to broaden her culinary horizons.

"Fried rice, though? Really?"

"What's the big deal if she doesn't like Korean food?" Kitty says.

"Korean food is our biggest link to Korean culture," Margot tells her. "Are we just never going to eat Korean food anymore because Trina doesn't like it?" Margot doesn't wait for us to answer. "I just hope she realizes that when she marries Daddy, she gets the whole package, and Korea's a part of that package."

"Margot, she knows that," I say. "And besides, we'll get to eat Korean food every day this summer." Every day this summer when I'm away from Peter.

"I wish Daddy and Trina were coming too," Kitty says.

"It's better this way," Margot says. "What would Trina even eat in Korea?" She's halfway joking but not really.

Kitty, who is petting Jamie, ignores her and asks me, "Who's going to take care of Jamie Fox-Pickle and Simone when we're all gone?"

"A dog sitter?" I suggest. My heart's not really in it. I'm

only halfway here. All I can think of is Peter. "We'll figure something out."

Margot looks around the room. Her eyes land on Trina's big armchair. "This house feels so small all of sudden. There isn't enough room for all of Trina's stuff."

Kitty says, "It doesn't feel that small when you're not here."

I gasp. "Kitty!"

All the color drains from Margot's face, and then her cheeks go splotchy. "Did you really just say that to me?"

I can tell Kitty regrets it, but she lifts her chin in her stubborn Kitty way. "Well, I'm just saying."

"You're a brat." Margot gets the words out strong, but I see her face as she turns to go upstairs, and I know she's going to her room to cry in private.

As soon as she's gone, I turn to Kitty. "Why did you say that to her?"

Tears leak from her eyes. "Because! She's been so mean to Tree for no reason."

I wipe her tears with the back of my hand. I feel like crying too. "Gogo feels left out, that's all. We know Trina, because we've had time to know her. But Margot doesn't know her at all. And Kitty—Gogo practically raised you. You don't talk to her like that."

Halfheartedly, she mutters, "I talk to you like that."

"That's different and you know it. We're closer in age."

"So you're saying you and I are on the same level?"

"I mean—no. Margot and I are almost on the same level, and you're on the level below us, because you're the youngest. But you and I are more on the same level than you and Margot. Just try and understand her. She doesn't want to feel like her place has been taken."

Kitty's shoulders hunch. "It hasn't been taken."

"She just needs a little reassurance, that's all. Be understanding." Kitty doesn't reply or lift her head, but I know she's hearing me. "You *are* a little brat, though." Her head snaps up and she lunges at me, and I laugh. "Go upstairs and say sorry to Gogo. You know it's the right thing to do."

Kitty actually listens to me for once. She goes upstairs, and then, sometime later, they both come down with red eyes. In the meantime I get a text from Peter, asking if I can come out. I tell him I can't, that I'm going out to dinner with my family, but I'll see him tomorrow night. The guys are meeting us at the karaoke bar after they have their steak dinner. I hope that by the time I see him, I'll know what to do.

In my room that night, I am painting my nails mint green for the bachelorette party tomorrow night, and Margot is lying on my bed looking at her phone. "Do you want me to do your nails too?" I ask.

"No, I don't care," she says.

I sigh. "Listen, you have to stop being in a bad mood about Trina. She and Daddy are getting married, Gogo."

Margot sighs. "It's not just Trina. Trina's . . . Trina."

"Then what?"

Margot chews on her top lip, something I haven't seen her do since she was little. "It's like I came back and there was a whole new family here that I wasn't a part of."

I want to tell her that nothing has changed, that she's still just as much a part of it as she always was, but that wouldn't be true. Life here kept going on without her, just like it'll keep going on without me when I leave this fall.

A tear rolls down her cheek. "And I miss Mommy."

My throat tightens up. "Me too."

"I wish Kitty could have known her." Margot sighs. "I know it's selfish . . . but I guess I just never pictured Daddy getting married again. I thought he'd date, maybe have a long-term girlfriend at some point, but married?"

Gently I say, "I never really thought about it either, but then when you left for Scotland, I don't know . . . it just started making more sense. The thought of him having someone."

"I know. And it's good for Kitty, too."

"I think she thinks of Trina as hers. I have my own relationship with Trina, but Kitty's had a special thing with her from the start."

"God, she's like a pit bull with Trina!" Margot laughs a shaky kind of laugh. "She really loves her."

"I know that's why you got so upset about Korean food today. You think that if Daddy stops cooking Korean food because Trina doesn't like it, Kitty won't have that connection anymore. And if we forget Korea, we forget Mommy." Tears are rolling down her cheeks, and she is wiping them away with the back of her sweatshirt sleeve. "But we'll never forget Korea, and we'll never forget Mommy. Okay?"

Margot nods and takes a deep breath. "God, I've cried

twice today! It's so un-me." She smiles at me, and I smile back, as brightly as I can. Her brow furrows. "Lara Jean, is something up with you? You've seemed sort of . . . I don't know, melancholy, ever since you got back from Beach Week. Did something happen with you and Peter?"

I want so desperately to tell her everything, to lay all my burdens upon my big sister, to have her tell me what to do. Things would be so much simpler if she would just tell me what to do. But I know what Margot would do, because she's already done it.

Don't be the girl who goes to college with a boyfriend. That's what my mom said. That's what Margot said.

36

FOR THE BACHELORETTE, KRISTEN DECIDED the theme of the night should be the nineties, because there's nothing Trina loves better than the nineties, so everyone has to dress up in nineties clothes. Honestly, I think the whole reason behind the theme is because Kristen wants to wear a crop top and show off her abs. She arrives at the house in a blue T-shirt that says SKATER GURL and baggy jeans, and her hair is parted down the middle. She's wearing dark brown lipstick, very matte.

The first thing she does is turn on a nineties station, which blasts all over the whole house. The girls are meeting here, and the boys (and Kitty) are meeting at the steakhouse. I'm glad, because I still don't know what I'm going to say to Peter.

We're still getting ready. I'm going with a floral babydoll dress I found on Etsy, and cream-colored knee socks and black platform Mary Janes. I'm brushing my hair into two ponytails when Kristen comes upstairs to do inspections, carrying a martini glass that says *Maid of Honor* in pink cursive. "Aw, you look cute, Lara Jean," she says, sipping on her cocktail.

I tighten my ponytails. "Thank you, Kristen," I say. I'm just glad my outfit is up to snuff. I've got a lot on my mind, and I would hate to mess up Trina's night.

Kitty and Margot are on the floor; Kitty is painting Margot's nails black. Margot has chosen to go the grunge route—a long flannel shirt and jeans and a pair of Doc Martens I borrowed from Chris.

"What are you drinking?" Kitty asks Kristen.

"Cosmopolitan. I have more downstairs in a Sprite bottle. Not for you, though."

Kitty rolls her eyes at this. "Where's Tree?"

"She's in the shower," I tell her.

Kristen tilts her head and squints at me. "You're missing something." She puts down her glass and digs into her clutch and pulls out a lipstick. "Put this on."

"Oh . . . is it the color you're wearing?" I ask.

"Yes! It's called Toast of New York. It was the shit back in the day!"

"Um . . . ," I hedge. Kristen looks like she smeared Hershey's kisses all over her lips and then the chocolate dried.

"Just trust me," she says.

"I was thinking about wearing this." I put down my hairbrush and show her a shiny pink lip gloss. "Didn't the Spice Girls wear lip gloss like this? Weren't they from the nineties?"

Kristen frowns. "They were more late nineties, early two thousands, but yes. I guess that'll work." She points her lipstick at Margot. "You need this, though. Your outfit isn't nineties enough." She watches as Kitty puts the finishing touches on Margot's nails. "I used to use a Sharpie," Kristen says. "You girls don't know how lucky you are to have all these options. We used to have to make do. Sharpies for black, Wite-Out for white."

"What's Wite-Out?" Kitty asks her.

"Oh my God. You children don't even know what Wite-Out is?"

As soon as Kristen turns her back to pick up her cocktail, Kitty bares her teeth at her and hisses silently.

"I saw you in the mirror," Kristen says.

"I meant for you to," Kitty says back.

Kristen eyes her. "Hurry up and finish with your sister's nails so you can do mine."

"I'm almost done," Kitty says.

A minute later the doorbell rings, and all three of them head downstairs. I hear Kristen yell, "You get the door; I'll get the drinks!"

Trina's sorority sister Monique is wearing a slip dress with big sunflowers splashed all over it, and a white T-shirt underneath, plus black platform Mary Janes that look like space shoes. Her friend Kendra from SoulCycle is wearing overalls with a pink ribbed cami and a matching pink scrunchie in her hair. A lot of the stuff people are wearing, the kids from school wear too. Fashion really is cyclical.

The nineties theme was the right call, because Trina is delighted by all of it.

"I love your dress!" Kendra says to me.

"Thank you!" I say. "It's vintage."

She recoils in real horror. "*Oh my God*. Are the nineties considered vintage now?"

Trina says, "Yes, girl. Their nineties are our seventies."

She shudders. "That's terrifying. Are we old?"

"We're geriatric," Trina says, but cheerfully.

In the car on the way to the karaoke bar, I get a text from Peter—it's a picture of him and my dad in their suits, smiling big. My heart lurches when I see it. How do I let a boy like that go?

We have a private room reserved at the karaoke bar. When the waitress comes around, Margot orders a pomegranate margarita, which Trina notices, but she doesn't say anything. What could she say? Margot's in college. She'll be twenty in a month.

"Is that good?" I ask her.

"It's really sweet," she says. "Do you want a sip?"

I would surely love a sip. Peter's texted twice from the steakhouse, asking how my night is going, and my stomach is tied up in knots. Furtively I look over at Trina, who is doing a duet with Kristen. She might not have said anything to Margot, but I have a feeling she will say something to me.

"In Scotland, the drinking age is eighteen," Margot says.

I take a quick sip, and it's good, tart and icy.

Meanwhile, everybody's looking through songbooks, trying to decide what songs to put in. The rule of the night is only nineties music. It takes a while for people to get warmed up, but then the drinks start coming fast and furious, and people are shouting out song numbers for the queue.

Trina's friend Michelle goes up next. She croons, "There was a time, when I was so broken-hearted . . ."

"I like this song," I say. "Who sings this song?"

Kristen pats me on the head indulgently. "Aerosmith, baby girl. Aerosmith."

They all get up and sing Spice Girls.

Margot and I sing "Wonderwall" by Oasis. When I sit back down, I'm breathless.

Trina's SoulCycle friend Kendra is swaying to the beat of whatever nineties song Trina and Kristen are dueting, her frosted martini glass in the air. It's acid green.

"What are you drinking, Kendra?" I ask her.

"Apple martini."

"That sounds good. Can I try it?"

"Yeah, have a sip! They're so fruity you can't even taste it."

I take a little hummingbird sip. It is sweet. It tastes like a Jolly Rancher.

When Kristen and Trina's number is up, they fall on the couch beside me, and Kendra jumps up to sing a Britney Spears song.

Kristen is slurring, "I just want us to stay close, you know? Don't be boring. Don't be, like, a mom all of a sudden, okay? I mean, I know you have to be a mom, but like, don't be a *mom* mom."

"I won't be a mom mom," Trina says soothingly. "I could never be a mom mom."

"You have to promise to still come to Wine Down Wednesdays."

"I promise."

Kristen lets out a sob. "I just love you so much, girl."

Trina has tears in her eyes too. "I love you, too."

Kendra's martini is just sitting on the table all alone. I take another sip when no one is looking, because it does taste good. And then another. I've finished the glass when Trina spots me. She raises her eyebrows. "I think you might've had a little *too* much fun at Beach Week."

"I barely drunk a thing at Beach Week, Trina!" I protest. I frown. "Is it drunk or is it drank?"

Trina looks alarmed. "Margot, is your sister drunk?"

I put my hands up. "Guys, guys, I don't even drank!"

Margot sits down next to me, examines my eyes. "She's drunk."

I've never been drunk before in my life. Am I drunk now? I do feel very relaxed. Is that what drunk feels like, when your limbs are loose, kind of silky?

"Your dad is going to kill me," Trina says with a groan. "They just dropped Kitty off back at home. They'll be here any minute. Lara Jean, drink a lot of water. Drink this whole glass. I'm going to get another pitcher."

When she returns a few minutes later, the bachelor party is in tow. She gives me a warning look. *Don't act drunk,* she mouths. I give her a thumbs-up. Then I jump up and throw my arms around Peter.

"Peter!" I shout above the music. He looks so cute in his button-down and tie. So cute I could cry. I bury my face in his neck like a squirrel. "I've missed you so, so very much."

Peter peers at me. "Are you drunk?"

"No, I only had like two sips. Two drinks."

"Trina let you drink?"

"No." I giggle. "I stole sips."

"We'd better get you out of here before your dad sees you," Peter says, eyes darting around. My dad is looking through a songbook with Margot, who is giving me a look that says, *Get it together.*

"What he doesn't know won't hurt a living soul."

"Let's go out to the parking lot so you can get some air," he says, putting his arm around me and hustling me out the door and through the restaurant.

We step outside, and I sway on my feet a little. Peter's trying not to smile. "You're drunk."

"I guess I'm a weightlight!"

"Lightweight." He pinches my cheeks.

"Right. Weightlight. I mean, lightweight." Why is that so funny? I can't stop laughing. But then I see the way he is looking at me, with such tenderness, and I stop. I don't feel like laughing anymore. I feel like crying. Look at the way he made my dad's bachelor party so special. Look at all the ways he loves me so well. I have to love him back just as much. I didn't know what I was going to do until this very moment, but now I know. "There's something I want to say to you." I straighten up suddenly and accidentally knock Peter in the collarbone, which makes him cough. "I'm sorry. Here's what I want to say to you. I want you to do what you're supposed to do and I want to do what I'm supposed to do."

He has a half smile on his face. Shaking his head at me, he says, "What are you talking about, Covey?"

"I'm talking about, I don't think we should be in a long-distance—a long-distance relationship."

His smile is fading. "What?"

"I think that you need to do all the things you need to do at UVA, like play lacrosse, and study, and I need to do what I need to do at UNC, and if we try to stay together, everything will just fall apart. So we can't. We just, we just can't."

He blinks and then his face goes very still. "You don't want to stay together?"

I shake my head, and the hurt on his face sobers me up. "I want you to do what you're supposed to do. I don't want you to do something for me. UVA is what you've worked for, Peter. That's where you have to be. Not at UNC."

He turns ashen. "Did you talk to my mom?"

"Yes. I mean, no . . ."

The muscle in his jaw twitches. "Got it. Say no more."

"Wait, listen to me, Peter—"

"Nah, I'm good. Just for the record, I mentioned UNC to my mom as a throwaway possibility. It wasn't anything definite. Just something I threw out there. But it's cool if you don't want me to come." He starts to walk away from me, and I grab his arm to stop him.

"Peter, that's not what I'm saying! I'm saying that if you came, if you gave up everything you've worked for at UVA, you'd only end up resenting me."

Flatly he says, "Just stop it, Lara Jean. I saw this coming a mile away. Ever since you decided to go to UNC, you've been saying good-bye to me."

My arm drops away from him. "What does that even mean?"

"There's the scrapbook, for one thing. You said it was to remember us by. Why would I need something to remember us by, Lara Jean?"

"That isn't how I meant it! I spent months working on that scrapbook. You're putting this all on me, but you're the one who's been pushing me away. Ever since Beach Week!"

"Fine, let's talk about what happened that night at Beach Week." I can feel my face flush as he looks at me with a challenge in his eyes. "That night you wanted to have sex, it was like you were trying to put a bow on this whole thing. Like you were putting me in your—your hatbox. Like I played my part in your first love story, and now you can go on to the next chapter."

I feel light-headed, unsteady on my feet. Peter, who I thought I understood so well. "I'm sorry you took it that way, but that's not how I meant it. Not at all."

"It clearly is how you meant it, because you're doing it right now. Aren't you?"

Is there some hidden truth to what he's saying, even a little bit? It's true that I wouldn't want my first time to be with anyone else. It's true that it felt right to have it be with Peter, because he's the first boy I ever loved. I wouldn't want it to be with some boy I meet in college. That boy is a stranger to me. Peter I've known since we were kids. Was I just trying to close a chapter?

No. I did it because I wanted it to be him. But if that's how he sees it, maybe it's easier this way.

I swallow. "Maybe you're right. Maybe I did want my first

time to be with you so I could close a chapter on high school. On us."

He freezes. I see the pain in his eyes, and then his face closes up like a shuttered empty house. He starts to walk away. This time I don't try to stop him. Over his shoulder he says, "We're good, Covey. Don't worry about it."

As soon as he's gone, I turn to the side and throw up everything I drank and ate tonight. I'm bent over, heaving, when Trina and Daddy and Margot walk out of the karaoke bar. Daddy rushes over to me. "Lara Jean, what's the matter? Are you all right?"

"I'm fine, I'm fine," I mumble, wiping my eyes and mouth.

His eyes widen, alarmed. "Have you been drinking?" He looks accusingly at Trina, who is rubbing my back. "Trina, you let Lara Jean drink?"

"She had a few sips of a pomegranate martini. She'll be fine."

"She doesn't look fine!"

Trina stands up straight, her hand still on my back. "Dan, Lara Jean's a young woman now. You can't see it, because you still see her as a little girl, but she's grown up so much in the time I've known her. She can handle herself."

Margot breaks in. "Daddy, I let her have a few sips of my drink—that's it. She really doesn't have any tolerance. Frankly, it's something she should work on before she gets to college. Don't blame Trina."

Daddy looks from Margot to Trina and back to Margot. She is standing shoulder to shoulder with Trina, and in that moment they are united. Then he looks over at me. "You're right. This is all on Lara Jean. Get in the car."

On the way home we have to pull over once so I can throw up again. It's not the pomegranate martini that's making me want to die. It's the look on Peter's face. The way the light in his eyes went away. The hurt—if I close my eyes I can see it. The only other time I've seen him look that way was when his dad didn't show up at graduation. And now that look is there because of me.

I start to cry in the car. Big sobs that make my shoulders shake.

"Don't cry," my dad says with a sigh. "You're in trouble, but not that big of trouble."

"It's not that. I broke up with Peter." I can barely get the words out. "Daddy, if you could've seen the look on his face. It was—terrible."

Bewildered, he asks, "Why did you break up with him? He's such a nice boy."

"I don't know," I weep. "Now I don't know."

He takes one hand off the steering wheel and squeezes my shoulder. "It's all right. It's all right."

"But—it isn't."

"But it will be," he says, stroking my hair.

I made the right choice tonight. I did, I know it. Letting him go was the right thing.

I can see the future, Peter. That way lies heartbreak. I won't do it. Better to part while we can still see each other in a certain way.

37

I WAKE UP IN THE MIDDLE OF THE NIGHT crying, and my first thought is, I want to take it back. I've made a huge mistake and I want to take it all back. Then I cry myself back to sleep.

In the morning, my head throbs, and now I'm the one throwing up in the bathroom, just like the girls at Beach Week, only there's no one to hold my hair back. I feel better after, but I lie on the bathroom floor for a while in case another wave of nausea hits. I fall asleep there, and wake up to Kitty shaking me by the arm. "Move, I have to pee," she says, stepping over me.

"Help me up," I say, and she drags me to my feet. She sits down to pee and I splash cold water on my face.

"Go eat some toast," Kitty says. "It'll soak up the alcohol in your stomach."

I brush my teeth and stumble downstairs to the kitchen, where Daddy is cooking eggs and Margot and Trina are eating yogurt.

"Rise and shine, little girl," Trina says with a grin.

"You look like someone ran you over with a truck," Margot says.

"You'd be grounded right now if it weren't for the wedding," Daddy says, trying to sound stern and failing. "Eat some scrambled eggs."

I gag at the thought.

"First eat some toast," Margot instructs. "It'll soak up the alcohol."

"That's what Kitty said."

Trina points her spoon at me. "And then, once you've put some food in your belly, you can have two Advil. Never, ever take Advil on an empty stomach. You'll be feeling much better in no time."

"I'm never drinking again," I vow, and Margot and Trina exchange a smirk. "I'm serious."

I spend the whole day in bed, lights off with the curtains drawn. I want so badly to call Peter. To ask him to forgive me. I don't even remember everything I said. I remember the gist of it, but the memory itself is blurry. The one thing I do remember so clearly, what I'll never forget, is the stricken look on his face, and it makes me hate myself for putting it there.

I give in. I text him. Just three words.

I'm so sorry.

I see the . . . on the other end. My heart pounds madly as I wait. But the reply never comes. I try calling, but my call goes straight to voice mail, and I hang up. Maybe he's already deleted me from his phone, like he did his dad. Maybe he's just . . . done.

38

CHRIS IS THE FIRST TO LEAVE. SHE COMES by the house that week and says, "I can't go to your dad's wedding this weekend. I'm leaving for the Dominican Republic tomorrow."

"*What?*"

"I know. I'm sorry." Chris doesn't look the least bit sorry; she has a huge grin on her face. "It's so crazy. A spot opened up for me at an eco-hotel, and there's no way I can pass this up. They speak Spanish in the Dominican Republic, too, right?"

"Yes. But I thought you were going to Costa Rica!"

Shrugging, she says, "This other opportunity came up so I pounced on it."

"But—I can't believe you're leaving so soon! You weren't supposed to leave until August. When do you come back?"

"I don't know. . . . I guess that's the beauty of it. I could stay for six months, or something else will come up and I'll go there."

I blink. "So you're leaving for good, then?"

"Not for *good*. Just for now."

Something inside of me knows that this really is for good. I don't see Chris coming back here a year from now to go to Piedmont Virginia Community College. This is Chris, the stray cat, who comes and goes as she pleases. She'll always land on her cat tippy-toes.

"Don't look so sad. You'll be fine without me. You have Kavinsky." For a second I can't breathe. Just hearing his name is like a dagger in my heart. "Anyway we're all leaving soon enough. I'm just glad I'm not going to be left behind."

That's how it would feel to her—staying here, going to a community college, working at Applebee's. I feel a surge of gladness that instead of that, she's off on an adventure. "I just can't believe you're leaving so soon." I don't tell her that Peter and I broke up, that I don't have him anymore. Today isn't about me and Peter; it's about Chris, and her exciting new future. "Can I at least come help you pack?"

"I'm already packed! I'm only bringing the essentials. My leather jacket, bikinis, a few crystals."

"Shouldn't you bring sneakers and work gloves and that kind of thing, just in case?"

"I'll wear sneakers on the plane, and whatever else I need, I'll get when I'm there. That's the whole point of an adventure. Pack light and figure the rest out as you go."

I thought we'd have more time, me and Chris in my bedroom, sharing secrets late into the night, eating chips in bed. I wanted to cement our friendship before she left: Lara Jean and Chrissy, like the old days.

It's all ending.

39

THAT NIGHT BEFORE THE WEDDING, WHEN my cakes are cooling on the kitchen counter and everyone at my house is setting up lawn chairs outside, I drive over to Chris's to say good-bye.

As soon as she lets me in, she says, "I'm not letting you in here if you cry."

"I can't help it. I feel like this is going to be the last time I ever see you." A tear slips down my cheek. There is a finality to this moment. I know it, I just know it. Chris is catapulting on to the next thing. Even if we see each other again, it won't be like this. She's a restless spirit. I'm lucky to have had her for as long as I did.

"You'll probably see me again next week when I fly right back home," she jokes, and there is the tiniest note of trepidation in her voice. Chris, with all her bluster and bravado, is nervous.

"No way. You're just getting started. This is it, Chris." I jump up and hug her. I'm trying not to cry. "It's all happening now."

"What is?"

"Life!"

"You're so corny," she says, but I could swear I see tears in her eyes.

"I brought you something," I tell her. I take the present out of my bag and give it to her.

She tears off the wrapping paper and opens the box. It's a picture of the two of us in a little heart frame, no bigger than a Christmas tree ornament. We are at the beach, in matching bathing suits; we are twelve, maybe thirteen. "Hang this up on your wall wherever you go so people know you have somebody waiting for you back home."

Her eyes tear up and she brushes them with the back of her hand. "Oh my God, you're the worst," she says.

I've heard people say you meet your best friends in college, and they're the ones you'll know your whole life, but I'm certain that I'll know Chris my whole life too. I'm a person who saves things. I'll hold on forever.

When I get back home, Trina's at SoulCycle. Daddy is still outside setting up the chairs, Margot is steaming our bridesmaid dresses, and Kitty is cutting paper flags for the bunting that will go over the dessert table. I get to work icing the wedding cake—yellow cake with buttercream frosting, just like I promised Trina. Daddy's groom's cake is already done, Thin Mints and all. This is my second try with the wedding cake—I scrapped the first one because I didn't trim enough off the tops of the layers and when I stacked it, the cake looked hopelessly lopsided. This second one is still a tiny bit uneven, but a thick layer of buttercream covers all manner of sins, or so I keep telling myself.

"You're putting enough frosting on that cake to give us all diabetes," Kitty remarks.

I bite my tongue and keep spinning the cake and frosting the top so it's smooth. "It looks all right, doesn't it, Margot?"

"It looks professionally done," she assures me, zooming the steamer along the hem of her dress.

As I sail past Kitty, I can't resist saying, "P.S., the last three flags you cut are crooked."

Kitty ignores me and sings to herself, "Sugar shock, whoa baby, that cake'll give us sugar shock," to the tune of that oldies song "Sugar Shack." It's probably my own fault for playing it whenever I bake.

"This is the last time it'll be just us," I say, and Margot looks over at me and smiles.

"I'm glad it won't be just us anymore," Kitty says.

"So am I," Margot says, and I'm fairly certain she means it.

Families shrink and expand. All you can really do is be glad for it, glad for each other, for as long as you have each other.

I can't sleep, so I go downstairs to make a cup of Night-Night tea, and as I run the water for my kettle, I look out the window and see the red embers of a cigarette glowing in the darkness. Trina is outside smoking!

I'm debating whether or not to forego my tea ritual and go to bed before she sees me, but as I'm emptying the kettle, she comes back inside, a can of Fresca in her hand.

"Oh!" she says, startled.

"I couldn't sleep," I say, just as she says, "Don't tell Kitty!"

We both laugh.

"I swear it was a good-bye smoke. I haven't had a cigarette in months!"

"I won't tell Kitty."

"I owe you one," Trina says, exhaling.

"Would you like a cup of Night-Night tea?" I ask her. "My mom used to make it for us. It's very soothing. It'll make you feel nice and cozy and ready for bed."

"That sounds like heaven."

I fill the kettle and put it on the stove. "Are you nervous about the wedding?"

"No, not nervous . . . just, nerves, I guess? I really want everything to go off—without a hitch." A giggle escapes her throat. "Pun intended. God, I love a good pun." Then she straightens up and says, "Tell me what's going on with you and Peter."

I busy myself with spooning honey into mugs. "Oh, nothing." The last thing Trina needs on the night before her wedding is to hear about my problems.

She gives me a look. "Come on, girl. Tell me."

"I don't know. I guess we're broken up?" I shrug my shoulders high so I don't cry.

"Oh, honey. Bring that tea over here and come sit next to me on the couch."

I finish making the tea and bring the mugs over to the couch and sit next to Trina, who tucks her legs under her and drapes a blanket over both of us. "Now tell me everything," she says.

"I guess things started to go sideways when I got into UNC. Our plan was for me to go to William and Mary and then I'd transfer, and we'd be long distance for the first year. But UNC is a lot farther, and when I visited, I knew I wanted to be there. Not with one foot in and one foot out, you know?" I stir my spoon. "I really want to give it a chance."

"I think that's a thousand percent the right attitude." Trina warms her hand on her tea mug. "So that's why you broke up with him?"

"No, not entirely. Peter's mom told me he was talking about transferring to UNC next year. She wanted me to break up with him before he messed up his life for me."

"Damn! Peter's mom is kind of a bitch!"

"She didn't use those exact words, but that was the gist of it." I take a sip of tea. "I wouldn't want him to transfer for me either. . . . My mom used to say not to go to college with a boyfriend, because you'll lose out on a true freshman experience."

"Well, to be fair, your mom never met Peter Kavinsky. She didn't have all the facts. If she had met him . . ." Trina lets out a low whistle. "She might've been singing a different tune."

Tears fill my eyes. "Honestly I regret breaking up with him and I wish I could take it all back!"

She tips up my chin. "Then why don't you?"

"I don't think he'll ever forgive me for hurting him like that. He doesn't let people in easily. I think I'm probably dead to him."

Trina tries to hide a smile. "I doubt that. Look, you'll talk to him at the wedding tomorrow. When he sees you in that dress, all will be forgiven."

I sniffle. "I'm sure he's not coming."

"I'm sure he is. You don't plan a man's bachelor party and then not show to the wedding. Not to mention the fact that he's crazy about you."

"But what if I hurt him again?"

She wraps both her hands around her mug of tea and takes a sip. "You can't protect him from being hurt, babe, no matter what you do. Being vulnerable, letting people in, getting hurt . . . it's all a part of being in love."

I take this in. "Trina, when did you figure out that you and my dad were the real thing?"

"I don't know. . . . I think I just—decided."

"Decided on what?"

"Decided on him. On us." She smiles at me. "On all of it."

It's so crazy to think that a year ago, she was just our neighbor Ms. Rothschild. Kitty and I would sit on our stoop and watch her run to the car in the morning and spill hot coffee all over herself. And now she's marrying our dad. She's going to be our stepmom, and I'm so glad for it.

40

THE AIR SMELLS LIKE HONEYSUCKLES AND summer days that go on and on. It is the perfect day to get married. I don't think there's any place prettier than Virginia in June. Everything in bloom, everything green and sunny and hopeful. When I get married, I think I might like it to be at home too.

We woke up early, and it seemed like there would be plenty of time, but of course we're running around like chickens with their heads cut off. Trina is flying around the upstairs in her silky ivory robe that Kristen bought her. Kristen bought pink ones for us bridesmaids, with our names embroidered in gold on the front pocket. Trina's says *The Bride*. I've got to hand it to Kristen. She's annoying but she has vision. She knows how to make things nice.

Trina's photographer friend takes a picture of all of us in our robes, Trina sitting in the middle like a very tan swan. Then it's time to get dressed. We compromised on Kitty's tuxedo—she's wearing a white short-sleeved button-down shirt, a jaunty plaid bow tie, and pants that hit at her ankle. Her hair is in Swiss Miss braids, tucked under and pinned up. She looks so pretty. She looks so . . . Kitty. I compromised by putting baby's breath in my hair but no flower crown. I also compromised on my vision of fairy nightgowns for Margot and me. Instead we are wearing vintage 1950s floral dresses that I found on Etsy—Margot's is cream with yellow daisies, and mine has pink flowers and straps that tie at the shoulder. Mine must have been owned by a short person, because we didn't even have to alter it, and it hits at the knees, right where it's supposed to, .

Trina is a beautiful bride. Her teeth and dress look very white against her tanned skin. "I don't look silly, do I?" She casts a nervous look in my direction. "Too old to wear white? I mean, I *am* a divorcée."

Margot answers before I can. "You look perfect. Just perfect."

My older sister has a way of sounding right. Trina's whole body relaxes, like one big exhale. "Thank you, Margot." Her voice goes tremulous. "I'm just . . . so happy."

"Don't cry!" Kitty screeches.

"Shh," I tell her. "Don't scream. Trina needs serenity." Kitty's been a nervous bundle of energy all day; it's like her birthday and Christmas and first day of school combined.

Trina fans her armpits. "I'm sweating. I think I need more deodorant. Kitty, do I smell?"

Kitty leans in. "You're good."

We've already taken a hundred pictures today, and we'll take hundreds more, but I know this one will be my favorite. Us three Song girls flocked in tight around Trina, Margot dabbing at Trina's eyes with a tissue, Kitty standing on a footstool fussing with Trina's hair, Trina's arm around me. We're smiling so big. Things are ending, but they are beginning, too.

As for Peter, there's been no word. Every time a car comes down our street, I go to the window to see if it's him, but it never is. He isn't coming, and I don't blame him one bit. But still I hope, because I can't help but hope.

The backyard is covered in Christmas lights and white paper lanterns. Granted, there's no wall of roses, but it still looks lovely. All of the chairs are set up; the runner is rolled out in the middle for Trina to walk down. I greet guests as they come in—it's a small group, under fifty people. The perfect size for a backyard wedding. Margot's sitting with Grandma, Nana, and Trina's dad and sister in the first row, keeping them company while I walk around saying hello to our neighbors the Shahs, Aunt Carrie and Uncle Victor, my cousin Haven, who compliments my dress. Throughout it all, I keep my eyes trained on the driveway, waiting for a black Audi that doesn't come.

When "Lullaby" by the Dixie Chicks begins to play, Kitty, Margot, and I get into our places. Daddy walks out and stands on the groom's side, and we all look toward the house, where Trina is making her way toward us. She is resplendent.

We cry throughout the vows, even Margot, who never cries. They go with the traditional ones, and when Reverend Choi, the pastor from Grandma's church, says, "You may kiss the bride," Daddy turns beet red, but he kisses Trina with a flourish. Everyone claps; Kitty whoops. Jamie Fox-Pickle barks.

The father-daughter dance was Trina's idea. She said she'd already been there and done that and didn't feel the need to do it again, and that it would be far more meaningful for us girls to do it instead. We practiced earlier this week, on the dance floor Daddy rented.

We planned the father–daughter dance to go Margot first, then I cut in, then Kitty cuts in. The song Daddy chose is "Isn't She Lovely," a song Stevie Wonder wrote for his daughter when she was first born.

Kitty and I stand off to the side, clapping to the beat. I know she's already relishing her moment to cut in on me.

Before Daddy releases Margot, he pulls her close and whispers something in her ear, and she gets tears in her eyes. I won't ask what he said; it is a moment just for them.

Daddy and I have practiced a few moves. The crowd-pleaser is when we dance-walk side by side and shimmy together in unison.

"I'm so proud of you," he says. "My middle girl." It's my turn for my eyes to fill. I kiss him on the cheek and hand him off to Kitty. Daddy swings her around just as the harmonica starts up.

I'm walking off the dance floor when I see him. Peter, in a suit, standing to the side, beside the dogwood tree. He looks so handsome I can hardly stand it. I cross the backyard, and he watches me the whole time. My heart is pounding so hard. Is he here for me? Or did he just come because he promised my dad?

When I'm standing in front of him, I say, "You came."

Peter looks away. "Of course I came."

Softly I say, "I wish I could take back the things I said the other night. I don't even remember all of them."

Looking down, he says, "But you meant them, right? So it's a good thing you said them then, because somebody had to and you were right."

"Which part?" I whisper.

"About UNC. About me not transferring there." He lifts his head, his eyes wounded. "But you should have told me my mom talked to you."

I take a shaky breath. "You should have told me you were thinking about transferring! You should've told me how you were feeling, period. You shut down after graduation; you wouldn't let me in. You kept saying everything was going to be fine."

"Because I was fucking scared, okay!" he bursts out. He looks around to see if anyone heard, but the music is loud, and everyone is dancing; no one is looking at us, and it's like we are alone here in this backyard.

"What were you so scared about?" I whisper.

His hands tighten into fists at his sides. When he finally speaks, his voice comes out raw, like he hasn't used it in a while. "I was scared that you were going to go to UNC and you were gonna figure out I wasn't worth it, and you were going to leave."

I take a step closer to him. I put my hand on his arm; he doesn't pull away from me. "Besides my family, you're the most special person to me in the world. And I meant some of those things I said the other night, but not the part when I said I only wanted to lose my virginity to you to close a chapter on us. I wanted it to be you because I love you."

Peter puts one arm around my waist, pulls me in, and, looking down at me, he says fiercely, "Neither of us wants to break up. So why should we? Because of some shit my mom said? Because your sister did it that way? You're not the same as your sister, Lara Jean. We're not the same as Margot and Sanderson or anybody else. We're you and me. And yeah, it's gonna be hard. But Lara Jean, I'll never feel for another girl what I feel for you." He says it with all the certainty only a teenage boy can have, and I have never loved him more than at this very moment.

"Lovin' in My Baby's Eyes" is playing, and Peter takes my hand and leads me out to the lawn.

We've never danced to this kind of song before. It's the kind of song where you sway together and make a lot of eye contact and smile. It feels different, like we're already older versions of Peter and Lara Jean.

Across the dance floor, Trina and Kitty and Margot are dancing in a circle, with Grandma in the middle. Haven is dancing with my dad. She catches my eye and mouths, *He's so cute.* Peter, not my dad. He is. He is so, so cute.

I will never forget tonight, not for as long as I live. One day, if I'm lucky, I'll tell some young girl all my stories, just like Stormy told me hers. And I'll get to live them again.

When I'm old and gray, I will look back on this night, and I will remember it just as it was.

Is.

We're still here. It's not the future yet.

That night, after all the guests have gone, after the chairs have been stacked back up, and the leftovers put in the fridge, I go up to my room to change out of my dress. Sitting on the bed is my yearbook. I flip to the back of the book, and there it is, Peter's message to me.

Only, it's not a message, it's a contract.

Lara Jean and Peter's Amended Contract

Peter will write a letter to Lara Jean once a week. A real handwritten letter, not an e-mail.

Lara Jean will call Peter once a day. Preferably the last call of the night, before she goes to bed.

Lara Jean will put up a picture of Peter's choosing on her wall.

Peter will keep the scrapbook out on his desk so any interested parties will see that he is taken.

Peter and Lara Jean will always tell each other the truth, even when it's hard.

Peter will love Lara Jean with all his heart, always.

41

THE NIGHT BEFORE I LEAVE FOR COLLEGE,
there is a Perseids meteor shower in the forecast. It's supposed to be a good one. Peter and I are going out to the lake
to watch. Kitty doesn't say so, but she wants to come too;
she's dying to. Her whole body is rigid with wanting and
not being able to ask. Any other time I would say yes.

When I say good-bye, her lips twist in disappointment for
just a second, but she hides it well. How hard it must be to
be the youngest sometimes, to be the one left behind.

In the car I feel sick with guilt for being so possessive
about my time with Peter. It's just that there's so little time
left now. . . . I'm a terrible big sister. Margot would have
brought her.

"What are you thinking about?" Peter asks me.

"Oh, nothing," I say. I'm too ashamed to say out loud that
I should have invited Kitty along.

When I come home for fall break, we'll do something the
three of us. Peter and I will take her to the midnight show at
the drive-in, and she'll go in her pajamas and I'll set up the
backseat with a blanket for when she falls asleep. But tonight
I want it to be just Peter and me, just this once. There's no
use lingering in the guilt and ruining the night, when I've
already done the selfish deed. And if I am truly honest with

myself, I would do it again. That's how covetous I am of every last moment I have left with Peter. I want his eyes only on me; I want to talk only to him, to be just him and me for this little while longer. One day she'll understand. One day she'll love a boy and want to keep him all to herself and not share his attention with anyone else.

"We should have let Kitty come," I burst out suddenly.

"I know," he says. "I feel bad too. Do you think she's mad?"

"Sad, probably."

But neither of us suggests turning the car around and going back to get her. We are silent, and then we are both laughing, sheepish and also relieved. Assuredly, Peter says, "We'll bring her next time."

"Next time," I echo. I reach over and grab his hand, and lock my fingers around his, and he locks back, and I am comforted in knowing that tonight he feels the exact same way, and there is no distance between us.

We spread a blanket out and lie side by side. The moon looks like a glacier in the navy night. So far I don't see anything out of the ordinary. It looks like the normal night sky to me.

"Maybe we should've gone to the mountains," Peter says, turning his face to look at me.

"No, this is perfect," I say. "Anyway, I read that stargazing is a waiting game no matter where you are."

"We have all night," he says, pulling me closer.

Sometimes I wish we'd met when we were twenty-seven. Twenty-seven sounds like a good age to meet the person you're going to spend the rest of your life with. At twenty-seven, you are still young, but hopefully you are well on your way to being the you you want to be.

But then I think, no, I wouldn't give up twelve, thirteen, sixteen, seventeen with Peter for the world. My first kiss, my first fake boyfriend, my first real boyfriend. The first boy who ever bought me a piece of jewelry. Stormy would say that that is the most monumental moment of all. She told me that that's how a boy lets you know that you're his. I think for us it was the opposite. It's how I knew he was mine.

I don't want to forget any of this. The way he's looking at me at this very moment. How, when he kisses me, I still get shivers down my back, every time. I want to hold on to everything so tight.

"The first sixth-grade assembly."

I look up at him. "Huh?"

"That's the first time I saw you. You were sitting in the row in the front of me. I thought you were cute."

I laugh. "Nice try." It's so endearingly Peter to make up stuff to try and sound romantic.

He keeps going. "Your hair was really long and you had a headband with a bow. I always liked your hair, even back then."

"Okay, Peter," I say, reaching up and patting him on his cheek.

He ignores me. "Your backpack had your name written on it in glitter letters. I'd never heard of the name Lara Jean before."

My mouth falls open. I hot-glued those glitter letters to my backpack myself! It took me forever trying to get them straight enough. I'd forgotten all about that backpack. It was my prized possession.

"The principal started picking random people to come on stage and play a game for prizes. Everybody was raising their hands, but your hair got caught in your chair and you were trying to untangle it, so you didn't get picked. I remember thinking maybe I should help you, but then I thought that would be weird."

"How do you remember all that?" I ask in amazement.

Smiling, he shrugs. "I don't know. I just do."

Kitty's always saying how origin stories are important.

At college, when people ask us how we met, how will we answer them? The short story is, we grew up together. But that's more Josh's and my story. High school sweethearts? That's Peter and Gen's story. So what's ours, then?

I suppose I'll say it all started with a love letter.

"I've had a splendid time," she concluded happily,

"and I feel that it marks an epoch in my life.

But the best of it all was the coming home."

—L. M. MONTGOMERY, *Anne of Green Gables*

Acknowledgments

I never thought I'd write another book about Lara Jean, so I feel lucky to have one last opportunity to thank everyone who's helped me along the way. With all my heart, I would like to thank my agent, Emily van Beek, and the team at Folio; my editor Zareen Jaffery and my entire S&S family, but especially Justin Chanda, Anne Zafian, Chrissy Noh, Lucy Cummins, Mekisha Telfer, KeriLee Horan, Audrey Gibbons, Katy Hershberger, Candace Greene, Michelle Leo, and Dorothy Gribbin. Thank you also to my film agent, Michelle Weiner; my publicist, Brianne Halverson; and my assistant, Dan Johnson. I would also like to thank Jeannine Lalonde from UVA admissions and Vincent Briedis from UVA's athletics department. Thank you to my friends and fellow writers for reading this manuscript and offering me amazing notes and cheering me on every step of the way—Siobhan Vivian, Adele Griffin, Jennifer E. Smith, Melissa Walker, and Anna Carey. I could not have done it without you.

And lastly, thank you to my readers. If not for you, I would not have written this book. Truly, this one is for you. My dearest wish is that you are happy and satisfied with the way Lara Jean's story ends. This time, I mean it—it really is the end for me and Lara Jean. But she'll live on in my heart, for there's always the bend in the road.

Jenny

Also available from Jenny Han

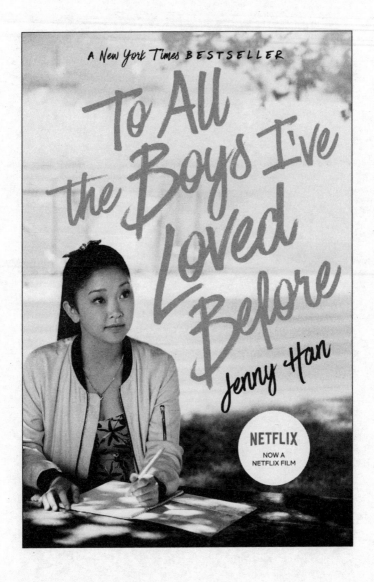

A *New York Times*
BESTSELLER

P.S.
I Still
Love
You

Jenny Han

NETFLIX
NOW A
NETFLIX FILM

SEQUEL TO THE NETFLIX FILM *TO ALL THE BOYS I'VE LOVED BEFORE*